COWBOYS IN SPACE

TALES OF BYANNTIA

by
C.J. Henderson
Bruce Gehweiler
James Chambers
Robert E. Waters
Jack Dolphin

Edited by
Mike McPhail

MoonDream
PRESS

AN IMPRINT OF COPPER DOG PUBLISHING, LLC

Cowboys In Space

Copyright ©2016 Copper Dog Publishing LLC

Published by Moondream Press, an imprint of Copper Dog Publishing, LLC
537 Leader Circle
Louisville, CO 80027

Visit our Web site: www.copperdogpublishing.com

Credits:
Cover and Interior Design: Helen Harrison
Edited by Mike McPhail
Authors: C.J. Henderson
       Bruce Gehweiler
       James Chambers
       Robert E. Waters
       Jack Dolphin

Library of Congress Control Number: 2016909526

ISBN: 978-1-943690-09-1

First Edition: June 2016

All stories copyright 2016 by the individual authors.

Printed in the United States of America

TABLE OF CONTENTS

INTRODUCTION

Bruce Gehweiler

MANKIND'S WANDERLUST WILL EVENTUALLY CARRY OUR SPECIES to the stars. Earth's explorers have always risen to the challenge of exploring our planet's remote rain forests, highest mountain peaks, deepest ocean abysses and deadly frozen polar caps. Answering the wanderlust deep within us is exactly what motivated the colonists of Byanntia to brave the dangers of space travel. Their reward is the opportunity to test their mettle against an alien planet—to explore an unknown environment and attempt to survive on their own terms. The mysteries of Byanntia unfold in these eight suspenseful tales. We welcome you as a fellow explorer to these sprawling vistas of the imagination contained in this book.

Science fiction has always brought together multiple genres to create fresh and exciting new fictional universes and the tales of Byanntia are no exception. As this great book takes its place among the best Space Western adventures ever written, let us discuss some of the history of this science fiction sub-genre.

By definition, the Space Western includes Western style stories told on far distant planets or in the distant future. A similar but different sub-genre is the science fiction story set in the old American West and not in outer space. Perhaps the best example of a space western is the

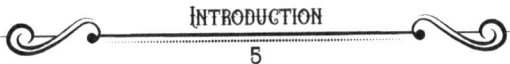

TV series *Firefly* which is set on distant planets in outer space. To date the best example of a science fiction story set in the old American West is the graphic novel and movie *Cowboys and Aliens*. Another related sub-genre is the science fiction steampunk set in the old American West. A steampunk is usually set in Queen Victoria's era of England, but recently it has been crossing the Atlantic. The steam powered engines, weapons, high-technology and exotic zeppelins are still present but the setting has moved to the old American West. Will Smith, Kevin Kline and Kenneth Branagh starred in the movie *Wild Wild West* based on the TV series of the same name starring Robert Conrad which is probably the most famous example of a steampunk science fiction western.

Some of the most popular books in the Space Western sub-genre of science fiction include;

Serenity: Those Left Behind by Joss Whedon which was followed by *Serenity: Better Days* and *Serenity The Shepherd's Tale*. This was a follow up to the *Firefly* TV series which is one of the most critically acclaimed TV series ever.

Trigun: Deep Space Planet Future Gun Action! by Yasuhiro Nightow
House of Cards (Star Trek: New Frontier #1) by Peter David
Storm Dogs by David Hine
Cowboy Bepop by Yutaka Nanten
Hellhole by Kevin J. Anderson and Brian Herbert

Gene Roddenberry, the creator of *Star Trek*, described his TV show as a Space Western since the goal of the U.S.S. Enterprise was to explore the final frontier of space. One of the latest and an excellent example of a Space Western is the book series *Hellhole* written by Kevin J. Anderson and Brian Herbert. Brian Herbert is the son of *Dune* creator Frank Herbert and Kevin J. Anderson is a prolific science fiction writer who also happens to be the highest paid sci-fi writer in the world. As you read *Hellhole* you will certainly see why this dynamic duo has garnered so much commercial success.

Some of the best Space Westerns on film include:

Star Wars Who can forget the memorable Mos Eisley Cantina scene and the bounty hunter Boba Fett?

Star Trek It's five year mission to explore the new frontier of space.

Outland Peter Hyams hired Sean Connery to make a great Space Western about the Marshall of a mining operation in deep space.

Westworld This is a fun science fiction western set in a future theme park where one gets to play cowboy and cowgirl with human-like robots.

Alien My favorite director Ridley Scott is known as a master of light and shadows and the best example of his genius is this Space Western that reveals the grim reality of living on the frontier of known space.

Battlestar Galactica Glen A. Larson created this Space Western about a lone flagship filled with the few surviving humans from distant colonies trying to find their way back home to the legendary planet known as Earth.

Babylon 5 J. Michael Straczynski created this excellent TV series and series of TV movies set on a space station at a crossroads of interstellar diplomacy and commerce. The spin-off series *Crusade* is also well worth watching.

Firefly Josh Whedon's critically acclaimed Space Western and the spin-off movies *Serenity* are definitely worth watching.

As you can see, you are more familiar with the Space Western and its cousins the science fiction western and the science fiction steampunk western than you previously thought. So strap on your laser pistol and saddle up an alien beast for the fictional ride of your life, as we take you on a journey to a distant planet called... Byanntia.

    –Bruce Gehweiler
    Dallas, Georgia USA

TIME OF THE GR'NAR

C.J. Henderson and Bruce Gehweiler

"**C**OME OUT, COME OUT, WHEREVER YOU ARE. LAST ONE TO show his face today gets to be steaks and chops tomorrow!"

Chad Matson floated above the muddy water hole on his hovercycle, searching the horizon for the kison that had wandered off from the main herd. When herding animals that pack-grazed in the tens of thousands, maintaining a head count was next to impossible. But Chad had a feel for the great dumb brutes that wore his father's brand. He could always tell when a few too many of them had strayed. And now, seeing the bottom silt of the last water hole before the vast Junsuka Desert that abutted the family farm churned and gray, he had all the proof he needed that some of them had strayed too far.

Can't have that, he thought. Not this close to round-up. Dehydration ships on their way, Earth hungry for meat—no, no, you ignorant beef bags, none of you are leaving your bones in the sand on my watch.

Chad shifted his weight, nudging his cycle closer to an outcropping of bluish rock jutting out sharply over the water hole. The strange, pancake-stack formations that dotted Byanntia's equator had never ceased to amaze the young plainsman. It had been his father's generation—The First, as they were known—which had discovered the rocks' life-saving secret decades earlier. The layered pores of the formations' surfaces absorbed water, storing it in hundreds of tiny internal pouches. Crushing a section of rock freed the trapped moisture, a trick that saved hundreds of lives when the planet was first settled. True, the result was an oily tasting moisture thick with sand, but drinking it was better than dying. Chad's father knew that fact all too well.

The rocks were actually a cross between mineral and vegetable life. A biologist who came out from Earth to see the formations described them as being something on the order of silicon based-sponges. Of course, he had not been able to explain why the rocks did what they did, or how they could be duplicated. Eventually he had left, taking whatever other diverting, but ultimately useless, knowledge he had with him, and life had gone on much as it had before his arrival.

Chad pulled a deep breath in through his nose, releasing it again through one side of his mouth. He was just about to make a looping circular pass out over the plains when something curious below caught his eye. A touch from his left foot sent his cycle in a measured drop, hanging him a scant yard above the still thinly-gray water.

"Goddamn," he whispered, more from awe than a need for privacy. "That looks like bones."

A numbing roar sounded behind the young plainsman, reverberating out over the desert. Chad down-thumbed his handlebar controls, sending his cycle into a reverse half spin that not only turned him around but sent him skimming rapidly backward out over the waterhole a measured thirty feet. The maneuver was a well-calculated move—one that allowed Chad to face whatever was behind him while instantly giving him a safe amount of distance. Or, so he had thought.

Chad believed he caught a glimpse of some kind of movement, but he could not actually see what it was that leaped from the outcropping toward him. A shadow stretched from the rocks to the hovering cycle in a fragment of instance, knocking the plainsman out of his seat. Chad's back hit the water at the same moment his riderless vehicle crashed into the rocks. His head broke the water, his hands clawing for his sidearm.

What in Hell have I ...

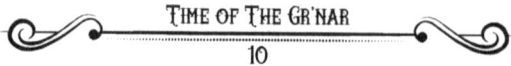

The thought died in the young man's brain as a devastatingly powerful blow smashed against his chest. Air crashed out of his body, his throat constricting, lungs flattening, their walls collapsing inward. Blood splashed out over the young rancher's shattered breastbone. His weapon fell from his suddenly useless fingers. His eyes blinked uncontrollably even as his knees buckled and his thoughts jumbled.

Dying, he realized. I'm dying. Have to warn—

A second blow collided with the back of Chad's head. Skin broke, bone snapped, blood flowed. Another roar sounded across the plains, followed by the sounds of a ruined hovercycle motor going into automatic shutdown. And then, a shadow pulled itself out of the water and moved toward the body floating face down in the water, its many teeth grinding in hunger.

***

"This world is such a halt," complained Stewart with the sneering righteousness of teenaged authority. "What could Dad have been thinkin' when he helped settle this pit?"

"Seal your mush-hatch, will you?" snapped Stewart's older brother Joseph. "My brain's baked from having to tune your damn frequency morning, noon and night."

"Bite one," snapped Stewart. "With all the planets in this galaxy, why'd we have to get born on the most boring pukeball ever found? No double sun, no extra moons, no rings—might as well be all the drok way back on Earth."

Joseph just shook his head. How many times did he have to say it? Anything extra in orbit around a planet causes changes in weather patterns. Satellites not much larger than Earth's moon had been known to virtually tear planets apart by causing endless quakes and volcanic activity, not to mention the monstrous tides such bodies could create. And that insane nonsense about double suns—did the goofy kid have to spend *all* his time scanning those cheap pulse thrillers?

"How stupid can Chad be?" asked Joseph finally, hoping to change the subject. "Going out stray tracking on his own, with his comm shut down, no less. He doesn't log a direction statement ... I can't believe Dad is going to let him start running the ranch next year."

"Why you always have to ragrip everything Chad does?" Stewart pulled his kisonboy hat down over his forehead. "He can take care of himself. He took his bolt thrower. He'll be back plowin' through a stack of ribs while we're still out here eatin' sand."

"I don't get mad at everything Chad does," answered Joseph, working to control his souring anger. "Just the stupid things. He's too damn unreliable to run Twin Feathers and I'd just like to know what makes Dad think he won't have us ass-deep in ruin after six months."

Knowing there was more than a little truth to what his older brother was saying, but not knowing how to defend Chad against it, Stewart changed the subject. "Whatever—why don't we try the comm again?"

"You do it," sighed Joseph. Removing his hat, the middle son of the Matson boys let his straight, dirty blonde hair billow in the slight breeze created by his cycle's forward motion. Staring out over the horizon, he tried to think like Chad would for a moment while his younger brother continued to call into his communicator. His dark blue eyes scanning the horizon, it was when he looked off to his left and spotted the dunes of the Junsuka that inspiration hit him.

"Follow me, squint. I've got an idea."

"Yeah," growled Stewart under his breath, "Ain't that just one of the things you're full of."

The two slammed outward above the still, thick grasslands, the stinger trees thinning rapidly as they approached the edges of Byanntia's great desert. Nearing the water hole Joseph had remembered as one of Chad's favorite location marks, he nudged his cycle to a lower speed, his eyes sectioning off and scanning the horizon block by block. After a moment, he said, "Hey, over there by that stinger ..."

Joseph gunned his engine, heading toward whatever he had spotted. Stewart followed his older brother, staring more at the dangerous plant than anything around it. Stinger leaves and the tree's younger branches made good eating while still green, but most of the planet's inhabitants

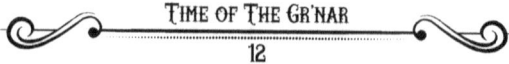

avoided them. They were far too wary of the tiny, spear-like barbs the plants could release at intruders to attempt to use them for even the occasional meal.

"Glory in the morning," mused the older brother. "What in Hell did that?"

At the base of the tree lay a scatter of kison bones—broken, sucked dry, blood splashed everywhere. Oddly, the bones were completely stripped—every vestige of muscle, cartilage and fat removed as if boiled away. Something more disturbing caught Joseph's attention. The ground was littered with stingers. Soil, grass, even the bones had been pierced. In the center of the fallout from the tree, however, there sat a semi-circle of clear ground. Untouched.

As if, thought Joseph, part of his mind refusing the notion he already knew must be true, whatever did this just sat there feeding ... like the stingers didn't bother it.

"So, where's the rest of it?" asked Stewart. "Jing me, I've never seen a kill this clean. Like the meat was vacuumed off the bones. What can do that?"

"Get back on your bike," answered Joseph, his voice cold and low, his eyes glued to the scatter of bones.

"You think the Kuzzi did it?" responded Stewart. "Doesn't look like it. I mean, they kill a kison, they bury it's heart near the kill. Don't see any dig holes here. Maybe it's not them damn aliens—maybe it's some them new settlers, tryin' to make trouble for Dad. What d'ya think?"

Joseph whirled around, confusion doubling his anger. "The Kuzzi were here first, you little shit," he snapped. "They're not the damn aliens—all right?"

"Drop it a notch, Joey."

"Shut up," barked Joseph. Climbing on his bike, the young rancher snapped a holo print of the bones and the curious stinger pattern. As the shock of what he had found began to wear off somewhat, Joseph noted several unidentifiable tracks near the vile scatter. Snapping another holo, a close-up of one of the prints, he brought them to his brother's attention.

"You see those tracks, Joe?" he asked. "You see how deep they are? How far apart they're spread? Does that give you some idea of how big this thing must be?"

Stewart's eyes went wide as realization began to seep into his consciousness. Backing toward his hovercycle in a stumbling half-shuffle, he tried to mount the bike without breaking off his gaze. When he slipped and fell, he found himself staring down the barrel of his brother's bolt gun.

"Sorry," said Joseph, changing the angle of his weapon but not holstering it. "When you yelled, I ..."

"No, no," answered Stewart quietly. "It's okay. Maybe we best just hug some cloud, huh?"

"Yeah," said Joseph. As the two took their cycles quickly to a safer altitude, the older brother checked his power box. He wanted to make certain he not only got proper storage on the holograms he snapped, but that he had enough juice for a non-stop flight back to the ranch.

"I-I hope Chad didn't run into this thing," stammered Stewart.

"I'm sure the others have already found him," lied Joseph. Eyeing the horizon nervously, he added, "But let's get back to the ranch anyway. It is getting dark."

***

"What d'ya mean, Doc?" Angry denial and fear scratched at Jacob Matson, tearing at him, struggling to reduce him to the minor stature of ordinary men. "You're sayin' I got some disease forty years ago from the flight here to Byanntia that's gonna kill me now?"

"That's roughly it, Jacob," answered the doctor, unable to comprehend how circumstances could have brought him to a moment where he would need to pity a man like Jacob Matson.

His patient fumed for a moment, lost in the struggle to understand what he had just been told. Matson was angry, yes—but not with his doctor. The rancher was angry with his own mortality, with the universe's incredibly bad timing, with the fact that his unbeatable luck had finally dried up.

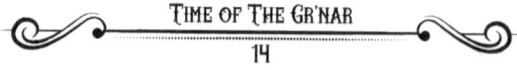

"So what's the solution?"

"There is none, Jacob," answered the doctor in a quiet voice. "There's just nothing we can do. Medical science didn't know about the effects of wave distortions forty years ago. You were the man on monitor duty while everyone else was shielded in their cyro-tubes. You took the hit."

"And these waves, they aged me thirty years? But I still looked ..."

"It was your organs, Jacob." The doctor wore his traditional white jumpsuit under his all-weather range coat. Standing on the porch of the Twin Feathers ranch house, he tried to make his patient understand what had happened to him decades earlier. "The distortions set off chain reactions within certain nucleoids in your tissues ... it caused them to burn up at twice their normal rate. Outside, yes—you're still a man of ninety-five ... not at all old by today's standards. But internally, you're pushing a hundred and fifty."

"Can't you fix them?" asked Matson, masking his growing desperation with his usual barking voice. "Transplants? Gimme a new heart, kidneys, whatever?"

"Jacob, even if you could survive the multiple transplants, which you can't—which a twenty year old couldn't—where exactly am I supposed to get an entire set of adult male organs? Try to understand—you're crumbling inside, Jacob. You've got a year—tops. And you're luckier than most to know about it this soon."

Well, it's good to know my luck hasn't deserted me, after all, thought the patriarch of Twin Feathers with mocking humor. Resignation dispelling his unaccustomed fear, the thin, white-haired man took his doctor's hand in honest gratitude.

"Thanks, Doc. At least it gives me a year to get Chad squared away on runnin' the ranch—and a year to make sure there's no diz'n squatters on my land when I'm gone." When the doctor gave his patient a stern look, Matson merely chuckled.

"Oh, boohoo—stare all you want. What're they gonna do, Doc? Put a dead man in the lock?"

The doctor was about to answer when Matson's wife Shelby came out onto the porch. Her long straight silver hair still caught the late afternoon sun the way it did when she was a teenager, thought her husband. He looked at her intently, staring past her kison hide tunic dress and native Kuzzi jewelry, wondering for a moment how many more times he would be able to see her this way—realizing his days for doing everything important were suddenly, abruptly, finite.

"Why, Doc Lieber," she said in a voice still rich with the twang of Earth. "I didn't know you were here. And, Heavens, with a set of empty hands yet." Shooting her husband a playful frown, she added, "You must think Twin Feathers' hospitality severely lacking. What can I get you?"

"Nothing this time, Shelby, I was just leaving."

"Oh, well then," answered the woman, understanding the looks on both men's faces, "why don't you take just a minute to tell me what brought you all the way out here from New Dodge if it wasn't my cooking?"

"I'll be deferring to the honorable Mr. Matson on that question, ma'am," answered the doctor as he slid his wide-brimmed hat back on his balding head. Buttoning his range coat, he said, "But I'll prime the pump by asking you to go easy on this old goat of yours."

The Matson's watched the doctor as he made his way down the functional, cut stone steps of the ranch house to his Terrain Hugger. The silver hovercar lifted to a standard nine meter height and then silently began the journey back to New Dodge City. Staring into her husband's eyes, Shelby Matson could see that something far worse than she could imagine was waiting for her.

Steadying herself for the worst, she asked, "All right, what's up between you and the Doc? And don't even think of passing on some of your usual runaround. I've been stuck with you too many years, raised too many kids and built this ranch up from nothing with you, so give it out and don't hold off on the bumpy parts of the ride."

"Plain and simple, bride, I've finally found that something I always knew was out there—that something I can't bend with my own two hands or think my way around." When white fire danced across Shelby's eyes, Matson told her, "Let's go inside ... we need to talk."

The two moved as one, the door closing silently behind them.

***

By the time Joseph and Stewart returned to Twin Feathers, the darkness outside matched the black moods in their young hearts. They were half caught up in worry over their older brother, half awash in terror that they might already know what had happened to him. The pair found their parents sitting on the sandboard couch in the den of the ranch's central house. Joseph noted that his mother had been crying.

"You guys are pretty worried about Chad, aren't you?"

"Yeah," answered their father, agreeing with the minor truth in order to keep his larger one concealed for the moment. "I take it you two didn't have any luck."

"No, sir," responded Joseph. "And it's too dark now to keep looking. You still didn't find anyone who's seen him?"

"Not yet," said Shelby as she rose from the couch, straightening her dress. "But I still think he's just wandered into Dodge to see his new girlfriend."

"Girlfriend?" exploded Stewart. "Don't tell me he's gone loopey over some squatter."

"Well," admitted their mother, "I don't think she's the daughter of any of the First—Chad said her name is Delilah Carter, which is not a name I remember from the *Triumphant's* logs."

"Jing me," sneered Stewart. "Chad dancin' dizzy over some tramp freighter whore ..."

"Stew ..."

"You're gonna defend him, Joey?" snapped Stewart. "For dinkin' with some runaway who jinked her family back on Earth. That's just what we need for Chad to bring home, some selfabsorb who's only claim to glory is deserting her own."

"Cool down, runt, we got more important business right now." Turning back to his father, Joseph said, "Dad, Stew and I found a fresh kison kill on the south range I think you'd better take a look at."

"Son," responded Matson with a edgy weariness, "I got a little more on my mind that ..."

"You're going to have to trust me on this," interrupted Joseph as he inserted the holo he had shot out on the plains into the computer console there in the den. With the tabbing of a few commands, Joseph filled the center of the den with a three-dimensional image of the grizzly scene.

"What in the world ..."

Jacob Matson's voice trailed off as he studied the image in the middle of the room. He scratched his head with wonder, his illness suddenly completely forgotten. Joseph tabbed for a new image, telling his father, "There's more."

A second holo he had shot of one of the footprints came into focus next to the first image. Matson sat back on his haunches, studying the image before him as closely as he would if he were in the presence of the real thing. His left hand strayed to his face, pulling at his clean-shaven chin.

"I helped map this world, catalog its life forms," he mused, his eyes never leaving the monstrously large track. "There's nothin' here anywhere near big enough to have done this to a full grown kison—nothing that leaves tracks like this." The patriarch turned to his wife.

"Not even a pack of yappers could've done this. Nothing cleans bones like this ... you know the Kuzzi better'n anyone, sweetheart. Could they have done this—maybe for one'a their ceremonies or somethin'?"

"Not that I know of," Shelby told her husband. "They only eat meat once a month—and that's just for religious observance. Besides, they don't have the technology to strip bone that clean. Jing, I'm not certain even we actually can do such things—out in the middle of nowhere I mean."

"Yeah," grumbled Matson. "And even if they did, they didn't leave that barkin' track. Did they?"

No one argued with the patriarch. Standing slowly, his eyes not leaving the holograms, Matson started giving orders. As was expected, everyone listened.

"Joe, alert the hands. Play 'em the holos. Then tell 'em we'll be standin' watch tonight. Get 'em to throw up the perimeter shields, too. Just a ten klik relay, for now—let's not start throwin' money away by the bushelful."

"Yes, sir," answered Matson's oldest surviving son. As Joseph headed out of the room, his father turned to his mother.

"Shelby," Matson ordered, "you call Sheriff Duncan. Let him know what's going on. Flash him a copy of the holos. Make sure he throws the image out onto the landholder relay, too—this is not the kind of thing we'd want to be keeping a secret. And see if he's got any word on Chad yet."

As she moved to the ranch's comm center, Matson told Stewart, "Boy, you make certain every man standin' watch has some iron to fill their fist. Pass out the repeller rifles—make those mushheads depo a thumbprint for 'em—and if those run out, break out whatever bolt throwers we have crated."

"Yes, sir," answered Stewart leaving the room at a run. Turning back to his wife, Matson told her,

"We'll form up search parties in the morning. We'll find Chad. And, if there's some thing out there, we'll find it, too. And we'll deal with it."

Shelby nodded in her husband's direction as she waited for the line to the Sheriff's office to clear. Staring at Matson, she could not help but be impressed anew with his grace under pressure. Never in the military nor ever elected to any kind of official office, still he was the kind of man who could think on his feet, who when he gave a command did not think twice about its being carried out. Shelby Matson knew the pressures tearing at her husband—concern about Twin Feathers, about Chad, about his failing health, and now this new mystery—and she marveled at how he could put his mind so coldly in order.

Then, Sheriff Duncan's rough, but smiling face suddenly filled the comm screen. Shelby Matson fought back the tears she knew would return soon enough, and quietly began letting the lawman know what had happened.

***

"Nope," said Sheriff Duncan into his commlink, "Pete hasn't seen Chad today, Mrs. Matson, nor anyone else, neither. I put the word out on the relay, but no one's called in. I'll put another pass on the system, though, make sure everyone on the vine keeps a scan out for him."

"Thank you, Sheriff," came Shelby's delicate twang over the lawman's office link.

"No, ma'am, our thanks to you and Mr. Matson for word on what your boys found. You'll pardon me, but I'm afraid this might be serious. I'd best be about getting busy and letting folks know about this."

Duncan and Shelby made their goodbye and then the lawman shut down his connection to Twin Feathers while keeping his link open. Turning to his second-in-command, Pete Dawson, a large man with a thick, black beard, the sheriff told him, "Well, you saw the same holos I did, let's get moving. We've got to put the town on alert—and the outlying spreads, too. Probably even more important they all understand what we know so far. Tell Bennie to find that hunter that checked into town last night—Sanders, in the Naha Palace—get him over here to look at this track."

"Sure, chief," responded Pete. "But why don't I just relay it over to him?"

"Because if he looks at it in his hotel room, then I don't get to study him while he studies it. Comprende, He-Who-Needlessly-Questions-Authority?"

The deputy nodded. The big man had to admit that the Sheriff was always one step ahead of him, if not two. His hand on the doorknob, he stopped to ask one extra question.

"Chief, it's just a thought, but isn't Matson in a land dispute with some new immigrants right now?"

"I see where you're going and it's a good point," admitted the sheriff, "but that's not Jacob's style." Pete pulled at his chin a moment, then agreed.

"That's true, I guess. If Jacob Matson wanted to put a scare into a bunch of tent squatters, he wouldn't have to invent no mystery critter. He's scary enough for that all on his own."

The sheriff laughed. His deputy smiled with deserved pride. It was not often he was that quick with his wits.

"Yeah," Duncan nodded, then paused to think. Turning back to Pete, he said quietly, "Of course, that means then that we're dealing with something weird enough to scare Jacob Matson."

Pete's eyes grew a touch larger. Duncan knew how he felt. Cutting off their conversation before more time was wasted, the sheriff ordered, "Better set up a perimeter curfew for the entire town. Let everyone know we'll be activating the shields at eleven."

His second-in-command nodded, his evening suddenly becoming something in danger of spinning beyond his control. Grabbing desperately at his imagination, Pete managed to get it under control enough to keep himself from shaking. Then, the sheriff added, "And Pete, before you go outside, strap on a repeller."

The bearded man nodded, shoving his hands deep within his pockets to stifle their vibrations.

***

Dim lights still glowed inside most of the tents, creating a rough circle of illumination in the vast blackness of the open range. Stars only vaguely dotted the night sky, most of those usually visible hidden along with the moon by an ever-thickening cloud cover. Still, the air was warm and sweet enough to make it a beautiful night—the kind that could make dreamers out of cynics, or lovers out of friends.

Delilah Carter stroked a comb through her golden hair as she sat on a folded blanket before the encampment's central fire. A small bolter strapped to her ankle broke the innocent beauty of her pose. Her friend, Lina Dotson, sat next to her on the blanket. The only other person still at the central fire was Joel Goldstein, a young man who had come out on the same freighter as the two women. The trio soaked in the warmth of the fire, dreaming of the land they had come so far to conquer.

"I wish we could've brought a dog with us."

"A dog?" asked Joel. "What for?"

"It just seems like there should be dogs here," answered Delilah as she stared past the lonely camp fire to the stinger grove beyond. "With the prairies so wide and open and all—this place just looks like it was built for dogs."

"Contradict," said Lina. "if there were dogs here, they'd be barking at every little noise in the night. You ask me, no yapping dogs was one of the few things this place got right."

"That and the opportunity for unlimited wealth," piped in a smiling Joel.

"Joel wouldn't care if we were ass-deep in wolves, as long as there was a credit to be made," teased Delilah. "Would you?"

"I'm sure some use could be made of the little puppies," answered the girl's fellow squatter. "It just takes a bit of entrepreneurial vision."

"Uh-huh," said Lina. "So, what're you going to call your big ranch when it finally gets built? Something native sounding?"

"Native, huh?" answered Joel with mock seriousness, as if actually considering the woman's words. "Guess I'll have to go ask the Kuzzi what a good name for my camp would be."

"Oh, sure," snickered Delilah. "You do that. I hear they're all nice and tucked away in their summer lodge now, up on the Northwestern side of Twin Feathers. Chief Bollatu's sure to help you. I hear he's real nice—for an alien, that is."

"Have you seen them?" asked Lina with a shiver. "The Kuzzi, I mean? What do they even look like?"

Joel interrupted. Folding his arms across his chest, puffing himself up like a family elder about to explain the secrets of the ages, he said, "The shopkeeps in Dodge say they look like a cross between Earth tigers and Barovian Arctic shamblers."

"And what," asked Delilah with a frown, "are Barovian Arctic shamblers?"

"Well, Barovia's an ice planet—I mean a real ice planet. Only life on it keeps to a pretty small band that runs around the planet at the equator. Which makes 'Arctic' something of a misnomer, I guess. Anyway, they're pretty ugly devils—sorta like gorillas, 'cept they're all white and completely covered with fur. Got like a dog snout 'stead of a mouth, good sense of smell, omnivorous ..."

"Ohh, big word," teased Lina.

"Ain't the only thing that's big about me," bragged Joel. Delilah gave him a rough push toward the fire that let him know his humor was not appreciated. Pretending not to notice, the young man continued with his semi-lecture.

"They're pretty intelligent, too. Level Two, on the Mondervian scale, really just one step beneath humans. They're tool-users—even actually construct temporary dwellings out of pack snow. They make domes out of it, then they burrow down into the soil underneath. It's how they hunt for tubers, small animals, that kind of thing. Supposedly they maintain pretty strict family units and even proper communities."

"Can you imagine being the explorer who first lived with those things to catalogue their biology and culture and the such?" asked Delilah with a laugh.

"Not for me," answered Joel. "I'll pass on livin' with overgrown albino monkeys."

"Me, too," agreed Lina. "With my luck they'd want to cross-breed and start a new species."

"Like you wouldn't cross mate with anything that had the right equipment and the price of a hot meal."

Lina turned her back on Joel. She was about to throw a playful insult back at him when she noticed the look on Delilah's face. Her friend was staring at the commlink on her wrist, lost in thought. Hoping to pull her back into the conversation, she guessed,

"Waiting for Chad to call?"

"I haven't heard from him all day. I hope he's all right."

"Probably lost track of the time, sitting up in his ranch counting all of Daddy's credits." Breaking out his cigarettes, Joel reassured his friend, "Don't worry about that nabob. He's got it bad for you. He'll be ..."

Joel went quiet as a strong, unknown scent wafted into camp. It was a pungent smell, a gagging cross between cinnamon and rotting meat. Joel held off lighting his cigarette, squinting his eyes as he tested the air, trying to catch another whiff of the odd aroma.

"What's wrong, Joel?" asked Lina.

"Not sure," answered the young man as he strained to see through the darkness beyond the ring of tent and campfire light. "Just a smell, I guess."

Joel turned back toward the two women. Lifting his cigarette once more to his still smiling mouth, he struck his lighter, saying, "Thought I saw a some kinda shadow moving out beyond the tents, but I guess—"

Words stopped. Joel's cigarette shot forward out of his mouth, propelled by a stream of blood and darker fluids. His eyes bulged, his voice spasmed a short scream, and then his chest erupted in three spots, more blood and bits of bone spraying across Lina and Delilah. The two women screamed at the scarlet touch.

Heads poked out of tents. The muzzles of bolt guns followed. As people watched in disbelief, Joel's body lifted off the ground and flew through the air, landing in the fire. The impact extinguished half the blaze instantly. In the remaining light, Delilah saw uniform, advancing puffs of dust rising from the trampled ground as if something were approaching her. The young woman stood frozen, even as two men ran up to her, demanding an explanation, intersecting the path of the oncoming billows.

The first man crumpled, his sides pushing inward, his head flying away from his body. As his mate turned toward the horrible sight, invisible blades seemed to pierce him with violent force. His body flew apart in huge bloody slices, his spine lifted out of his body then catapulted into the air.

Delilah ran. A terrible roar split the night behind her, followed by scream after scream that she recognized, all of them silenced abruptly one by one. Gun shots exploded. Children wailed. Then, before she had gone twenty yards, Delilah was hit in the side of the head by something flying through the air.

She did not know what it was—just something small but heavy that stunned her so violently she could not keep her feet. Stumbling into the torn remains of someone's tent, she floundered in the canvas rags, then stumbled off into the darkness. She wandered dazed into the night, then finally succumbed to the throbbing pain in her temple.

At the edge of an embankment the young woman fell in a sad tangle, blackness sliding over her mind. Sliding down the gentle slope, all she heard as she slipped into unconsciousness were more gun shots, and the pitiful screams of the dying. Before she passed out, though, even those had faded, replaced by the rhythmic snorting of something large— something that slurped and belched and chewed far too loudly.

***

Sunrise was still several minutes away as the Matson's ate breakfast. Eggs, bacon, biscuits thick with honey and butter and crisp potatoes spiced with sliced peppers and onions sat in platters spread across the synthetic oak table there in the kitchen. Twin Feathers was a working ranch, a place that demanded a full day's work from everyone—hard work that required full loads of calories. None of the Matson's seemed to be able to work up their regular appetites, however.

"I'm sure the sheriff will send some men to search the squatter's camps for Chad at first light, sweetheart," said the elder Matson, trying to cheer his worried wife.

"He'd better," answered Shelby, her jaw muscles tense, taunt. "I'm worried about my boy."

"He's no boy, anymore," said Matson softly, encircling her left hand with his right. "He's twenty-one and growin' bigger every day and he's bustin' to let the world know who he is. He'll be all right."

The elder Matson tried to sound reassuring, but the effort was telling. The lines in his old face were deeper that morning than ever. It was obvious he had not slept well. Attempting to put his wife at ease, he told her,

"At worst he had some trouble with his hovercycle ... had to spend the night using his range coat as a tent. Hell, why not? That's what the things are for—right? Do him some good, toughin' him up some more."

"And a range coat is going to protect Chad against that thing that's out there?"

"Now," answered Matson, cautiously, not wanting to upset his wife but seeing no logical way around doing so, "we don't know what's out there. All we have is a footprint and some skinned bones that could've ..."

"My boy is in danger," shouted Shelby, her normally sweet voice suddenly thin and ugly. "And all you want to do is waste time feeding your face."

Jacob Matson's head moved back as if stung. Coldly, he dropped his knife and fork onto his plate as he rose and headed for the door without a word. Scrambling up from the table, Joseph and Stewart hurried after their father.

Grabbing up his kisonboy hat, Joseph said, "This is just typical Chad behavior, Dad. Impulsive, self-centered—it's why he'll never be able to run Twin Feathers. He's got no sense of responsibility—not to mention the fact the range hands won't ever respect a word he says."

"Then they can find somewhere else to work if they don't like who I put in charge of my ranch."

"What about Stew and me?" asked Joseph. "We have to live here, too."

Matson stopped in his tracks, his head sinking to his chest. Stifling the boil of rage festering within him, he turned slowly toward his son. His eyes hard slits, he growled his words in a low, dark voice.

"You'll get your share of Twin Feathers when you're of age. 'Til you're twenty-one, you'll be Chad's responsibility."

"Chad's gonna be the boss of me?" exploded Stewart. "I got no bang with Chad, but what's the deal? Why would I have to take orders from him? What are you gonna do, Dad, whittle a rocker and just go dreamy on the front porch or somethin'?"

Matson ground his teeth for a half a moment, anger pounding the inside of his skull. He was worried about his son, worried about his wife and what her fears were doing to her, worried about how Twin Feathers would survive with him dead. Now his other boys wanted to give him something else to worry about. Putting his hand on the front door's bolt, he drew it and opened the door full as he said,

"You two go back and talk with your mother. Let her tell you where I'll be when you're ungrateful asses turn twenty-one!"

"Jezz, Dad ..."

"I didn't ..."

"Jacob, don't—"

Matson put his head up, the burning glare in his eyes silencing his family. Staring at his wife, he told her cruelly, "Sorry, Shelby, I'd love to tell them all about the Doc's visit, but I wouldn't want to waste any more time while your boy might be in danger."

Matson stormed out of the ranch house slamming the door behind him. Both Joseph and Stewart were hesitant to follow him. Turning to their mother for some kind of answer, both stared at her while Joseph asked, "What did he mean, Mom?"

Shelby Matson tried to contain herself as her sons approached. She looked from them to the table, her gaze resting on her husband's plate. She stared at his half-eaten breakfast, at the knife and fork tossed carelessly into the cooling food, and then she noticed his biscuit.

She had made his favorite type that morning—standard white flour pan-biscuits with a slice of cheese melted in the center. Matson's mother had made them for him when he was a boy back on Earth. Every few weeks, Shelby surprised her husband with a pan of them. He always lathered one with butter and jelly and then let it sit on his plate until he was finished with everything else.

The biscuits were his special treats, and he enjoyed them like nothing else. Shelby Matson looked at the biscuit there on her husband's plate, smeared with butter and jelly—cold and untouched. Then, while her sons watched in confusion, the woman raised her hands to her face and began to cry.

***

Sheriff Duncan and Alan Sanders led the lawman's five deputies out onto the range, leaving the familiar surroundings of New Dodge City behind.

"We'll check all the most likely places the squatters might have set up shop for the night," said the sheriff.

"Good thing about lots of people," answered the hunter, "they leave lots of tracks. Should make things easy."

"I think so," agreed Duncan. "We'll find 'em before noon—guaranteed. Now, maybe Chad tried to go out and give them a little trouble and got in over his head. Most likely, what with the rumors about a certain blonde in this new batch in from Earth, he's probably gotten himself mixed up in something, but it's probably nothing we have to worry about."

"Naw," added Pete Dawson, "not until Chad's a daddy and his mom starts screaming about whoretrash being shipped out on the next freighter."

"Don't see why we gotta babysit some rich snot brat, anyway," added Ben Fogerty.

"Ben," the sheriff said quietly to his youngest deputy, "the Matson's pay their taxes, and therefore your salary, just like everyone else. They file a missing persons report, we follow up on it. You got a problem with doing your job all of a sudden?"

"No, sir," answered Ben with a hasty gulp.

"Fine." The sheriff kicked his hovercycle into a low gear and headed upward to a standard cruising elevation. As the others rose up beside and behind him, he added, "Well, with no further debate being necessary, let's see if we can't get this over with clean and fast and easy."

All seven of the men rode in silence after that, each of them scanning the grasslands around them in all directions. None of them said anything further about Chad Matson. None of them mentioned the holograms they had studied before leaving, either. They all kept their eyes peeled, though. And one hand on their weapons.

∗∗∗

Shelby Matson pulled her dark brown range coat tightly around herself as she stepped from the ranch house porch. Her hovercycle was waiting at the bottom of the steps along with two others. Joseph and Stewart stood alongside, waiting for their mother.

"Are you sure we should be doin' this, mom?" asked Joseph.

"Yes, son. I do. I've studied the Kuzzi since your father and I first got to this planet. Chief Bollatu is a friend of mine. Maybe he'll have some idea about where Chad is. Maybe he'll know something about those bones and that track you found. And if they don't know anything, well ..." Shelby took a deep breath as she slung her left leg up over her hovercycle's seat, "if nothing else at least we'll be doing something."

Shelby's foot came down with practiced ease, kicking her cycle into gear. Elevating quickly, she shouted, "You two coming or not?"

Then she leaned into a curve, spinning herself smoothly around the side of the ranch house, heading for the Northwestern boundary of the ranch. Whether her boys were following or not, she really did not care. Right then all she wanted was the feel of air rushing against her face and body. And to see her eldest son. She would never stop wanting her son to come home. Despite the fact that she was already certain he would never come home again.

∗∗∗

The usual spew of blue dust fled from the approach of Jacob Matson's hovercycle as it neared the ground. The sun was halfway across the sky, but still the rancher had seen no traces of Chad. The patriarch had moved across Twin Feathers in an orderly fashion, making a methodical sweep of his land. Frustrated by the lack of results practicality was producing, Matson swung his cycle around, heading south instead.

It had suddenly dawned on him that on the day before, Joseph and Stewart had been heading for the southern watering hole to look for Chad when they had been sidetracked by the discovery of the bones and the bizarre tracks. Checking the level on the waterhole had been one of Chad's duties the day before.

Not exactly rational, Jacob, the back of his mind whispered to the elder rancher. Why the water hole? With a grim note of despairing finality, Matson told himself;

"Even monsters have to drink."

Another thirty minutes put the rancher within visual range of the waterhole. Light reflecting above the water line told Matson he was on the right track. He sounded his cycle's horn on the way in, but no response was forthcoming. As he neared, he could see that what he had spotted was a hovercycle. This one seemed to have hit an outcrop of rock near the waterhole, then flipped over backward and fallen into the pool.

The rancher slowly circled the remains of the hovercycle twice. Once he was certain that it was his son's vehicle, and that no one was pinned beneath it, he backdropped his own cycle to the shore, unholstering his bolter as he landed. The half dozen kison ranged along the shore continued drinking, undisturbed by neither the machine nor its rider's approach.

At first Matson inspected the ground near the edge of the waterhole, hoping against hope that he might find some tracks that would give him a clue as to what had happened. As he expected, the ground, long baked by the dry winds constantly coming in off the Junsuka offered nothing in the way of information. With a long sigh, Matson waded into the warm water to retrieve the downed cycle, hoping it might offer some sort of explanation.

Halfway there, his boot came in contact with something hard—something that hadn't been on the bottom of the waterhole long enough to be sucked down into its grasping, muddy bottom. Jacob Matson closed his eyes, his chest jumping involuntarily. His mouth a thin, tight line, he bent toward the water, his head shaking softly as his fingers closed on whatever he had kicked. When the rancher finally opened his eyes again, he stared at the object in his hand—a dripping, human skull stripped of its meat.

Sinking to his knees, Jacob Matson cried the tears for his son that the day before he could not find for himself.

***

Alan Sanders rode nearly a half a kilometer out in front of the sheriff and his deputies. While those following him were maintaining a safety height of some thirty feet, Sanders stayed less than four feet from the ground, his cycle barely skirting the high grass. The hunter was searching for clues, true enough, but it was not the reason he was doing so in such a risky fashion. Sanders was a hunter. A decade earlier he had left his family and friends and all he knew behind on Earth to seek the thrill of tracking new and different life forms. He lived for the hunt. It was his life, his reason for being.

Sanders did not necessarily have a need to kill those things he hunted. It did not bother him, of course, spilling the blood of brute animals, but slaughter held no great thrill for him, either. Plunging into oceans, ranging across mountain tops, tracking all manner of beasts in forests, lakes or through the skies, it was the chase that filled the hunter with passion. Rooting them out, finding them no matter how they hid themselves, beating creatures designed by the whimsical natures of a thousand different worlds at their own games—that was what Alan Sanders lived for. It was why he had come to Byanntia in the first place.

This is it, he thought, his lips unable to keep from curling into a smile. The old rummer was right. This is going to wrap the past in a ball and trash it. The whole droking universe is going to know my name after this.

Sanders could not forget his good fortune. Months earlier he had run into one of the few Kuzzi warriors that had ever left Byanntia. For the price of three drinks, the old alien had told the hunter the story of the Gr'nar. Sanders had not been certain he believed the trembling sot, but he was a good judge of beings—human or not, sober or drunk. Even if he was being misled, Byanntia had promised to hold enough new creatures to at least give him some well-needed practice. Zoos, scientists, collectors—there was always someone looking for something different. He knew he could force a profit out of any new planet. Then, on his second day on-world, he had been called by the local lawman who had shown him the footprint—a mark revealing design characteristics common in creatures possessing both strength and speed. The footprint screamed to him—carnivore. Predator.

And, he speculated, if even half of what that wrinkled drunk told me is true, this is ...

Sanders stopped speculating, his mind going instantly on the alert. Something still and bright had caught his attention, something living, but motionless, perched halfway down a sloping ridge off in the distance. The hunter raised his arm to indicate to those following that he had found something, then gunned his engine heading straight for it at top speed.

As he drew nearer, the distance setting of his goggles focused on the object. It was a blonde woman in a yellow jumpsuit laying face down in the scruff. Sanders studied the terrain as he closed on the unmoving figure. His instincts told him it was safe to approach. He could feel that nothing was lurking nearby waiting to pounce.

The hunter rolled the woman onto her back, brushed the hair out of her face. Her pulse was normal. She was alive, but her breathing was shallow. Fearing she might be in a coma, Sanders pulled his canteen from his cycle and splashed her face, washing away the caked blood smearing her forehead.

"Is she alive?" asked Duncan as he set his hovercycle down next to the pair.

"Yes," acknowledged Sanders. Pointing toward the woman's head, he said, "As best I can see so far, she only has a single wound on her left temple—here—as if she was struck a blow. She's lost blood, but I her color's good, so I don't think it was much. She's probably not too badly off."

"Was it the thing?" asked Pete.

"No," answered the hunter. Pointing up the slope, he said, "look at the scuff marks. That's her trail. She slid down over the edge from above. Probably fell during the night. She got here on her own, then collapsed."

Duncan sent two of his men up the hillside to see where the tracks came from. The two started up the gradual slope carefully. The hillside was a mixture of baked clay and sand. One wrong step would send a climber sliding back to the bottom in an unstoppable rush. Knowing it would take his men a few minutes to make their ascent, the sheriff turned his attention back to the others. As he did, the girl suddenly responded to Sander's ministrations. She sat up quickly, then yelped as she winced from the pain in her head.

"You'd better take it easy," cautioned the sheriff.

"It killed them," she said simply in a quiet monotone. "Tore them all to pieces. Threw them around like dolls. It smashed them and cut them and, and, and it, it ..."

Then the blonde woman went silent once more. Leaning against Sanders, she stared forward unblinking, either lost in thought, or in the avoidance of it. The hunter asked Duncan, "Any idea who she is?"

"Delilah something or other," answered the sheriff, searching his memory. "Squatter. Bunch of about thirty came out together from Earth a couple of months back. Romantic idiots, in love with the notion of the Old West, or something. Thought they were all goin' to be range kings in six weeks. Mostly they've just been sort of a nuisance to the real ranchers. This one don't have any family if I remember correctly."

"Brave kid," said Sanders, sympathetically, "coming out here on her own."

"From what I hear tell, she didn't have much choice. Step-father back on Earth taking advantage, mother not sticking up for her ... just decided one day that anything was better than that, and she joined up with a group that needed another body to tally their bulk passage."

Sanders did not feel the same level of disdain for the girl that the sheriff obviously did. With a modicum of admiration in his voice, he said, "Still, when you're in a bad situation, it takes guts to do something about it instead of just taking it. Even running away is better than doing nothing."

"It came into our camp last night," the girl said in a droning voice. Still unblinking, unmoving, she rambled, "It killed everyone. Everyone.

Blood everywhere." Then, she turned her head, her eyes seeming to focus on Sander's face.

"We couldn't do anything to stop it—stop the blood. Nothing can stop it."

"Delilah," Sanders spoke slowly and clearly in a friendly, fatherly tone. "Why couldn't you stop the creature? Was it too large? Too strong? Too fast?"

"Don't know."

"You don't know what, Delilah?"

"Don't know how big, or fast. Don't know anything about it."

The sheriff's eyes closed to slits. His look caught Sander's eyes, but the hunter did not turn his attention away from the girl nestled against his arm. As she continued to look up at him, Sanders asked, "Why, Delilah? Why don't you know anything about the creature?"

"Couldn't see it."

"Because it was so dark?" suggested Duncan.

"No," answered the girl calmly. "Plenty of light from the fire. Just couldn't see it."

Suddenly the sheriff's attention was drawn to the top of the ridge. His men had reached the top and were signalling frantically for the others to join them. Duncan headed for his hovercycle, calling up to his deputies as he walked across the plane.

"What is it? What d'ya find?"

"It's a camp, sheriff. What's left of one. There's bodies everywhere. Bones, too. Human. Lots of 'em. It's pretty fierce up here."

"We couldn't see it."

Sheriff Duncan stopped and spun around at the girl's voice. Angrily, he growled at her, "Listen up, you little fool. Start makin' some sense. What the hell attacked you people? What was it? Tell us, for God's sake. You said there was plenty of light. Well, if there was plenty of light, why couldn't you see what it was that killed all your friends?!"

"Because," answered Delilah in the same cold, absent voice. "It was invisible."

***

Shelby Matson and her sons flew through the entrance to the Valley of the Twelve Peaks. Ahead of them, two Kuzzi tribesmen stood guard over the narrow passageway. Even after more than twenty years on Byanntia, Shelby still felt her breath catch at the sight of the native warriors. The pair on guard were typical specimens—both roughly eight and a half feet tall, with short coats of horizontally striped fur covering their bodies.

The blue, black and grey markings were a natural camouflage that blended well with the alien landscape. The male's heads were surrounded by a thick and glossy black mane. A single stripe, usually black, parted their foreheads and muzzles while other colors varied across the individual Kuzzi's faces. Their chins and jaws were covered with the longer black fur of their mane, setting off their muzzles which were accented by hard, blue lips.

Most Kuzzi males had very broad shoulders as well as chests that rippled with layers of muscles. They were generally short-waisted, with powerful, backward jointed legs. Their forward facing feet were quite human in design, save for their feline toes and claws. Their hands followed along much the same lines.

The two Kuzzi on guard were using their hands at the moment, holding their purjungs—long spears with multiple curved blades—to the ready. Shelby and her boys knew what their poses meant. Dismounting their hovercycles, translator headsets already adjusted and in place, the trio bowed formerly, then Joseph and Stewart stood back as their mother addressed the guards.

"I am Shelby Matson, come with my sons to seek an audience with Chief Bollatu. We desire his council on a most important matter which not only concerns us, but the Kuzzi nation as well."

"Wait here," answered the taller of the guards who turned and walked into the valley. The other warrior's nostrils twitched. He sniffed the air, seeking clue about the visitors' intentions. His yellow and black eyes never strayed from the trio. He knew the human woman—had seen her in council with Bollatu more than once. Her familiarity meant nothing to the guard, however. Humans were not to be trusted without caution. It had been a hard-learned lesson years earlier for the Kuzzi. There were none who wished to learn it anew.

Shelby pretended not to notice the guard's examination, choosing instead to look upward at the white and clear crystal peaks stretching hundreds of feet upward there at the edge of the valley. Sunlight was pouring through the massive quartz-like formations, creating a dazzling abundance of rainbows throughout the valley. The refracted light help disguise the entrance to the Kuzzi's fortress home, just one of the natural defenses that had made the valley the perfect shelter for the Byanntian natives for countless centuries.

The first guard returned after several long minutes. He waved Shelby and her sons inside, then escorted them through the valley to the Kuzzi marketplace. Female Kuzzi, the races' artisans and merchants, were on all sides of the quartet, buying, selling and bartering their wares. Byanntia's indigenous sentient females usually ranged from seven to eight feet in height. They were similarly marked as the males of their species, but they did not share their mates' manes or massive shoulder structure. Their smaller bodies were still layered with sinewy muscle, however.

Stewart stared at several of the females for a moment—specifically at the three pairs of small breasts that lined the chest of each. All Kuzzi went naked throughout the year, their short fur being all they required in the way of protection from the elements. Even the jewelry they crafted was mostly cerimonial and reserved for only certain times of the year. The human custom of clothing oneself confused and amused the Kuzzi. The only material used by the natives, for their pouches and litters and their great nomadic tents, came from the skin of a callosal fish that lived mostly in the northern seas. The Kuzzi word for the leviathans was unpronounceable by nearly all humans, so the Firsts had settled for renaming the great fish Melvilles.

Joseph studied the draping walls of the tent to which he and the others had been lead, looking for the telltale vein lines in the fabric. Like most humans, his contact with the Kuzzi was limited, and the idea of living in fish skins had always fascinated him. He turned his attention to their host, however, as they all entered the main chamber of the tent.

Shelby and her sons were led to the center of the room where a number of Kuzzi—male and female—sat in a circle on round mats woven from various wild grasses. As one the natives all stood and faced the ranchers. Shelby and the boys made the proper bow to which the Kuzzi responded by bowing in return, then returning to their seats. At that point, a female stepped forward from behind those seated and approached the Matsons.

"What wisdom do you seek from great Bollatu?" she asked.

"We seek several things. First, of greatest importance to me, we are searching for my son, Chad Matson. He has been missing for more than a day. We were hoping some member of the great Kuzzi tribe might have seen him."

At that point a male—older, larger than the others—stood and approached Shelby.

"No Kuzzi see your cub these past two suns, Shelby Matson." As the rancher made to interrupt, the male continued. "No Kuzzi leave the summer lodge since beginning of the summer cycle."

"But," questioned Joseph, half-confused, half-suspicious, "the Kuzzi always hunt heavily in the summer months. What's so different about this year?"

"This," answered Chief Bollatu, "is year of the Gr'nar."

"What's a grrrr-nar?" asked Stewart, repeating the foreign word as best he could.

"Gr'nar is evil god of the Junsuka. He come forth every eighth handful of cycles."

Joseph did the math quickly in his head—the Kuzzi's four-fingered paws had lead them to create a numbering system in base eight. Every sixty-four years, he thought.

"The harmony of the plains is destroyed at his approach. Blood flows. Terror fills the skies as tears flood the plains." .

Joseph did not believe a Kuzzi god was killing his father's kison—but it was a big universe. It was possible something lived on Byanntia the settlers did not know about yet. Something that followed a longer cycle than the seasons of the year.

That means, thought Joseph, if Bollatu is onto something here, the last time this happened was sixty-four years ago—decades before the First arrived.

Shelby's commlink hummed. She punched the uplink button, announcing, "Shelby Matson."

"It's Jacob, sweetheart—you got the boys with you?"

"Yes, we're at the Kuzzi summer lodge."

"Get back to Twin Feathers—now! I'll explain everything when I see you at home. Keep your guns handy and stay high off the ground. The shield will be up at the ranch, so give a drop-call at the perimeter."

"Jacob, I don't understand."

"I'm with Duncan and his deputies—we met up out at the south waterhole." His command voice softening, Matson explained, "There's something loose on the plains, Shelby. Something murderous. Warn the Kuzzi, but leave now—please."

"The Kuzzi already know."

Shelby Matson's commlink went quiet for a moment. Then her husband's voice returned, colder than before.

"I should have thought of that," he said cryptically. "You go home—take the boys with you. Tell Bollatu to expect me. I'll be there in twenty minutes."

Shelby's comm went quiet once more.

***

Sanders moved across the range by himself, his spectrum goggles constantly shifting the available light bands. Now that Duncan and his men knew the creature was invisible the hunter saw no reason to continue pretending he did not know, either. Not that the lawmen realized he had come to Byanntia equipped with prior information. Sanders had not pulled the goggles out until he was alone. The sheriff and his men had been tied down by the discovery of the slaughter at the squatters' camp. As much as the sheriff might have wanted to continue on with the hunter, his duty held him at the disaster site. The terrible attack had to be investigated—the dead catalogued.

Duncan had ordered Sanders to remain on-comm, however. The hunter was to report any sightings, as it were, of the thing that had left the barest remains of some thirty human beings on the plain above the spot where Delilah Carter had been found. The lawman had not veiled his threat of taking action against the hunter if he did not comply.

Sure, Sheriff, thought Sanders with a smirk, I'll get right to you, as soon as I've got an invisible carcass to take off this rock with me.

It had been some hours since the hunter had set out on his own, following what few tracks the thing had left behind. They had faded quickly, however, leaving Sanders to simply guess at which direction the horror might have taken. So far he had not found any indication he was getting closer to the monster of the plains. Delilah's story had put the attack on the squatter camp more than half a day previous, making what few claw prints and broken grasses Sanders had found to follow an extremely cold trail. The hunter did not mind, though. He had a plan.

The information Jacob Matson had commed to the sheriff had helped Sanders immensely. The hunter had been told by the old Kuzzi warrior that his tribe moved away from the desert into the northern mountain canyons whenever the Gr'nar was to return. Generally, the creature preferred to hunt where it was warmest. The slaughter of the squatters had taken place at an extreme southern latitude from the Twin Feathers ranch, close to the Junsuka. Matson had confirmed that his son had been killed at an extreme southern latitude from the Kuzzi summer lodge. Which meant that the creature had moved east, away from the Kuzzi lodge—toward New Dodge.

Interesting, mused the hunter. With the Kuzzi safe in their lodge for the duration, could this mean the Gr'nar knows about the changes that have taken place in its world since it last went to ground?

Spotting a shattered copse of stinger trees, Sanders dropped his hovercycle down to investigate. In the center of the ruined grove he found what he expected—the glimmeringly clean skeletal remains of half a dozen kison.

"You sure are one hungry son of a bitch," said Sanders aloud as he surveyed the carnage. The monster had eaten tons of meat in the last few days. Bending over one of the larger piles of bones, he asked, "When the hell do you stop for a breather?"

More to the point, wondered the back of the hunter's mind, when do you take a dump? Where does this thing leave its spoor? Does it ever? And how does it move about? It always leaves tracks at the kill sites, but nothing you can follow anywhere. It just shows up, kills, eats, and ...

"Disappears."

Sanders' mind dragged him back to the bar where he had met the elderly Kuzzi. That was what the alien had told him. That was why he had left Byanntia. The Gr'nar came every sixty-four years. It ate everything in sight—slaughtered every living thing in its path until the summer ended—then disappeared for another sixty-four years.

"But he said you disappear after every attack, too." Sanders spoke aloud to the fields all around him.

"So how do you do it?" he called out as he stood up from his examinations. "What's your secret? Do you fly? Burrow? Swing through the trees? Curl up into a ball and roll across the land—what? What's your gimmick?"

And then, suddenly, the ground beneath Sanders trembled slightly. As grains of sand bounced between the blades of grass, the hunter stepped quickly to his hovercycle. Pulling his over-sized Hoffman Brothers Wide-Bore from its sheath, he tabbed the sideprime calling for explosive rounds. Doing a rapid but thorough perimeter swing, Sanders scanned the grasslands in every direction, looking for some sign of the great beast.

"Come on, I know you're here somewhere," whispered the hunter, his nerve ends tingling with his favorite thrill. "It's all over now, Gr'naree. So, why don't you just come on out and make this easy on both of us so I can head back to New Dodge and start buying rounds of drinks for the house?"

With nothing moving in any direction, Sanders closed his eyes for a moment—listening. He threw his senses outward in all directions, straining to catch some tiny scrape or tread or whisper that would identify his target. The hunter could tell the creature was somewhere nearby—could *feel* the proximity of his target as he had hundreds of others on a score of other worlds. Licking his lips, he opened his eyes and whispered;

"So where are you, you bastard?"

And, as if in response, the ground beneath Sanders opened and massive, invisible fangs separated the hunter's legs from his body.

* * *

"Damn fool," cursed Duncan. Staring down at Sanders' stripped remains, he asked the stark scatter of bones, "Damn, greedy, arrogant stupid son of a bitch—how's it feel to be dead?"

When the hunter had not responded to any comm messages, Duncan had traced the retrieval signal from his rented hovercycle. Communicating with Jacob Matson on his way to search for Sanders, Duncan invited the rancher to meet him along the way.

"How's the interrogation going, sheriff?"

"Don't start on me, Jacob," snarled Duncan. "Bad enough everything else that's happened. Now I got me a dead offworlder. If you think I want a squad of Rim agents pokin' around here, you've been punchin' kison too long."

"Might be welcome," offered the rancher, spreading his hands to indicate the carnage all around them. "Considering ..."

"We'll handle this ourselves," snapped the sheriff defiantly.

"Yeah," answered Matson with a weary sigh, "we've been doin' a bang-up job so far."

Duncan stared at the elder rancher, but said nothing more. He knew Matson was not blaming him for anything. The old man only wanted to see dead the thing that had murdered his son. Deciding that continuing his investigation would be more profitable than further bickering, the

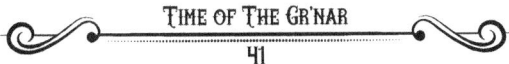

sheriff returned to studying the bones of Alan Sanders. Scratching at his head, he noted;

"I'm not sure what this means, Jacob, if anything—but did you take any notice of the fact that this yahoo's legs are far off from the rest of him?"

Matson had noticed that, but had made nothing of it. Now, at the sheriff's questioning, he turned his attention to it once more.

"All right, so the thing took his legs off first," said the rancher. "So what? What's that tell us?"

"I'm not sure it tells us anything."

"Everything we see tells us something. The question is, is it anything we need to know? Like, did you check his weapon? Did he get a shot off at this thing?"

"Nope—the entire clip still registers solid."

Matson took the weapon from the sheriff, turning it over in his hands. Making a gesture with his eyes that indicated he did not know what to make of the loaded weapon, the rancher slid it into the side sheath on his hovercycle. After that, both men stopped to think. The creature was invisible—it was possible the hunter never had a chance to frame a shot. But still, even if the thing were quiet enough to sneak up on Sanders, it might have taken a chunk out of his back, or taken off his head, or possibly an arm in its attack. But his feet?

Jacob Matson went slightly pale. Turning to Duncan, he ordered the lawman to mount his hovercycle even as he did the same. As the two men took to the air, the rancher explained.

"Look for a depression, in the ground, I mean. A hole, or burrow ... anything that looks like it was just recent filled in." It only took the two men a moment to find what they were looking for—a sunken spot in the ground nearly two feet across. Sand and loose soil had already begun to blow over it. Indeed, if the range grass had not been somewhat smashed in that area, the men would not have noticed it. As the two landed near it, Matson said, "When you reached me I was out at the Kuzzi lodge. Wanted to question them about this thing. Figured they should know more about it than we do."

The rancher broke out the short utility shovel from his hovercycle's tool bin. As he started to dig into the depression, he said, "Damn furheads didn't know shit, really—or at least they weren't sayin'. But one thing struck me funny. Whenever they referred to the thing, the translator would spit out the word 'snake.' I didn't think much of it then ..."

Suddenly, Matson's shovel hit something mixed in with the sandy soil. Less than two feet from the surface, a black core of manure began, one filled with bits of cloth.

"Well," said the rancher, his eyes narrowing to dark slits, "now we know why it doesn't seem to leave too many tracks."

***

Matson returned to Twin Feathers alone. Duncan had been forced to stay behind with Sanders' remains—an offworlder's death meant plenty of United Rim paperwork to be processed before the next Enforcement ship made port.

Well, that's his concern, thought the rancher as he landed his hovercycle in the main stable yard of his spread. I got other things on my mind. Like takin' care of the son'va bitchin' thing that killed my son.

Leaving his flier where he landed, Matson headed into the stables. Going straight to the last stall, the rancher called out to his favorite horse.

"Okay, girl—I've got a job and a half for us today. Are you ready?" The large, grey and tan saddle horse gave a nod of its head that coaxed a thin smile from Matson. As the rancher pulled down his no nonsense working saddle, he congratulated himself once more on insisting in the early days of their expedition that horse embryos be included in their cargo.

Most of the other members of the First had been happy to rely on groundcars and hovercycles, but Matson had known better. Despite their programmability, mechanical transports were not the answer to every problem presented by ranching on Byanntia. The kison were often easily spooked by machines of any kind, and hovercycles had proved disastrous on inclines of any great steepness, let alone inside the cool, but narrow range passes the kison headed for whenever the summer temperatures began to climb.

As Matson finished with his saddle's cinches, he whispered to the mare, "Besides, you're smarter than any damn computer, ain't ya, girl?"

Again the horse nodded. Matson's mouth drew to a tight line, his smile grim, lips pursed, as he nodded in return. Grabbing up Alan Sanders' Hoffman Brothers Wide-Bore, he slid it into his saddle's sheath even as he hung a good length of plas-hemp line over the horn. Then, throwing himself up into the saddle, he headed south out into the open range—ready to end things one way or the other.

***

It did not take Shelby Matson long to piece together what was happening from the clues she had. When she saw her husband's abandoned hovercycle in the main yard, then discovered his favorite mount, Dancer, missing, she knew Jacob had ridden out to track the beast. What she did not understand was why he would trade his flier for a horse. Getting Sheriff Duncan on the comm had explained that to her. Instantly she called her remaining sons to her.

"Stewart, I want you to get the hands together. Tell them that thing is still out there and moving toward New Dodge. I want Twin Feathers on triple watch tonight—every man on a cycle and scatter patrolling—full lights."

"Spit," answered the boy. "That's a lot of credits. Cheaper to run the shields at full."

"Besides being invisible, apparently the damn thing travels underground, Stew. Shields won't stop it. Tell the men to be prepared."

As both boys adjusted to the new information, their faces showing their obvious discomfort, Shelby told her oldest boy, "Your father's ridden out to find the creature. I think he ..." her voice catching, her words clogging in her throat, the woman veered off from her thought, saying instead, "you and I are going after him."

"Dad won't like us interfering with whatever he—"

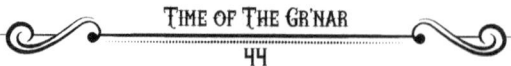

"Joseph," snapped the woman as she pulled her personal bolt thrower from a drawer in the living room desk, "I've been interfering with your father's plans whenever I damn well felt like it for a hell of a lot longer than you've been around to warn me about it. And right now he's got a pulling long lead on us, so if you want to see your father alive again I suggest we get moving."

And with that, Shelby Matson headed for the front door without bothering to look to see what her boys were doing. She knew them both. She knew what they were doing. Just as she knew what she was doing.

***

All right, you damn bastard, thought Matson, where the Hell are you, anyway?

The rancher sat atop Dancer while the mare drank from the southern water hole. Matson frowned that Chad's flier was still there, uncollected.

Well, why not? the rancher asked himself sadly. My boy's remains are still here. What difference does it make if his cycle is still here?

Matson had ridden the northern edge of the Junsuka for several hours, waiting for the Gr'nar to show itself. His assumption was that the creature had stumbled across Chad at the water hole by accident. It had wanted a drink and had found a meal instead. Chad was the only victim who had been airborne when killed. The various kison, the squatters, Sanders—all of them had been on the ground when attacked.

Duncan and his deputies and Sanders, the bunch flew over the whole area all day without a stir. But, the hunter lands for five minutes and he's dead. That damn thing can hear through the ground.

Matson pulled back on his reins, forcing Dancer to rear, making the mare stamp the ground several times hard.

"You want something to hear," he said, "hear that."

The rancher repeated the maneuver several times. Then as he paused to listen, Dancer suddenly backed off from the watering hole. The horse began spinning in short, nervous circles, throwing her head this way and that. Matson smiled. Taking the reins in one hand, he snapped them meaningfully, starting the horse toward the blue outcropping nearby.

"Knew you'd sense the damn thing, girl," he said soothingly. "Knew you wouldn't let me down."

The rancher lead the mare up onto the sloping pancake-shaped rocks, hoping he was getting the beloved animal out of harm's way. Then, he slid out of the saddle, pulling Sanders' Hoffman Brothers Wide-Bore from its sheath. The weapon held two hundred rounds, ammunition that could be primed to different functions as required. Assuming he needed real stopping power, Matson tabbed the sideprime calling for explosive rounds. Then, he dropped to one knee and waited.

The rancher kept his eye to the weapon's roving sight, watching the ground for movement. He nudged the viewfinder's automatic scanner to its highest setting, waiting for the slightest unnatural tremor in the grass. The seconds ticked by, forming one minute, then another. Matson let his eyes dart to the side for an instant, looking at Dancer. For a moment he wondered if he had misread the animal's panic. Then suddenly, he knew he had not.

A trilling roar echoed up out of the ground. As Matson wheeled in the direction of the muffled growl, the earth split open, a wide spew of soil and sand flying outward on both sides of the cavity. Closing one eye, the rancher tightened his finger on the trigger.

"Die."

Five rounds erupted from the Hoffman Brothers rifle. Matson spaced them out along a line at roughly one foot intervals. Only two of them missed their target.

"Great, jumpin' Jesus ..."

The air filled with a wild series of shrieking bellows. Spews of dark fluid erupted from seeming nothingness, splashing up and around in all directions. Dancer screamed with fear, scrambling futilely in an attempt to gain higher ground. Earth and rocks flew through the air in response to the creature's thrashing. A sizeable chunk of stone slammed into the side of Matson's head, knocking him over. The rancher did not let the injury stop him. Crawling to his knees, he fired another series of five shots. With the creature now out of the ground and thrashing wildly, only two shells of the second volley found their target. The explosive rounds blasted huge slabs of muscle and fat out of the creature's sides. The Gr'nar began to take shape as its blood coated its body, giving Matson a rough idea of the thing's form. Its body was elongated, punctuated along the sides by a series of jointed legs. The forward-most legs seemed to have the ability to lift off the ground, as if they could be used as pincers, putting the rancher in mind of an Earth scorpion.

Having a definite target, Matson fired again, carefully lining up his shots, pumping round after round into the beast. Each explosion rocked the creature, sending it staggering backward. The rancher did not shoot rapidly, but calculated each blast, firing slowly, savoring his revenge. He purposely did not fire for its head, preferring to draw out the thing's suffering. That was a mistake.

As the rancher paused to wipe the sweat from his brow, the Gr'nar threw itself to the ground, rapidly digging its way beneath the surface. Matson fired off thirty rounds in less than a second, but it was too late. The creature had disappeared from sight.

"Damn!" shouted Matson, cursing his reckless actions. "Goddamned stupidity. Idiot."

Not smart, Jacob, he thought. You had that thing—had it cold. Now what are you going to do?

Indeed, he wondered. What could he do? Dancer was still clawing away at the porous stone wall behind him, wild with fear. Could the Gr'nar dig its way upward through the rocks? Could it reach them from below? How fast could it heal? Had he done it serious, permanent damage, or had he only blown away excess outer layers—an action that might only madden the beast?

For a moment the rancher considered following the Gr'nar down its hole, but that avenue was denied to him. The walls caved in behind the creature as it retreated, explaining why none of its other burrows had been discovered without a search.

"All right," he whispered, "That won't work. So what else can we try?"

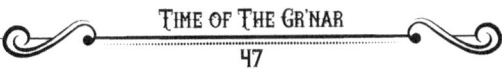

Remembering Chad's downed hovercycle, Matson decided to see if the flier was still operational. He stared at it from his position high on the outcropping. The hovercycle was still out in the waterhole, resting on its back. The rancher stood, only to go dizzy from the action. Touching the side of his head, he found it horribly tender and covered with blood. Clutching desperately to consciousness, Matson grabbed the loop of rope hanging from Dancer's saddle. Taking one last look out over the surrounding area, he hopped down to the ground in four short, careful leaps, then staggered lightly to the edge of the pool.

The front of the cycle was crunched inward, but the body of the flier seemed intact. Matson stood still for a moment, listening for the Gr'nar. No sound reached his ears except that of the hot wind washing over the prairie. Even Dancer had begun to calm down. Carefully, Matson stepped out into the pool, heading for the hovercycle. Reaching the craft in only six steps he grabbed onto its starboard runner and pulled, testing to see if it had become mired in the bottom.

Not yet, he thought as the cycle rolled over, responding fairly easily to his efforts. Checking its control array, Matson could see that the flier may have crashed, but that it was still workable.

"Don't know how much life you've got in you," he told the dripping machine, "but I'm willin' to bet you might be able to help me out here."

A touch kicked the starter to life. Bringing the hovercycle up to only a few inches above water level, Matson maneuvered the flier to the shore. Then, he set to work rigging his rope out as a snare. The rancher worked carefully, stopping every few seconds to pause and listen for his enemy. He was fairly certain the monster was not yet moving, but he could not be sure. The ringing in his ears was growing worse, his vision blurring.

Mopping the blood on the side of his head with his shirt sleeve, the rancher grabbed the hovercycle's remote control, then stepped away from his trap. Slowly, he raised the flier to a height of ten feet off the ground. Satisfied the hovercraft could hold its position, he returned to the rocks where a now quiet Dancer waited, eyeing him cautiously.

"Don't blame you, girl," he said slowly, hearing the dangerous slurring in his voice. Ignoring his injury, Matson sat down heavily on the blue rocks and once more took up the Hoffman Brothers wide bore. Tabbing the sideprime, he switched to small caliber rounds. Then, the rancher took careful aim at the center of the noose he had spread out on the ground.

A trigger pull and a small spray of sand lifted in the center of Matson's trap. The rancher counted to five then fired again.

"Com'on, you bastard. Com'on up."

Again he counted and fired. Counted and fired. Again. And again. He ignored the slick feel of blood dripping from the side of his head to his shoulder. Paid no attention to the feel of it sliding down his back.

Again he counted and fired. Again. He blinked to drive away the blurring creeping into the corners of his vision. Then he fired again. Waited and fired again.

The ground split asunder in the center of the noose. The Gr'nar broke through the surface of the ground, biting and snapping, hunting for the prey the bullet's impacts told him was there. Matson fumbled for the hovercycle's controls, instantly depressing the preset control that would lift the flier straight into the air.

The Gr'nar screamed as the noose jerked tight around its body. As the creature bellowed, the hovercycle ascended, dragging the horror up out of the ground and suspending it in the air. Dropping the flier's remote control, Matson again raised his weapon to his shoulder. The sideprime switched back to explosive, the rancher took aim as best he could and fired. His first round blasted into the body of the Gr'nar, dragging more monstrous bellows from the terrible thing. Another round followed, then another—ten more.

"That's for my boy, you piece of shit," screamed Matson. Tears filling his eyes, he screamed, "for Chad!"

He fired again, but this time no explosion met his ears. He had missed. Blinking, working desperately to focus his failing eyes, Matson saw why. Unable to escape his bond, the creature was climbing the rope upward to the hovercycle.

"No, Goddamn it!"

Matson fired again and again, but he missed the beast with most of his shots. It was moving too furiously. With much of its previous blood and soil coating scraped away when it had retreated underground the rancher could not get a bead on it. The creature was not nearly as exposed as before, and Matson's vision was clouding over. The rancher knew he might slip into unconsciousness at any moment.

"No," he growled defiantly. "If I go, you come with me!"

Then, raising his weapon higher, Matson took aim on the hovercycle's engine and put two rounds into its power chamber. The flier exploded with a roar that shook the countryside. Burning metal and plastic rained everywhere. The Gr'nar was ripped through in two score spots by the explosion. A black and purple cloud blasted across the skies as the remains of the hovercycle fell from the air, dropping the Gr'nar to the ground. Jacob Matson did not witness the event, however.

A large section of the flier's stabilization unit had struck the rancher in the chest. Matson went down on impact—hard—six ribs cracked, two shattered. Blood poured over his lips, slashing down across his chest. The rancher floundered on his side, trying to right himself. Pain tore through his body, clawing at him, dragging him back toward unconsciousness once more. Pushing the urge to surrender aside, however, Matson began to make his way slowly to the monster's side.

Wandering through the broken wreckage of the hovercycle, the rancher reached the Gr'nar only to fall to his knees when he arrived. Biting back the pain, he stared at that much of the hateful creature as was made visible through its coating of blood and dirt and soot. He was not afraid to get so close to the monster. The Gr'nar's bellows had been reduced to quiet whimpers. The thing was dying—helpless.

Matson stared into the thing's face, trying to read its expression. The rancher lifted his weapon once more while at the same time the Gr'nar made weak scrabbling motions, trying to dig its way back beneath the surface. Matson cocked his weapon. The creature responded to the audible click, staring up the barrel of the Hoffman Brothers special.

Matson hesitated, staring back at the beast. His legs shaking under him, he held his fire for a long moment, then finally he lowered his weapon and spoke softly to the Gr'nar.

"Go on," he croaked, his hate draining quietly away. "Get out of here."

Then, the rancher turned his back on the bleeding, dying horror and slowly made his way back to the outcropping where Dancer waited. Matson sat down heavily, his weapon slipping from his fingers—forgotten.

The Gr'nar was finished. He knew it. He could see in its eyes that it could only return to its hibernation in the hopes of being reborn again in its next cycle.

"Go ahead," muttered Matson. "With me dead, this place is gonna need some kind of son'va bitch in the background to keep it from goin' soft."

Maybe he was crazy, he thought, but life needed adversity. If he could handle the Gr'nar, so could whoever held Twin Feathers sixty-four years later.

"And if you can't," he spat a wad of blood defiantly into the sand, "then you don't deserve her."

The rancher could hear the whine of his wife and son's hovercycles approaching just before he passed out.

YOUNG AS THE MOUNTAINS

C.J. Henderson

"The tragedy of age is not that one is old,
but that one is young."
—Oscar Wilde

BOLLATU STOOD AT THE WATER'S EDGE, STARING OUT TOWARD the horizon. The sun had just begun to shatter its edge, spilling across the vast Northern Ocean of Byanntia. Dawn—not the best time to push out in search of the great fish. But then, that had only been an excuse, anyway.

They voted nay, thought the old chief. *All of them.*

Bending his back, the Kuzzi warrior threw his still-powerful limbs into the job of sliding his hunter's skiff across the hard-packed blue sand and into the water beyond. He reached the lapping waves by instinct, his eyes not seeing the ocean before him, his conscious mind not actually concerned with the hunt. Throwing himself into the moving boat with accustomed ease, Bollatu landed in the center lightly, managing the maneuver without wetting any of his fur.

What did you expect, he asked himself with a bitter tone. *That they would accept the judgments of a failure forever?*

The chief was the oldest of the Kuzzi, a proud warrior who in his elder years still stood an even eight feet high. A short coat of horizontally striped fur covered his body, as it did all of his people. The blue, black and grey markings were a natural camouflage which allowed the Kuzzi to blend well with the planet's landscape.

Bollatu did not differ from the rest of the Kuzzi in any remarkable ways. His head was surrounded by the same thick mane, the usual single black stripe parted his forehead and muzzle. His chin and jaw were covered with the typical longer fur of the Kuzzi mane, setting off his muzzle and hard, blue lips like the rest of his fellows, his shoulders broad and chest rippling with thickly layers of muscles.

But Bollatu felt different that morning. As his skiff followed the morning tide out to sea, for once he felt much older than the rest of his tribe. He felt tired. Weary. Betrayed.

It's you that's betrayed them, his mind whispered in dark recrimination. *Led them astray, forced them to eat the lies of the past. Murdered them—*

"Enough!"

The chief sat back in his boat, closing his eyes, letting his mane cushion his head against the rear panel seat. Still close to shore, the current rippled gently against the sides of the skiff. The sound was smooth and pleasant—relaxing.

They voted nay, the voice from the back of his mind repeated. *What do you have to relax about?*

Bollatu sighed. His was a nomadic warrior race that had lived on their planet since the beginning of time. Their cherished story cycle gave them a history extending back through a hundred and twelve thousand cycles. Over all that time the Kuzzi had formularized their way of life. Their population had always remained small due to the ravages of the Gr'Nar, frightful beasts that returned from a generational hibernation to destroy everything in sight. Over the centuries the Kuzzi had learned to calculate the coming of the creatures. They knew when to move to avoid their coming and to where. When the Gr'Nar arrived they would slaughter the plainsherd, but never the Kuzzi. The nomads were too clever.

When others had come, outsiders from the stars—the Earth'ings. They had come to Byanntia to build permanent homes. They went where they wanted, did what they wanted, acting like children lost in the dark. Some of the younger Kuzzi had been concerned. The Earth'ings would swallow their world, they said. But Bollatu had said, no, leave them be. Soon will come the Gr'Nar and the Earth'ing bones will litter the sand.

All had agreed. Of course, Bollatu was correct. None could resist the Gr'Nar. The greatest Kuzzi warriors—even in groups of a thousand—had been devastated by the great god beast.

Let the Earth'ings plow and build and roam. In twenty-two cycles they will all be dead. It had been a time of great laughter.

But the years had passed and the Gr'Nar had come, and it had not destroyed the aliens. It's arrival had not even driven them away. A few pawfuls only did it kill. Pawfuls! It usual cycle of blood had been reduced to a few days. A single Earth'ing had stopped it—cold and final. And then, the alien had not even shown the Gr'Nar the dignity of slaying it. He had turned his back on the god beast, allowing it to slink off to its lair.

"You knew it would come back to plague your land and sons, Jacob Matson," snarled the warrior in confused contempt, "and yet you let it live. Knew its death would have washed you in glory. And you let it live."

Bollatu sat upright in his skiff. Rage boiled his blood, steamed the water within his brain. He had been so certain, positive the Gr'Nar would sweep the plains free of the Earth'ings. But, he had been wrong. And now for the first time in all of Kuzzi history, a chief had been removed from his station.

Bollatu stared out across the endless water. Only a pawful of times had there ever been a vote. Seven times throughout all their generations. Seven times the entire nation had been brought together to cast their stones—blue to retain their chief, black to send him out. Not one blue stone had been cast for Bollatu. Not by his smoke mates, his sister, his children—not even his wife had thrown for him.

Why should they?

Bollatu frowned. Why was it his fault the Earthlings had triumphed? Millennia of tradition said they would fail. None could stop the Gr'Nar-ten thousand grandfathers wagging their collective fingers down through the centuries had said so—

And you listened to them ...

Disgusted, the former chief threw aside his thoughts. It was over. Fine, let the next chief do better. Tired of self-pity, annoyed with simply drifting, Bollatu picked up the double-bladed oar next to him and thrust it into the water. A smooth stroke pushed him forward, followed by another the next second. The oar shifted from side to side, silently slicing the water, the skiff effortlessly gliding faster and faster toward the horizon.

"Good day for fish," whispered the elder Kuzzi, as if fishing were what he sought from the Northern Ocean that day. In a tone still thick with anger, he looked over the side of his skiff and muttered, "Are you hungry down there?"

Setting his oar aside, Bollatu pulled up his line and cast. Securing the cast's handle in its notch in the cross brace before him, the Kuzzi held the hooked end of his line up for examination. Having not really come to fish he had, of course, brought no bait. A thin laugh grumbling through him, the elder worked his mouth, pulling together a thick wad of mucus and phlegm. Spitting it onto his hook, he cast the wicked curve of barbed metal into the ocean, shouting—

"Well, eat this!"

And then, Bollatu laughed. No sooner had his hook sunk but a few feet beneath the surface when his line jerked. Something had taken him at his word, impaling itself on his invitation.

Everything dies that listens to you

Laughing again at his own cynicism, the elder warrior watched as coil after coil of line dashed out over the stern. Something big and fast had decided to challenge him. Reaching for his hauling gloves, he told his hidden foe—

"I accept."

His heavy, resin-woven gloves in place, Bollatu hauled on the line. Of course, he was not trying to drag whatever had taken his hook to the surface. This was only the opening lunge in a duel he expected would take the next half hour or more. The rate at which the coils of line had snaked overboard told him he had something big, a fellir, a houlta—twenty pounds worth, at least. Whatever it was, it had to be made aware that it was in a struggle. The Kuzzi's opening tug would let it know there was a new force in its life, and then the battle would truly begin.

As the elder warrior worked his line, easily letting a few yards play out, hauling them back in, letting them out again, he began to relax. The sun was warm on his fur, the occasional splashes churned up by his struggle refreshing. The fish began circling the skiff, going deeper and deeper, trying to find a direction from which it could not be pulled back. Bollatu easily kept the line from tangling against any of his vessel's edges, his still strong muscles easing the line around and around.

Slowly the elder's cares were being left behind—forgotten. The contest had shifted his focus away from the internal. As his fingers stiffened, he would hold the line secure with one paw while flexing the fingers of the other. Then he would let his line play again, pulling the fish short with his refreshed paw while loosening the rest of his fingers.

Then, finally, the line went slack. Bollatu's hidden adversary was heading for the surface. The warrior's forehead ridged, his lips smiled. He had tired his foe to the point where it could think of nothing else to do but to run straight toward its captor.

"Come to me, swimmer. We'll prove I'm not dead yet."

The water broke, shoved to both sides by a leaping form. Water caught the light, surrounding the fish in reflected dazzle. Bollatu marveled at his prize.

"A geldiffa—this close to land."

The elder laughed, pleased with himself. Seeing his enemy, he could tell the great fish weighed forty, forty-five pounds easily. Then, in the background, Bollatu noticed the distant shore, discovering he had traveled much further than he had realized. The warrior did not care, however.

What could that matter? Forward, toward the end of his line, that was where his attention was demanded. The geldiffa, all blue and yellow stripes, hit the water again cleanly, gliding below its surface, racing for the bottom.

He's trying to throw the hook—he's done this before.

A real adversary, decided Bollatu with a grunt of admiration. A worthy foe. This would be a battle worth fighting.

The Kuzzi found himself repeating the steps he had already made. First playing out and hauling in the line, working it around his skiff as the fish went deeper and deeper, constantly switching directions as it again tried to find some space of ocean that did not connect him to Bollatu's line. The warrior smiled with a child's sincerity. He had not been so happy in many a year.

Then, once more his line went slack. Again, the geldiffa was racing to the surface. For a moment Bollatu's breast swelled with pride. In his moment of despair, the gods had sent him a challenge, a sign, an opportunity for redemption within his own eyes. It was a small thing, but life was assembled from small moments, and he was in no position to argue. Then, his split-second of joy was dashed.

Instinct sent his free paw to the bottom of his skiff, feeling for vibrations. His eyes scanned the water around him. Something was wrong. To his left, the ocean was beginning to swell. It was a signal—the geldiffa was returning to the surface. No longer trying to escape Bollatu, instead it was running from something else.

"What in all the gods...?"

Bollatu's mouth froze open in amazement as the geldiffa broke the water once more, not merely leaping this time, but shooting straight upward into the atmosphere. Before his prize catch had begun to sink back below the waves, the water beneath the fish boiled and then split apart, shattered by the arrival of a black and massive form.

"Chuln'fa'ulu!"

Bollatu sat in his tiny skiff, his boat and himself dwarfed by the incredible monster swallowing the ocean before him. So gigantic were the chuln'fa'ulu that their skins were used by the Kuzzi to make their central meeting tents. The nomads did not hunt the great fish, of course. They only salvaged their carcasses on those fortunate occasions when one of their dead drifted into shore. Even the Gr'Nar-killing Earthings had been impressed by the size of the largest creature Byanntia had to offer. Unable to pronounce the beast's Kuzzi name, they had labeled them "Melvilles," claiming the word to be a compliment.

There was no way to stop chuln'fa'ulu. The records spoke of insanely daring bands of Kuzzi, twenty, thirty boats worth, going out with spears and throwers, looking for the glory of being the first mortals to slay a godfish. None had ever succeeded. Few had ever returned.

All these things flashed through Bollatu's mind as he watched the chuln'fa'ulu break the surface. He smelled the terror of the geldiffa—*his* geldiffa—as it struggled upward, flopping desperately, only to fall pitifully back toward the ocean and the waiting jaws below.

"*Nooooooo!*"

The godfish's jaws came closed, Bollatu's prize disappearing from sight. With a casual shrug the massive beast turned and headed back beneath the waves. The elder warrior stared, his mind numb, emotions racing. He had been so at peace, actually happy, and then ... there was no sense he could make of the moment playing out before him.

Had he been given his purging moment only so that he might be punished further? Was he naught but a toy of the gods? Was he to be scorned by not just his tribe, but by all life as well? To have snagged the geldiffa as he had, surely it had been a chance at redemption. Now, was it so easily taken away?

Is what you allowed so easy to walk back from? The elder winced, his stomach churning with fury. *Was your mistake that minor?*

At his feet, his line was disappearing once more. Second after second more coils disappeared over the side, leaping into the air two, three at a time. Without thinking, Bollatu's paws reached out.

"No," growled the Kuzzi, his anger smashing reason. "Not this day. Not to me."

His left paw grabbed at the disappearing line, carefully catching a straightened segment, not one of the snapping loops which could slice his paw in half with a motion. The elder gave the line careful jerks, testing the great fish, gauging how far down it intended to sink. The line stopped.

"Not far," muttered Bollatu. As the line limped, he asked himself, "Coming back so soon? Why?"

The warrior reeled his line back in as quickly as he could. Four hundred yards he returned to the floor, refusing the notion of cutting it, of backing away from the challenge he had made.

Retreat, the back of his mind questioned with a sneer. *To where? Why?*

He sensed tension in the line. Knowing the geldiffa had already been chewed to bits, he realized his hook had reestablished itself somewhere within the chuln'fa'ulu. Perhaps it was lodged in some swollen abscess, wedged between two teeth where it was striking some nerve, serving the great fish a pain it had never known.

"Not used to being hunted, eh?" taunted Bollatu.

The warrior's mind reasoned quickly that it was impossible for the chuln'fa'ulu to understand what was happening. Unlike the geldiffa which had been harvested from the ocean for eons, the godfish had no instinct for such impunity. Still retrieving his line, Bollatu watched the water, waiting for the chuln'fa'ulu to return.

Again the ocean boiled as the great mass broke the surface, hurling water in all directions. The elder left off gathering his line, his paws closing on his spear. Made as a boy, carried throughout his life, it had served as his staff of office for more than thirty cycles. Carved from the straight trunk of a young stinger tree, it possessed weight and cutting power. Filled with authority and memory, it spread confidence throughout its owner.

The godfish made a wide circle, then began moving toward the skiff. Was it somehow following Bollatu's line back to the boat? Did it know they were enemies? Did it matter? Pulling back and planting himself as best he could on the pitching floor of his vessel, the warrior shut one eye, watched his foe's progress, gauged his moment, and then threw.

The spear dashed forward, slamming through the thick black skin of a monstrous eye, sinking nearly two feet into the vision of the onrushing horror. Terrible as the attack was, however, if the chuln'fa'ulu noticed any pain, it was but a moment's distraction at best. Onward came the godfish, jaws wide as a cavern, water rushing over the terrible rows of broken teeth.

"And so it ends," whispered Bollatu. Still standing, balled fists at his sides, he waited for the monster. His skiff rocked wildly as it tipped upward over his foe's lower jaw, Kuzzi and vessel flipping inside the massive mouth. The skiff swirled, twisted by the miniature whirlpool created within the godfish's maw. Then, motivated more by anger than either desperation or self-preservation, Bollatu suddenly jumped to the back of his craft with force, pushing its prow upward into the roof of the great mouth. The sharp edge dug deep into the soft lining, the skiff's transom wedging against the bottom of the gullet.

The elder was thrown sideways as the godfish thrashed against the sudden pain. Bollatu instinctively sank his claws into the side of the chuln'fa'ulu's mouth, hanging on against the churning current. His oar fell from the skiff, bouncing off his shoulder. Grabbing out, the warrior snatched it from the air. Digging its pointed blade into the chuln'fa'ulu's throat, Bollatu pushed himself toward the great mouth before him.

The warrior laughed as he staggered forward. He had jammed the godfish's mouth open, and now it could not dive for fear of drowning. A fish, he though, afraid of drowning. The idea made him giddy even as he fell repeatedly, thrown about effortlessly by the chuln'fa'ulu's panicked thrashing. Water crashed against Bollatu as he struggled toward the flapping lips before him. Despite the wedge blocking its throat, the chuln'fa'ulu still strained to close its great mouth. Reaching the doubled rows of the godfish's horrible teeth, the elder found his line once more. He could not see its end, buried somewhere beneath the constant rush of ocean falling in and out of the open mouth—could not determine why the creature had noticed his hook.

Nor did he care. At that moment, all that mattered to the warrior was escaping the beast's gullet before he followed his geldiffa to its bottom. Poised to dive out into the ocean, however, the godfish thrashed once more, sending Bollatu falling against its lower jaw. Eleven spikes tore into the elder's side, the great teeth ripping skin, piercing muscle. Blood sluiced out of him, the taste of it sending the chuln'fa'ulu into wilder spasms.

Bollatu dug his oar into the godfish's mouth, pushing himself off the tearing rows. None of his wounds were terribly threatening, but several were deep and all were painful. Pushing himself erect, however, the warrior sneered—

"Best you can do?"

—and then dove outward into the welcoming ocean beyond. Bollatu landed feet first, dragging his oar behind him far under the waves. The chuln'fa'ulu passed overhead, plunging the ocean into darkness for the long moment it took to glide by. Not having taken in a deep enough breath before jumping, the Kuzzi struggled his way back to the surface. When his head broke the water, three things caught his attention instantly. The first was that he was now much closer to shore. The second was that the end of his line was floating several yards in front of him. The third was that the chuln'fa'ulu was no where to be seen.

What happened?

Had the skiff come dislodged? Had the tremendous pressure of the godfish's straining jaws finally snapped the vessel? Had his hook come loose as well? The warrior reached out for the floating line before him.

"Where are you, thing?"

As if in response, the godfish's great body shattered the ocean's surface some distance to his right. Such a quick return told Bollatu that his wedge was still be in place. He reasoned that the chuln'fa'ulu must have dived in an attempt to clear its throat with a rush of water. Unable to remove the blockage, it had hurried back to the sky for another breath.

Bollatu bobbed in the water, taking in his own deep breaths, watching his adversary. The chuln'fa'ulu floated with the current. Although its remaining good eye was trained directly at him, it made no move to continue their struggle. It did not try to submerge again, nor did it attempt to make for the open sea. As the warrior's strength began to return to him, he looked upon the godfish for the first time without anger.

The monstrous beast glistened in the sunlight. As its gasped one short breath quickly after another, the elder realized what must have happened. He could see that the chuln'fa'ulu's mouth had reached the point where it could almost close. Bollatu knew his skiff had shifted, perhaps even shattered. Now it was wedged within the godfish's throat. The elder knew in was only a matter of time before his adversary would swallow one wave too many and choke to death.

Suddenly, his anger drained, numbness gone, Bollatu felt a great surge of pity for the dying beast before him. Graping his line tightly, he began pulling himself toward his victim. Sad, sorrowful notes trembled from deep within the beast, drifting across the ocean. Reaching the chuln'fa'ulu's side, the elder pulled himself upward—paw over paw—until he reached the bristling rows of teeth once more. Straining with all his remaining power, trying not to excite the still flowing wounds along his side and abdomen, the warrior pulled himself up onto the hardened ridge which served as the godfish's lower lip.

"And what would you all say," wondered Bollatu of his former tribe members, "if you could see this?"

Half jumping, half falling, the warrior cleared the jagged teeth by inches. Standing, he made his way backward through the dark gullet until he found the blockage. Indeed, his skiff had been dislodged by the chuln'fa'ulu's dive, but that had only made things worse for the godfish. The vessel had followed the downward water flow and wedged itself further back in the creature's throat, leaving only the slightest of air passages.

Bollatu shook his head sadly. Not caring what might come next, laughing at his former inability to understand Jacob Matson, he whispered to himself—

"No wonder they all threw black." Looping his line around the still solid center spar, the elder added, "If I could have seen this moment, I would have thrown black, too."

Pulling against the horrible weight, the elder strained to free his shattered vessel. The movement tore at the lining of the godfish's throat. Blood oozed as the creature exhaled harshly. Bile rushed up from its stomach in cascades. Bollatu ignored the smell, ignored the pain in his own body, ignored the derisive laughter within his head. Instead he merely struggled—step by step—toward the thin line of light so far away. A great cough shuddered the beast. The warrior fell to his knees, almost losing hold of his line. Fighting to maintain the tension he had created, the elder felt his left glove finally eat through. Blood leaked from his paw, but he refused the accompanying sensation. On his knees, he crawled onward, dragging at the skiff.

"Move, damn you. Move. Move."

Digging his heels into the floor of the chuln'fa'ulu's mouth, Bollatu drew his remaining line into a loop and tossed the loop end forward. Snagging it around one of the godfish's teeth, he threw his weight into pulling on the line, using the great fang to increase his strength. For a long moment the warrior strained, his eyes fast shut, heart racing, breath held deep. And then, the godfish coughed once more.

Instantly Bollatu was thrown from the chuln'fa'ulu's mouth. The elder hit the water at a bad angle. His left side going numb, he sputtered violently, gasping for air. The Kuzzi floundered, his good arm tangled in his line. Something was attached to it, weighing him down, dragging him under. Then, a shadow appeared over Bollatu's head, and the remains of his skiff were returned to him along with a shattering flood.

***

Max L. Kornev, captain of the U.R.S. Canton, was an insatiably curious man. When he noted that passage had been booked on his vessel for an alien being, he saw an opportunity to not only brighten some of the dull travel hours ahead, but to accomplish what he had come to space to do in the first place—to meet another life form for himself.

"That's a hell of a story." His tone not revealing whether or not he believed what he had been told, he added, "back on Earth we'd called it a 'whopper.'"

In the grand tradition of the ocean-going vessels of his past, Kornev had requested Bollatu's company at his table that evening for dinner. The chief had accepted, knowing that if he were to travel amongst humans, he would have to learn to deal with them. Attempting to do so, he inquired, "Is that a good thing, or a bad one?"

"Depends, I guess," answered Kornev honestly. "Probably good this time."

Bollatu nodded. When he had awakened on the beach, he had laughed for a long time. How he had managed to drift all the way back to shore without drowning, he did not know. Nor could he say why his bleeding wounds had not attracted any predators. Perhaps, he had thought, he had endured enough bad blessings for one day.

"Can I ask you a question?" Bollatu nodded in response toward the captain. "I noticed your ticket was purchased by a Jacob Matson. Isn't that the guy you said killed your Gr'Nar?"

"Yes," answered the old warrior. When Kornev gave him a look even the Kuzzi could interpret, the elder answered, "for some reason I can not explain, once I realized I had survived I felt it necessary to tell the tale to the man who had destroyed my ability to lead my tribe. He asked me what I was going to do now that I was no longer chief."

"What'd you tell him?"

Bollatu made a "tsking" sound moving his tongue against his teeth. Giving the captain a look the man understood, the old warrior answered his question.

"I told him that on the morning I had gone to the sea, I felt old. I had left my people—gone to the ocean to die. The ocean spit me back. Thus I was free to do as I might."

Bollatu answered Kornev's next question before he could ask it. "The big tooth, the one that snarled my line, it washed up on the shore with me. I traded it to Matson for passage on your vessel."

Kornev raised an eyebrow. "He bought you a Rim Circle Trip. That's a lot of ticket for a tooth."

"He came, took my world. I told him that I would leave to take his heavens."

The captain smiled. Did the alien know how much this Matson had done for him?

Then again, thought Kornev, considering what Bollatu did for Matson by sitting back and letting humans get establish on his planet, maybe the price wasn't all that steep.

The captain paused for a moment, staring out the observation port built into the close wall of the dining room. In many ways it was a senseless luxury, but it was one he delighted in. Staring out at the endless sea of stars, he thought that, maybe, he knew what the alien before him was feeling.

"There was a poet on my world," said Kornev, pouring himself and his guest another drink, "Emerson, they called him. He once said that 'few envy the consideration enjoyed by the eldest inhabitant.' Good thing you're just a kid, huh?"

Bollatu smiled.

"I do feel young," he answered, surprise in his voice. "As young as the mountains."

Man and Kuzzi laughed, banged their glasses together, drained them, then laughed once more.

THEY WERE THE WIND

C.J. Henderson

"**S**O," ASKED THE HUMAN, THE OUTSIDER. THE ONE WHO DID not know. "What the hell *was* that thing?"

A Kuzzi warrior stood next to the human, thinking how to explain. Though the one called Joseph Matson was tall, over six of their feet, the Kuzzi stood more that two feet taller. His short coat of horizontally striped fur had thinned for the summer, the blue, black and grey markings of his skin showing through, a natural camouflage that blended well with the alien landscape during the hot months. The male's head was surrounded by a thick, glossy black mane, a single gray stripe cutting its forehead and muzzle to the chin.

"They were the wind," answered the warrior.

Matson wondered if the Kuzzi were speaking metaphorically, as its kind often did, or not. It certainly sounded like a poetic description, but the young man knew much of Kuzzi speech patterns, and Matson would have sworn his companion meant the statement to be taken literally.

"Bentelii," he asked, "speak plain now, or with layers?"

"Speak with plain layers," the warrior answered. "No other speak possible."

Matson grunted. He wanted an answer, a simple, uncomplicated set of words wrapped around an idea he could accept. His companion's answer, however, told him there was nothing simple or uncomplicated about his question, no matter how straight-forward it might have seemed to him. Setting his repeller on the ground, the young man made a motion with his head the Kuzzi understood as a request for the full explanation. Both males sat, one cross-legged, the other with arms wrapped around knees, and the one who was not an outsider spoke.

"Long before your people come this place," it said, sinewy arms in motion, "long before Kuzzi people even, there were the Fa'Lun. They exist, learn to hunt and harvest, to speak and write and build and dream. They name Byanntia, teach Kuzzi speak, know whole world as old race while Kuzzi only children."

"So, that thing could talk?" Matson asked his challenging question with wonder in his voice, and Bentelii nodded, equal wonder in the motion. Then, it continued.

The warrior told the human of the Fa'Lun's fascination with flight. The race might have been ancient, but they had always remained nomads, had never built permanent shelters. The humans would find no artifacts of a Fa'Lun empire. They had never been a race interested in great populating numbers. No, the Fa'Lun, the story went, decided early on that the best way to deal with predators was not to try and construct defenses, or to cover the land with great numbers of their kind. Instead, they had a different idea.

"They wanted to fly. Their thought was that the safest place was in the sky, and so they went there."

Joseph Matson shook his head in fascinated confusion. He questioned his friend as to what he meant. How did someone simply *choose* to fly?

Bentelii explained that the Fa'Lun were quite adept at breeding. It was they that had crossbred the early kison, an at-the-time stringy, tenacious beast, until they had perfected the slow-moving, fat and juicy breed the humans had discovered upon their arrival on Byanntia. To the Fa'Lun the answer to their quest had been simple.

"If they wanted to fly, they would simply make themselves fly."

The Fa'Lun, a people who had made almost a religion out of genetics–who had never over-extended their population in fear members would break off and form their own tribes, tribes that might turn on one another–turned their amazing talents on themselves. Quite simply, they began to breed themselves into a race which could take flight.

"It took them thousands of years," Bentelii said with a flourish, a sound like pride in its graveled voice. Matson wondered if the Kuzzi was telling the tale in a bragging sense–home town clan makes good–to let the human know that not only his race could make things happen when they set their minds to it. "But slowly, eventually, they succeeded."

Matson looked into the sky, his mind filled with questions. How was it no one had mentioned any of this to a human before? Why had a Fa'Lun never been seen before now? How did Bentelii know all he told? The Kuzzi continued its story.

"Bones got lighter, hollow. Skin stretched, flaps extended, ankle to wrist, hair thickened, hardened, grew into feathers, not like bird, different, their own. Feathers enough to take the Fa'Lun to the skies."

Bentelii's command of the human's language was quite good, but still the warrior stumbled as it tried to explain the transformation of Byanntia's first race. The Kuzzi, it seemed, had begun to reach for sentience just as the Fa'Lun began to reach for the clouds. The older ones refused to hinder the dangerous carnivores as they obviously began to come into their own as thinking beings. Instead they used the event as fuel, a prod to keep them working toward their goal.

Let the Kuzzi learn to hunt with tools, they decided with an inordinate generosity, let them learn to plant and built and spin and carve and create. By the time they are a force that can oppose us, we will be gone to where they can not reach.

"Are you saying the Fa'Lun named, ah, your people? 'Kuzzi' was a Fa'Lun word?"

"Yes. All words are Fa'Lun."

Bentelii explained that while the Fa'Lun had sought flight above all things, still they had remained a part of the world. Not wanting to exterminate a predator, they had instead helped the Kuzzi along, adopting them, gearing the younger race to take their place as caretakers of the planet. By the time the Fa'Lun had streamlined themselves to the point where tools and tribes were no longer of any use to them, they had left their language behind in the stewardship of the Kuzzi, as well as anything else the younger species desired to claim as their own.

"They had been flying for some time by then. By the point Kuzzi understood, really, what the Fa'Lun were, had been, were doing ... I mean ..."

"I understand," whispered Matson, his tone quieted by the awe tingling his senses. "Go on."

"By that time, the Fa'Lun disappeared. They used to fly and land, like the birds, fly to escape danger, fly to search for food, land to sleep, to make nests ... but that stopped. By the time Kuzzi became a true race, the Fa'Lun went to the skies and did not return."

Matson was speechless. He could not comprehend it all. Oh, he could accept the story as a scientific thought, as an idea, a suggestion. A possibility. But as a reality, as a tangible notion with weight he could test against his own beliefs—no.

No, it was too large an idea, too foreign.

Too *alien*.

"It is hard for us to accept as well."

"But," Matson countered, "your people had time to accept this, they saw it. Talked to the Fa'Lun ... ah, I, er ... do you still ... does anyone still talk to them?"

Bentelii shook his head.

"Not for stretch after stretch. Last person I know to talk with a Fa'Lun, many long stretch ... in my grandfather's grandfather's grandfather's grandfather's time, healer Baww'ja, they say he friend with one Fa'Lun. The last Fa'Lun that would come down from the sky. They would talk and Baww'ja would tell him of Kuzzi."

The Fa'Lun of whom Bentelii spoke had no name, or at least never gave one to the healer. Over the years of their relationship, the Fa'Lun grew more and more distant. His eyes began to stay constantly trained on the sky. Finally, after Baww'ja died, the Fa'Lun were never seen again.

"Their minds different," the warrior explained. "Life on land forgotten, social rules forgotten, everything left behind, not just things, but ideas, concepts, maybe even thought itself."

Matson shifted uneasily. The more his friend tried to make the concept of the Fa'Lun clear, the more impossible understanding them seemed to become. An entire race that just up and changed themselves—herdsmen who got it into their heads one day to leave the ground behind, who abandoned thought itself for flight.

"They really stopped thinking?"

"The last Fa'Lun, Baww'ja's visitor, it was said he became harder and harder to communicate with, that toward the end of Baww'ja's days, it seemed the creature only came back to hear his voice. It is said the healer had a most pleasant voice."

Matson shuddered. The story he had been counting on to make him feel better, to diminish his guilt, had instead multiplied to become a weight he could barely stand. He turned his head, looking back at the mangled corpse splattered against the rock wall behind them. Not some monster from the skies, at all, but a thing of grace and wonder, a self-made angel which he had snuffed out through a panicked moment of careless fear.

His mind fell backwards, rushing his memory to the moment not so long ago where he had heard the noise in the sky. He had wheeled around, had seen the great, glorious wingspan spread across the heavens, and his first thoughts had been colored with awe. The young human had watched the soaring object as it spun and looped and floated its way in and out of the clouds. He had no idea what he was looking at, did not care. He had stumbled across yet one more of Byanntia's marvels and was simply happy to be witness to another miracle discovered.

And then, everything had changed. The flying form had taken note of Matson, had changed direction, diving straight for the young man. He had grown frightened. The thing was moving straight for him, flying directly at him at what seemed an incredible speed.

Matson had lifted his repeller, the creature had screeched defiantly, charging on, sweat had stung the trembling human's eye, and with a single action, it was over.

Suddenly the sky was blotched by an explosion of fluff and flesh and blood, and the ruined sack of what had been a living being slammed down out of the blue and destroyed itself against the solid rock of the mountainside upon which Matson still sat. His eyes glued to the shattered remains, the young man whispered;

"That might be the last of its kind, for all we know. And I killed it."

The air hung dark with grief between the two friends, regret curling itself around Matson's neck and biting away at his skull, burrowing into his brain. The human could not bring himself to look his friend in the eye. At least, not until the Kuzzi spat;

"Good."

Matson's eyes blinked hard in shock. He swallowed, his head jerking, first sideways then backwards. The motions were violent, but slight. The human asked;

"What do you mean?"

"Fa'Lun foolish, cowardly people. Run away from life instead of embracing it."

"But they taught themselves to fly."

"Taught themselves to hide. Afraid of everything, they go to the sky and never return. Tell me, Joseph, what good is flight without destination?"

"But I killed it."

"Dove at you out of sky, screamed and came for you. What were you supposed to do? What do you think it was coming for?"

"I, I don't know ... but ..."

The big Kuzzi smiled. Its mouth opened past the point of humor to where Matson knew the lion-like alien was laughing at him. Placing a paw on the human's shoulder, Bentelii said softly;

"You humans, you could never understand the Fa'Lun. And perhaps," the Kuzzi's yellow eyes went soft for a moment, "perhaps it is best that way."

The two friends gathered their things then, and prepared to make their way back down the mountain. They had climbed to the height they had merely as a diversion and had been rewarded with far more than they had ever expected. As they started their trek back to the pass where their decent would begin, Matson asked one last question.

"You said the Fa'Lun, that they were the wind. What did you mean by that?"

"They were the wind," Bentelii repeated, muscles rippling as he ambled down the steep incline. "They were there, but then they were gone."

Joseph Matson's eyes scanned the horizon, searching the sky endlessly as he and his friend worked their way down the mountain through the heavy heat of the late afternoon. He wondered about the Fa'Lun, as well as the Kuzzi's casual dismissal of them. He thought on what he had done, punishing himself diligently, and on how Bentelii had felt about it and had seen no damage in his actions.

Then, a breeze cooled his brow and he sighed in relief, grateful for the slight but comforting gust.

THE LAW OF THE KUZZI

James Chambers

THE BOYS HUNKERED LOW ON THE SHEET-METAL PLATFORM and waited for the next chromatic eruption to illuminate the night. They were not supposed to be there, high up on the narrow catwalk that topped one tower of the New Dodge dew wells. The fragile array of thermal reactive sheeting, strung on hinges between several makeshift framework structures, captured condensation and funneled it into low, squat tanks in the valley below. The settlers had salvaged the sheeting from the *Triumphant*'s massive cooling system, yet durable as it was, its reactive coating eventually grew stale with wear. After more than four decades on Byanntia, they had little left unused in storage. Bad enough it was dangerous for the boys climbing around on the lightweight structures untended in the dark, but lately, the dew wells had proven barely adequate to bolster the water supply of the community. Damage to even one tower could jeopardize lives.

Such thoughts, though, were as far from the boys' minds as Byanntia was from Earth. Tonight was a celebration, and the trio had been anticipating the promised fireworks through months of hard toil and rigorous schooling—ever since Thom Horton and Mick Busco had announced finding the necessary raw materials to make explosives. In each boy's pocket nestled a rare cigar, pilfered with care from the storehouse where they had spent the past several decades in nulltemp storage, doled out in miserly fashion to celebrate new births and other momentous occasions. Despite some of the farmers' efforts to cultivate tobacco crops, the addictive weed would not take root in the Byanntian soil. Thus, they could only obtain fresh smoking supplies on the periodic trade vessels from Earth. The next ship, due in two weeks, would replenish the humidor. The boys hoped the new stock would cover the three missing stogies. It was a calculated risk, but then, so was everything on Byanntia.

Although they knew the importance of the dew well arrays, the boys felt confident that they could come and go without harming them. Not only did the tower offer a secret place where the three friends could savor their booty free of adult interference, but it provided the best unobstructed vantage point for the pyrotechnics. Up here, the boys were eye-level with the fireworks.

A screaming whistle sheared the dry air, then went silent while sparks of gold fire scintillated across the black sky. They blotted out the endless twinkling stars above and left afterimages floating in the boy's eyes.

The next rocket shrieked upward, producing a palpable concussion and a rainbow of shimmering, metallic flickers.

The third turned the world crimson and tangerine and illuminated the landscape like a miniature red sun.

That's when Frank Duncan spotted the long, dark shape trundling over the eastern hills. "Hey," he said, jamming his elbow into Colt Bukowski's ribcage. "You see that?"

"See what?" asked Colt. "Fireworks are damn near burning out my retinas."

"Man, quit griping, already, will you?" snapped Grant Drasinovich. "It's always something with you."

"Well, we're not even supposed to be up here," nagged Colt. "We get caught, and you know we're spending the next month digging trenches for the irrigation system overhaul."

"No one's going to find us," Grant grumbled.

Three rockets erupted with a rhythmic crackling, their green and amber light painting the air.

"There it is again," said Frank, pointing. "Way out there. Up in the hills."

"I don't see anything," Colt answered.

"Wait," interjected Grant. "I see it. Up on the ridge near that willow sapling, right? Looks like some stray kison calves—oh, damn, I just lost them."

"No, not there. Lower," Frank said. He palmed the back of Grant's head and turned it.

"Oh. Coming down the eastern trail. Yeah, I see it. Looks like a Crawler," Grant said. "Is that smoke coming out of it?"

Frank squinted and shielded his eyes with his hand as an electric, champagne burst brightened the shadows and thrust the damaged Crawler into stark view. It was headed toward New Dodge. A column of dark smoke wafted from its rear section. The gentle burbling of its motor reached across the plain.

"Who could be out there? Everyone's in the town square for the party," said Colt, now seeing the vehicle. "We better tell your Dad about this, Frank."

"Yeah, you're right," Frank agreed. "Let's go."

"But what about the fireworks? And the cigars?" pleaded Grant. "It's probably just someone coming in late from Verdi's Plain. Geddy McCarthur herds his kison out that way sometimes, and you know he's always late for town events."

"No way, man. I saw Geddy dipping into the punch with old man Matson before we left." Frank raised an eyebrow and pitched an impatient glare his friend's way. "Besides, that Crawler look like any model you've ever seen before?"

The Crawler was larger than any of those in New Dodge: heavier, with stronger treads, and reinforced siding. The boys had seen that much in the tide of light coming from the steady bombardment of cheerful explosions. Grant shook his head and grunted his concession. "No."

A moment later, the boys were scrambling down the latticework toward the dusty earth. They leapt the final four feet to the ground, each rolling to his knees for an instant, before they raced off toward the lights and voices of New Dodge.

***

In the foothills, the Crawler continued its slow progress toward the settlement. Behind it, tall, slender figures crested the ridge, topping the lone, young willow there by several feet. They stood in silent appraisal of what filled the once-empty valley: the building and lights of New Dodge, all of it as alien and unwanted as the short, baldish creatures that dwelled there. They were disturbing, these beings who draped their bodies in patches of cloth and fiber, who worked the land in strange ways, grappling and struggling with it, forcing it to their own ends, rather than living in accord with the natural rhythms. Even the cycle of the Gr'nar, among the most powerful natural forces on Byanntia, had not been enough to cow the obstinacy of these brash and defiant beings called "men" and "women." Tonight would be different. So it had been decided in the hearts and minds of the stealthy watchers. On this night, the frail human parasites would glimpse the real soul of Byanntia, and then their true measure would be taken.

***

Far from the darkness of the hills, picnic tables cluttered the town square. The people of New Dodge feasted on fresh kison, whole grain breads, young stinger leaves, and cakes and pies baked with the meager surplus of sugar, cream, and dried fruit donated by the surrounding ranches and farms. From the walls of the school, the medical center, and the administration building, which most people called "Town Hall," hung strings of cold, glowing lanterns dripping soft light onto the festivities. A makeshift band of fiddle, guitar, horns, and drums played a fast-paced song that set many party-goers to dancing.

The entire day had been spent this way, given over to the arduous effort of eating, drinking, relaxing, and laughing. It was a rare occasion in the hardworking community, one that delivered an invigorating break from work and routine. It was a true holiday, a fête of distinctly Byanntian nature, different from those times small groups of settlers paid their respects to their origins by observing the holidays they had carried with them from Earth. This day, this observance, could only be celebrated on Byanntia and only by the people of New Dodge.

Back on Earth, before the settlers left, before even the *Triumphant* had been built and their equipment gathered, their journey charted and planned, their lives uprooted and cast upon a new course, scientists and researchers had issued an analysis of their chances for survival. It came in the form of a one-hundred gigabyte document that contained instructions, guidelines, and databases designed to increase their chances of founding a permanent settlement in thirty-seven different environments. Among all that information, a single statistic imprinted itself on the minds of the settlers: the scientifically derived fact that their chances of success rose from 22.7 percent to 64.3 percent if they lasted for eighteenth Byanntian months.

Today marked the forty-first anniversary of the first Turning Point, that historic first day of the settler's nineteenth month on Byanntia, which had marked a new phase of hope and optimism that carried them through many of the bleak times that had followed in the ensuing decades.

Even the dour Stuart Duncan felt the high spirits electrifying the crowd tonight. At a table near the edge of the square, he craned his neck upward to take in the pyrotechnics display and considered the hardships the people of New Dodge had overcome—the missteps and the close calls, the friends and family members lost and put to rest in the semi-arid soil of their adopted home. He thought, too, of the many laid in the ground for whom this planet was the land of their birth, for only those who had come on the *Triumphant*—the First—could rightly call this place adopted, and when they lost one from among the second or third generations, the tragedy always seemed somehow greater than losing a member of the First. Still, they carried on. Each of the settlers shouldered part of the burden, but Stuart felt its pressure more than most in his post as sheriff.

He knew these were good people who surrounded him, every one of them, but disagreements were inevitable. Differences of opinion were as common here as they had been on Earth. Such things could poison a place like New Dodge, a town barely past its infancy for all its years on the ground, and now, finally, taking its first steps toward a greater permanence. Duncan and the town leaders did their best and so far it had sufficed. They had guided the town to another Turning Point. But with one weight lifted from his shoulders, Stuart knew that others waited in the days ahead.

Sharon Duncan hooked her arm through the crook of her husband's elbow and twined her fingers around his, rubbing their deep calluses. She leaned toward him and whispered, "Lighten up, Stu. Relax. It's a party, remember?"

"I am relaxed," he claimed with a broad smile.

"Uh-uh. I know that look. It's one hundred percent pensive. There's not a slack muscle in your body. So, you listen to me. If there's anyone here who has earned a night off, it's you. It's the Turning Point, and you got us here through another year. Now, enjoy it for a couple of hours, because tomorrow, it's back to business as usual for everyone," Sharon said.

Duncan scooped the back of his wife's head with his broad, thick-knuckled hand, and pressed her lips to his, holding her there for a long moment while the warm breeze passed between them. Breaking away, he said, "You're right, you know."

"Of course I am, darling," Sharon purred. "When was the last time I was wrong?"

Stuart knew the best answer to that question, but the teasing reply dissipated at the sound of a familiar voice calling to him—Frankie, hollering from the far edge of town. He turned and saw his son racing across the outskirts of the buildings, his two best friends hard on his heels, all of them pounding their legs like the Gr'nar was breathing down their necks. Stuart shifted around on the picnic bench and waited.

"Bet I know where they've been," he said to Sharon, his expression hardening.

"That boy," Sharon muttered as she felt her husband's shoulders draw tight. "Don't let him ruin your night, Stu."

"It's not my night about be ruined," he replied.

"Dad!" Frankie yelled again. He stumbled to a stop, skidding to one knee in the dirt, and knelt there panting, trying to speak. "Dad!"

Grant and Cole pattered up behind him, the two boys bending over and sucking air. The run into town had lasted just over a mile, but the boys had covered the distance like a sprint, bounding and leaping over rocks and gullies, pumping their legs to maximum speed, ignoring the blood pounding behind their eyes.

"Dad!" Frank belted out between gasps. "We got company! Someone's driving a Crawler down the east trail. We've never seen it before. It's on fire or something."

"What are you talking about, Frankie?"

"We saw it, Dad, coming this way. A strange Crawler. Smoke coming out of it," Frank huffed. "Coming down the east trail."

"So, you three were up in the well towers?" Duncan barked. "No other way you could see the east trail at night."

Frank grimaced. "Yeah, Dad, yeah, we were. I know we're not supposed to be messing around up there. We just wanted to see the fireworks. But listen, that Crawler we saw will be here soon. You can count on that. It's already inside the shield perimeter."

Frank's quick admission snapped Duncan into focus. Under other circumstances, the boy would have hemmed and hawed, searching for a way to avoid the punishment he knew he was due for disobeying his father and breaking the law. That Frank had owned up without skipping a beat made it clear how alarmed he was by what he had seen and that he was doing his best to warn the town. Duncan respected that. It was the kind of behavior he'd tried to teach his son, the kind of thinking it would take for New Dodge to survive over the long haul.

"All right, I believe you, Frankie. You did the right thing by telling me," Duncan said. "Don't get it into your heads that any of you three are off the hook for being up in the towers, but I appreciate what you've done.

Now, listen, I got a job for you. Whoever is coming into town, it's probably best if we go out and meet them halfway, and until we know what we're dealing with, we don't need any diversions. So, I need you three to get down to the south clearing fast as you can and tell Thom and Mick to cut the fireworks short until they hear from me. Got it?"

All three serious-faced boys nodded.

"Then get going!" Duncan barked.

The trio took off at a dead run toward the town square and the meadow on the far side of New Dodge.

Duncan walked to a neighboring picnic table where the Matsons and the Hughes sat. Jacob Matson and Garris Hughes had broken off talk with their wives, distracted by Duncan's conversation with his son. The last few weeks had been nerve-wracking, for New Dodge suffered through its third drought this year, and the two men had watched the arrival of Frank and his friends with worry. The town had been teetering on a knife's edge of survival, and the settlers had come to despise unwanted intrusions. Bad enough the skirmishes with the Kuzzi they had weathered a few months back. Up until that bloody episode with the Gr'nar, the Kuzzi had more or less ignored them for years. But after Jacob Matson had single-handedly just about killed the legendary, invisible beast that came out of hibernation only every 68 years, the creatures had deposed their leader, the moderate Chief Bollatu, and tensions had flared. The conflict had settled down to a workable coexistence for the time being, but it was a long way from a permanent solution, barely enough to hold the lid on if nothing upset the balance.

Sheriff Duncan watched Jacob Matson rise, and he felt a pang about asking the man to exert himself. The lawman and the rancher were both well on in years, but Jacob had recently been diagnosed with a terminal illness and was already living and breathing three or four months beyond Doc Lieber's best expectations. And Jacob had lost his son Chad about fourteen months back, one of the first human victims of the Gr'nar. Chad had been meant to take over running Twin Feathers, the Matson's ranch, but that responsibility had now fallen to his brother Joseph. Duncan told the two men and their wives what Frank had reported.

"So, I need you fellows to raise the Guard. Figure our better halves can spread word to the crowd to keep it low key while we set up a blockade out on the east trail. I don't want that Crawler rolling in here until we know who's driving it and why. Bad enough the damn thing already made it inside shield range," Duncan said.

"Smart thinking, Stu," Matson agreed. "I'll go over to Town Hall, open the weapons vault, and prep some repellers. Want me to sound the alarm?"

"No," said Duncan. "Let's see if we can do this quietly. If it turns out to be nothing, I want folks to have a shot at getting back to the party."

"In that case, I'll round up the men, and we'll meet you on the trail," said Hughes.

Frank nodded and loped off toward the eastern end of town.

***

Elsewhere, the three boys elbowed their way through the crowd, jostling settlers and stepping on toes. They carved a pathway of surprised yelps and scolding shouts until they broke free on the other side. They flew downhill, letting the incline carry them until each step was almost a bound, covering far more ground than the boys' natural strides. They yelled and waved their arms the whole way. Thom and Mick paused at the sight of the trio, then lit a fresh rocket that blasted overhead, where it unleashed a ring of blue sparks. Mick pointed his lighter toward the fuse of the next round, but Grant plowed into him at full speed, knocking them both into a tumble on grass.

"Grant!" shouted Mick when they stopped rolling. "What the hell is your problem, boy? You trying to kill me?"

Frank filled them in on the situation while Thom helped his partner back to his feet. The two men set aside the next firework shell and squinted into the eastern blackness. Thom raised a pair of field glasses from their strap around his neck and peered through them toward the east.

"Don't like this," Thom commented. "Running a Crawler at night without lights is a good way to pitch yourself into a ditch. Must have a good reason for wanting to keep a low profile."

"More likely, it's a bad reason," said Mick. "I told you I saw someone over the ridge past Verdi's plain the other day. And there's no call for anyone to be out there this time of year."

"And I told you it must have been Kuzzi," Thom retorted.

"I know the difference between an eight-foot tall striped monster and a man," snapped Mick.

"Well, whatever it is, I can't say I'm ready to roll out a hearty welcome. Guess we better grab our repellers and hustle our rumps up there with the rest of the Guard," Thom decided.

"You fellas stay here and keep watch on the works," Mick said to the boys. "Not a good idea to leave them unattended. But don't even think about playing around with them. Need to be a trained professional to do it safely."

"No, you don't. It's easy," chided Grant. "Just hold the damn lighter to the fuse then duck. Hell, you can do it, I can do it."

Mick slapped Grant in the back of the head. "Don't even think about it. Mess with my fireworks, and I will make it my personal obsession to see you on waste reclamation duty for the rest of your pathetic childhood. I do not need to hear it from your father for the next ten years if you blow yourself to smithereens."

Thom doffed his field glasses and handed them to Frank. "Here, you can hold onto these, too. Was using them to spot our aim. They got night vision."

"Cool, thanks," Frank said.

With that, Thom and Mick dashed up the hill toward the town center.

Already, three men were marching to the eastern edge of town, armed with repellers and bolt throwers. The boys watched their silhouettes cross the steady glow from the lights at the power plant. A larger group of men trailed them, carrying picnic tables, which they turned over on their sides and set in the dirt to form a crude roadblock across the path, about fifty yards outside of town. Next came Garris Hughes and Richard Finch, shuffling along with shoulders bowed under the weight of a heavy noonlight that had once been part of *Triumphant*'s signal array. They planted it beside the tables. Finch swiveled the light's drum around and activated it.

Icy illumination painted the trail, turning it to afternoon for more than a hundred yards. As far away as they were, the sudden light still hit the boys with a sharp, harsh glare. The rumble of the Crawler drew closer while their eyes adjusted, and by the time they could stare straight on toward the arc of the noonlight, they could see the Crawler rolling across the edge of the shadow and nosing to a stop just inside the range of the light. Black smoke, coarse and oily in the brightness, drifted from the back engine compartment.

"Man, talk about timing," said Colt.

***

For a cold minute, nothing happened.

Stuart Duncan, Garris Hughes, and the Joseph Matson stood thirty or forty feet out in front of the makeshift checkpoint, repeller rifles hanging loose and ready in their hands. The Crawler idled, its engine gurgling and belching forth occasional bulbs of black soot that smelled of burning engine fluid. In the town square, the people of New Dodge grew silent and the band set down their instruments. The eyes of every settler turned toward the east, where spillover from the noonlight bounced and rippled on the flapping thermal sheeting of the distant dew wells. A stray wind caught some dust from the trail between the men and the Crawler, lifted it, spun it in a miniature cyclone that held for a moment, and then dropped it back to the ground.

With a mighty creak, the forward hatch of the Crawler swung outward and a man emerged, one hand cupped across his brow to take the edge off the artificial brightness. He took three steps down the trail and then stopped. One hand fumbled inside his coat until it emerged with a pair of desert sungoggles that he donned to protect his eyes.

He cleared his throat, and the sound carried through the silence.

"Well, Hiya," he called. "See you brought out the welcoming committee. Not necessary, but much appreciated. My name's Barnes Mungelson. My crew and I apologize for dropping in unannounced, but we could sure use some help."

Mungelson wore loose-fitting clothing of the kind favored by rangers and desert researchers for its comfort and protection from the sudden, swirling sandstorms that plagued the Junsuka. Several days' growth of beard spotted his jaw line. He looked tired and his left arm shook.

"Always happy to lend a hand to a neighbor," responded Duncan. "It's just that, well, pretty much every human who lives here on Byanntia happens to be down in the town square tonight. So, I think you can understand our intense *interest* in a new face. What business brings you our way?"

"Well, there's damn few humans on this ball of dirt and even less civilized living, that's no lie you're telling. I guess this must be the famous town of New Dodge," said Mungelson.

Duncan's eyes narrowed and he tightened his grip around the stock of his repeller. "Mr. Mungelson, I asked you a question," he stated.

Mungelson bristled.

"So you did, so you did," he muttered. He stuck one hand behind his back and waved two fingers toward the Crawler. "Doing research out in the damn desert brings me to Byanntia. Collecting samples, monitoring weather patterns, looking for signs of new and interesting life brings me to Byanntia. And given our current situation, I'd just as soon I had never set foot here. We hit a sinkhole coming across some dunes and slid into some submerged rocks. Banged up the Crawler real well. Our pickup isn't scheduled for another week, but we caught a bead on your satellite beacon and figured you were close enough for us to pull in to make some repairs."

"What outfit you with?" asked Duncan.

"LunaTech," said Mungelson. "Got all our papers and permits in the Crawler. Be happy to show them to you, though I have to say, I wouldn't mind knowing your name first."

"I'm Sheriff Stuart Duncan," he said. "I expect we'll be able to help you fix that Crawler. We got some spare parts and half-a-dozen crack mechanics. But I'll take you up on that offer, I think. So, let's see those papers, meet your crew, and have a look at your cargo."

"Sure, sure, Sheriff," Mungelson said. He rotated, waving for Duncan to follow him. "Come on with me, and I'll introduce you to my guys. One of them is injured. Sprained his ankle digging the Crawler free. He'll be all right, but I suppose he wouldn't mind some painkillers if you have a doctor in town."

"We do," said Duncan. "We'll see to his injuries as soon as we take care of business."

"All right, then," replied Mungelson. He reached up to the hatch and pulled himself back into the Crawler.

Duncan looked over his shoulder at Garris Hughes, and whispered, "You catch that signal he flashed back to the Crawler?"

"I noticed it," Hughes said.

"All right, then," said Duncan. "Keep us covered. I'm not back in a reasonable amount of time, pull everyone into the square and get ready to blast this bunch to dust and debris if they cross the town line."

Hughes nodded.

***

Through the field glasses, Frank saw his father's subtle wave, hand at his side, in silent signal to Joseph Matson and Richard Finch. The two men broke off from the group, outside of the range of the noonlight, and disappeared into the night. Frank tried to track them, switching the glasses back to night vision, but the plume of smoke flooding out of the Crawler obscured his view.

"I don't believe it!" blurted Colt. "Your dad is going into the Crawler."

"Yeah," Frank said, dangling the field glasses from his neck. "Guess he wants to make sure everything is all right before he lets these people into town."

"You think that's a good idea?" asked Colt. "Going in alone?"

"What do you think they're going to do, Colt? Kidnap him and run? Where would they go? They obviously need our help. It'll be fine. You know my Dad. Has to have everything signed on the dotted line before he so much as takes a leak. He's just being careful."

"That Crawler has seen better days, I'll tell you," observed Grant. He took the field glasses from Frank and scanned the vehicle. "Look at those scratches and gouges. Must have been some pretty sharp, hard rock to take chunks of metal like that out of it. Back tracks are off alignment. Probably leaking fluids under there, too."

"Well, I figure we can get it fixed for them," Frank said. "As long as we got Choi and Tomlinson around, there's not much mechanical work we can't do."

"You think your dad is going to have our hides for being up in the dew towers?" wondered Grant. "That was pretty damn stupid, I guess. Not that we hurt anything."

Frank shrugged. "He won't let us off, you know that."

"Look, he's coming out!" blurted Colt.

***

Duncan emerged from the cabin of the Crawler. The stranger followed. The two men shook hands in the vehicle's shadow.

Duncan returned to the checkpoint. "They back, yet?" he asked Hughes.

"Nope," Hughes said. "So, what do you make of these guys?"

"Everything seems to be in order. Got the papers from LunaTech, just like he said, notarized by a duly appointed representative of the United Rim. And he showed me a few bins of samples they got stored. Still, something doesn't feel right," Duncan explained. "That Crawler has taken a beating, something more than just tipping over on some sandy rock, I'd say. And there's a strange smell in there. Faint. Can't place it, but I know I've smelled it before."

"Papers can be forged. Samples can be faked," Hughes noted.

"Sure can," acknowledged Duncan. "And I'm no soil scientist to say whether their rocks and dirt are the genuine article or not."

"Want me to send Pete Dawson to fetch Professor Ridley? He'll tell you in a second if the stuff is genuine," suggested Hughes.

"Already thought of that," Duncan said. "And I see it this way—if they're on the up and up, no problem. If they're not, the sooner they think we're onto them, the sooner this could turn ugly. I think we should get them under control, separate them from that Crawler, and then we can get down to the nut of this on our terms."

"Why don't we just send them packing?" said Hughes.

"Broken down and injured? They need a place to go. Can't be sure they'll leave if we tell them to. They could just linger around out in the foothills and make trouble for us. Or worse, they might find their way into the squatter camp and rile that bunch up. More trouble we don't need. Better to keep them where we can see them," Duncan said. "And, Hell, who knows—maybe they're just who they say they are."

"I kind of doubt it, but all right; we'll clear the trail another sixty yards or so to the vehicle shed. That Crawler ought to be able to make it. I can post fifteen, twenty men to block the path toward the square," Hughes said.

"Do it," said Duncan.

The sheriff approached the Crawler and waited for Mungelson. He surveyed the odd damage to the vehicle, the scratches and dents left as if something had raked across the hard shell and tried to pound its way into the interior. A hairline crack ran through the windshield, and Duncan pondered a dozen scenarios that could have broken glass made to withstand an avalanche. He felt satisfied by none of them.

Mungelson ambled out of the Crawler and met Duncan at the center of the trail.

"Have your guys follow my men to the garage. Then we'll get you squared away and see about some food and sleeping quarters for the night," Duncan said.

"That sounds better than fine, Sheriff. I'm grateful to you, my new friend," replied Mungelson, a toothy smile creasing his broad face.

"Now, just hold off on all that," clipped a clear, stern voice from the darkness beyond the edge of the trail. Joseph Matson and Finch emerged into the light, their repellers up and cocked, one aimed at Mungelson and the other at the Crawler. Something coarse and wet dangled from the crook of Matson's arm and flapped in the half-hearted wind. The men's expressions lit an anxious fire in Duncan's gut.

"Whatever line of bull this scum has been feeding you, Stu, forget it. Him and his men are dirty poachers and liars. There's blood all over the back tracks of this Crawler, and we found this in a broken storage compartment back there," Matson said. "Thing is full of them."

He hurled the fresh skin to the ground.

It fluttered in the tepid breeze and unfurled, its blue, black, and gray striping unmistakable, as were the dark red patches of blood spotting it. A caustic odor rose from the dead flesh, the same scent Duncan had sensed in the Crawler, but stronger, an odor he now recalled from when men had fought and killed for the right to keep this stretch of ground they called home.

"Kuzzi hide," uttered Duncan.

Cold dread filled him then melted away to searing rage.

Duncan swung once, the blow so unexpected and fast that Mungelson took it flat in the center of his face without quite knowing what had hit him. He doped it out seconds later after he had dropped to the ground, rolled once, and came to rest on his back. Duncan lurched over him with his repeller aimed at the poacher's heart. His knuckles were numb, but he felt confident his fingers could still squeeze the trigger.

***

Back in the clearing, Grant, still watching through the field glasses, cried out, "No way! Your dad just decked the guy, Frankie."

"Give!" Frank ordered, seizing the field glasses, raising them to his eyes. "Oh, man, that's a Kuzzi skin on the ground. These guys are hunters!"

"Outlaws," Colt said. "Then that means they're armed."

***

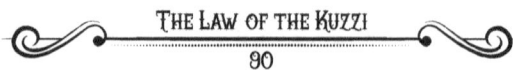

Looking down at the wounded man, Duncan brimmed with venom. "Give me one good reason not to blast a hole in every single one of you sleazy sons of bitches," he growled.

The vengeful edge in his voice shocked his friends as much as it did Mungelson. Hunting Kuzzi was illegal, punishable on Earth by life in psychiatric rehab, but that had not stopped a black market for the creature's hides and organs from springing up. People who measured their souls in wealth and power had proven more than willing to spend small fortunes for the pride of owning secret items made of genuine Kuzzi hide, or for the pleasure of consuming the tiny clusters of glands in their chests that contained a rare chemical that was hallucinogenic in humans. There was more than enough money in it to tempt men like Mungelson, ample lucre to pay for their ships, bribe officials, and purchase the equipment needed to land in the wilderness. A week's hunt could garner a hundred hides for clever, stealthy hunting parties, though the Kuzzi often proved dangerous prey. Career poachers were a rare breed. One who survived more than four hunts earned the tag of veteran, and those few who lasted six often earned enough to retire for the balance of their lives and live like kings. Not many did, though.

Everyone waited for Mungelson's answer, their attention fixed to the steady black hole at the end of Duncan's repeller.

Mungelson wiped his blood on his sleeve and cleared his throat. "They're jes' animals," he slurred. "Not human."

"They're intelligent," Duncan retorted.

"By whose standards?" burbled Mungelson. "They're savages! Wild beasts! Dirty creatures roaming the hills with no more sense of social structure than a pride of lions. Sophisticated, yeah, but not like men. Way I heard it, the whole lot of them have just been biding their time waiting to see you killed by the Gr'nar. And yet, here you are, defending them?"

"This is their world, not yours," Duncan said. "They're not supposed to be like men. It doesn't mean we're free to murder them."

Mungelson laughed. "It ain't murder, and I really don't care what you have to say. I thought we might work out an arrangement like reasonable, worldly men, Sheriff, but I'm just as happy to do this the hard and unpleasant way. Now, throw that repeller over here or I'll have my men lob a *blisterbomb* into your happy little gathering down the road there."

The top hatch of the Crawler clanked open and a dirt-matted figure popped up, a broad launch tube poised on his shoulder. The glow of its targeting display colored his face a pale green. He pointed the weapon upward, indicating the arc that would carry its projectile into the town square. Duncan recognized the gun and knew its range, knew what it meant for the settlers.

The missile would cover the distance in less than two seconds, then explode twenty or so feet overhead, dispersing a liquid sheet of death that would drench anyone below it, burning through clothing to coat their body with thick, caustic oil. Within seconds, the settlers' skin would turn bright red and erupt with plump pustules and heavy blisters. The fumes would travel into their lungs and the same process would begin internally. Within a minute they would be lying on the ground, writhing, unable to move, barely able to breathe, and then the inflammations and lesions would swell and burst, carrying flesh away in great swaths shed like a snake's skin. In less than three minutes, all those caught in the blast spray would be dead and reduced to bone and molten meat. Duncan played it out in his head. He thought of Sharon, pictured her body decomposing inside and out while he stood by helpless to save her.

"I got a bead on this prick, Stu," said Finch, steadying his repeller on the man atop the Crawler. "Let me take him out, and end this right here."

Finch was a top marksman, but if he missed or failed to kill the poacher in one shot, it could mean a painful death for many of the settlers. "Just hold off there for now, Rich," Duncan said. "Now that we have the truth, I want to hear what Mr. Mungelson really wants."

The satisfied smirk on Mungelson's face burned Duncan, but he saw no option other than to stall until an opportunity presented itself. He activated the safety on his repeller and threw it to the ground. The poacher stood and brushed dirt from his clothes. He sniffled, produced a stained handkerchief, and pressed it to his face, shivering as pain shot through his head and down his neck.

"One hell of a punch you got there, Stu," he snarled as he groped around for the repeller and found it. "Impressive for an old fart. Any harder and I'd be breathing out the back of my neck."

"Let's hear it, Mungelson. What do you want?" Duncan demanded.

The poacher shook his head. "Damn fool you are. You and all your friends here. Trying to find a way to live with those foul beasts out there while Earth stews in its own filth, suckling at the meager teat of clean meat and produce you send back. Men could take this world, make it our own, and live like we were meant to—free! Instead you choose to scrape and sweat, spill your blood into the soil so it can drink it up in a heartbeat like it never even existed. You make me sick, *Stu*."

Mungelson pulled the handkerchief aside, opened his mouth and stuck two fingers in while he mimed gagging and choking.

"Just tell me what you want," Duncan said.

"Fine," said Mungelson. He drew himself up inches away from the sheriff and leaned in close to his face. "We want protection and shelter until our ship comes to take us away. And then we want use of your landing facilities. Those miserable Kuzzi are getting smarter. They caught wind of us early this time and they were waiting. Came at us in a horde while we were stowing our take from one of their hunting parties. Got some new, heavy weapon, battering ram kind of thing, like a redwood trunk. Nearly broke their way into our Crawler, except the thing is built like a tank. We limped away from them, but they've been following us for two days. Thing is, we can't spend another week exposed in the wild and we can't risk them interfering when our ride comes. So, you and the rest of New Dodge are going to put us up until then, fix our Crawler, feed us, hide us from the Kuzzi, and then help us lift off. Got it?"

"If the Kuzzi have been tracking you, Mungelson, then they know you're here," Duncan said. "You're asking me to put New Dodge at risk."

"Understand something, here, Sheriff—New Dodge is already at risk. We used a fair number of blisterbombs fighting off the Kuzzi, but we got more than enough left to deal with your little shithole town here. So, I'm not asking you for anything, Stu. I'm telling you," Mungelson said.

"Think it through, Sheriff," Joseph Matson warned. "Even if we cover these animals for a week and then let them leave, the Kuzzi will know we helped our own kind get away with slaughtering their kind. They'll never trust us after that. Won't matter a bit that it was under duress."

"I know that, Joseph," Duncan said. "But what choice have we got?"

"Just take a minute to give it some thought, Sheriff. That's all I'm trying to say," Matson continued, and Duncan picked up on the young man's unspoken message—*buy some time*. Something had been set in motion. Duncan did not know what to expect, but he had faith in his friends.

"Go on and let me take the shot, Stu," pleaded Finch. "I'm telling you, I got this bastard dead to rights."

"Yeah, maybe you should," Duncan said, putting on a show of ambivalence. "Figure we don't take our chance now, we're just delaying the inevitable. We either fight this ragtag pile of kison turds or thousands and thousands of Kuzzi. Maybe we'll get lucky with these losers."

"Uh-uh," Mungelson said. "You listen to me before you do anything rash, Stu, because my associate atop the Crawler is but one member of my crew, armed with the firepower necessary to cripple your little tin-walled happyland here at the push of a button. Go ahead and kill him. Kill me if you think you're fast enough. You'll be signing death warrants for a lot of people and your own at the same time. Well, you got the facts. Rest is up to you, Sheriff."

"You're putting me in one hell of a spot here, Mungelson," Duncan said.

"Quit stalling. I ain't got time for shooting the breeze," the poacher spat back.

Duncan began to reply, but the blazing report of a bolt thrower cut him short.

The shot had come from the rear of the Crawler, the portion still cloaked in night, and the flash had pointed toward town. The poachers had a sniper mounted back there, out of sight, equipped with an infrared viewer and a long range weapon. Duncan cursed his stupidity for not anticipating such a maneuver as he whirled around and looked for the gunner's mark. A second shot fired. Through the narrow spaces between buildings, the sheriff saw Mick Busco and Thom Horton laid out on the ground at the edge of the town square. Jacob Matson knelt beside them, a pile of discarded repeller rifles at his feet, scattered alongside those dropped by Mick and Thom. Each man had been carrying an armful of weaponry. A small group, led by Doc Lieber, broke off from the gathering and rushed to help the fallen men. Across the distance Duncan could not tell if they still lived.

Mungelson sneered. "Well, now, that's about the saddest attempt to fight back I ever did see."

Duncan looked to Joseph Matson and Finch for explanation. Both men's faces had gone pale. The marksman lowered his weapon "Damn sniper," Finch grumbled.

"I'm sorry, Stu. Dad thought Mick and Thom would get through with the guns, get the crowd spread out to defend the town," Matson said. "We set them up before we reported back to you. Figured it was worth a shot."

Duncan shrugged. "I suppose it was at that."

"Well, what's it gonna be?" Mungelson prodded. "As if I don't already know."

A knot tightened in Duncan's stomach. Every one of his muscles trembled with the desire to clutch Mungelson and beat him into silence. But there was nothing he could do. He hated his helplessness. If it had been only his own life at stake, he might have sacrificed it, so long as he could take Mungelson with him. But he had others to watch over and protect.

"Keep your shirt on, Mungelson. I may be ornery, but I know when I'm licked," Duncan said.

Mungelson's face broke into a wide, self-satisfied smile, but it faded fast.

A sanguine howl filled the moonless sky: a long, anguished accusation, answered by other voices joining it in a discordant chorus that rose together and meshed into a single outpouring of pain, injustice, and anger. It thinned the blood of all those who heard it. The tall, dry grass that grew off the trail rustled with movement beyond the range of the electric light. The guttural wailing continued, increasing in volume as it drew closer, and achieved a shrill, painful pitch before it ceased as abruptly as it had begun.

Mungelson seized Duncan by his shirt. "We got no time left!" he screamed. "Order your men to protect us. Now!"

Duncan ignored the poacher's frantic pleas. His attention fixated on the lithe form taking shape in the shadows by the rear of the Crawler. The towering figure stepped partway into the realm of the noonlight, where its powerful striped legs identified it as a Kuzzi warrior. The auburn embers of its eyes, still shrouded in darkness, conveyed its disposition. Muscles and sinew twisted and flexed and a bulky shape flew across the air. A poacher, his hands still wrapped around a bolt thrower, crashed to the dirt. A long spear angled with multiple blades and points protruded from between his shoulders.

A second Kuzzi joined the first, this one taller and stronger, its eyes enflamed with fury, its teeth bared and glowing in the dark. It stamped the dirt beside its wide taloned paws with the haft of its *purjung*, a spear identical to the one embedded in the sniper.

"Must be a hundred of them out there," said Finch.

"More," added Matson.

Guardsmen crouched behind the flimsy protection of the blockade, their weapons raised, their nerves buzzing with anticipation.

"Shoot! Shoot already," cried Mungelson. "What are you waiting for? You'll let them kill us all. Give the order, Sheriff, by the count of three, or I will have my man burn your town to extinction."

Mungelson leveled the repeller toward Duncan and began his count. He never finished it.

At "two," an explosion ripped across the air directly above the men, followed half a second later by two more. Even the noonlight paled in the sudden flash of colors that bit the men's eyes and turned their movements into strobed pantomimes of activity. In the increased illumination, Duncan saw the ranks of the Kuzzi spread out in semi-circles on each side of the trail, two or three deep in places, their lines stretching into the foothills and beyond sight. Their long, creamy fangs, slicked with saliva, protruded from black gums; the dark lips of their muzzles were drawn back in shallow snarls. Their eyes narrowed to bores of ferocity, and their shiny, black manes stood erect and pointed along the backs of their skulls and down the line of their spines. Each one clasped a twelve-foot *purjung*, arrayed with three or more blades.

There were not a hundred, but hundreds, possibly thousands stretching deep into the foothills, as if the entire Kuzzi nation had turned out in witness for the events of this dark night.

A gunshot cracked, but Duncan could not tell who had fired. The clashing glares tricked his vision. A second report snapped. He ducked in fear of stray shots, but no other gun spoke, and he crouched, uncertain whether to run or defend himself. He rubbed his eyes as the parti-colored flares faded, giving way to the steady clarity of the noonlight. What had happened had taken only seconds.

Mungelson lay sprawled in the trail, blood spattered across his leather tunic, his chest pumping in erratic gasps for breath as consciousness bled from him.

The poacher armed with the blisterbomb hung from the hatch of the Crawler, his rocket launcher lost in the dust beside the machine's tracks. Half a dozen men from the Guard, who had been further back and away from the full intensity of the explosions, had already surrounded and entered the vehicle, taking control from the stunned poachers inside. The men tried to ignore the fierce Kuzzi warriors, who watched and waited.

"You all right, Stuart?" someone asked.

A reassuring hand pressed Duncan's shoulder. It was Finch.

"Told you I had the bastard dead to rights," he said.

Duncan rubbed his eyes. "So you did."

"Your eyes will recover. One of those fireworks went off right over your head. Another practically set that man on top of the Crawler's hair on fire," Joseph Matson said.

Duncan scanned his men as his vision cleared and wondered who had ignited the fireworks. He thought he already had a pretty good idea, but he wasn't quite sure how he felt about it.

The Guardsmen led the poachers from the Crawler and lined them up in a row in front of the vehicle. There were five of them, all dirty and tired-looking, with expressions ranging from frightened to defiant. Duncan felt cold hatred for these men, who were themselves more like beasts than the Kuzzi they hunted. The hum of leathern paws scuffing brown grass and coarse dirt snapped Duncan back to the moment. The Kuzzi tightened their ranks, moving into the light and closing the half-circle they had formed around the Crawler. Duncan could not interpret their reserve during the brief firefight. Why had the Kuzzi not taken the opportunity to sweep in and overwhelm the men with their numbers? He searched their alien expressions, but no face among them divulged a single clue.

The tall one he had noted earlier broke ranks and approached him.

Better than eight feet in height, he loomed over Duncan, a giant of muscle and bone and fur, the kind of beast fit to spawn a thousand legends back on Earth. The Kuzzi nodded and dipped his muzzle in a traditional greeting and then it growled a low rumbling sound that rolled on for a full minute. The other Kuzzi echoed him. They stamped the posts of their *purjungs* against the ground, the dull thumping building to a thunderous roar as more and more of them joined in, found a common rhythm, and turned the arid plain into a massive, muted drum that throbbed with fury and heartache. And then Duncan understood their discipline, their purpose.

How Mungelson or anyone else could consider these creatures less than human was something he would never understand.

With all the power they needed to enforce their will at hand, the Kuzzi had chosen to make known their desires and then wait to see what their human neighbors would do. Duncan knew the people of New Dodge were being tested tonight in more than one way. The standoff with the poachers had been defused, and now the Kuzzi had laid their claim. The hunters had broken the law, and Duncan knew he could imprison them, hold them until the Rim Authority could send a transport to take them back to Earth to stand trial. But Earth law was not the only law they had transgressed. Certainly, it was not the first law they had broken. Didn't the Kuzzi have an even greater right to satisfy their need for justice? Kuzzi blood had been spilled, not human. The people of New Dodge had been unwilling players in the eternal conflict between hunter and prey, though Duncan could not say for sure precisely which role fit the Kuzzi and which the poachers. Not that it mattered. The way was clear to him now.

The sheriff crouched and retrieved the hide Joseph Matson had thrown to the dirt. He carried it to the Kuzzi leader, cradling it across his forearms, and then he knelt and presented the skin as though handing over the corpse of a fallen friend.

"My name is Sheriff Stuart Duncan, and I'm deeply sorry," he said to the Kuzzi, not knowing if the creature understood. "I'm sorry for all this, for everything men like these here have done to your kind. That must sound hollow, and I know it's no comfort, but these are bad men. We recognize that. They're outlaws and murderers, and we do not associate ourselves with them."

The Kuzzi took the hide and nodded once, a wet rumble rolling over in his lungs.

Duncan rose. "I imagine you have ones like them among your own people, ones you single out for punishment. I hope you understand what I'm saying."

He gestured for the men guarding the Crawler to stand down, and as they moved aside, Kuzzi warriors took their place. A line of Kuzzis entered the Crawler, and after a short time, reemerged, each one carrying a share of skins in their arms, the remains of their fallen. Other Kuzzi raided the rear storage compartments, producing more hides, and soon the lanky warriors were stealing away into the darkness, the striped furs draped across their shoulders and hands. They moved in silence. Duncan's heart sank at the number of skins reclaimed. He knew, measured in money, they would amount to enough to buy a city, but he could not comprehend that kind of bargain.

When the Kuzzi had completed their work, the sheriff ordered his men to take the empty Crawler into town and leave the poachers for their new captors. As he turned back to New Dodge, he found Jacob Matson blocking his way, the old man's chest bucking from his jog out from town square.

"You sure about this, Stuart?" Matson asked. "You remember that day out past Morgan's Bluff, back when we were charting the land? You know the place I mean? Way out on the edge of the frontier? Long time ago, I know, but we were both there. I can't believe you've forgotten. That's what you're sentencing these men to. You prepared to do that?"

Duncan had already considered the sheer rock of the bluff, the gentle, sloping valley beyond it, and the terrible sight it had contained. He and Matson had been with ten or twelve other men scouting the outlying reaches of the region on hovercycles when they came to it—a thicket of *purjungs* and sharp pikes planted in the earth and draped with the skins and bodies of dead Kuzzi warriors, laid out there by a rival tribe that most likely had ambushed them coming south along the bluff. The stink of rotting flesh had been repellant, but even worse were the faces, the flayed skin with eyeholes and muzzles still intact, flapping in the wind from the tips of broken spears.

"Yeah, I know what it means for them," said Duncan. "I'll never forget what we saw out there, but I'm not the one sentencing them. We're not the ones most wronged by these men. It's the Kuzzi, and the fate of these men is up to them. Way it's gotta be, Jacob."

"But it was horrible," prodded Matson.

Duncan looked his friend in the eye. Matson recoiled from the stark wetness he saw there. "More horrible than what they did to the Kuzzi?" Duncan asked.

The Crawler grumbled down the trail toward the vehicle shed. The poachers hollered and swore as half a dozen Kuzzi took position around them. They cursed the men for leaving them, but their pleas went wasted. Poking the men with the flat of their spears, the Kuzzi marched them toward the foothills. Soon only Duncan and the Kuzzi leader were left, face-to-face in the middle of the trail, their people withdrawing on both sides, stillness returning to the night.

"I hope neither of us ever meets men like that again," Duncan said.

The Kuzzi leader snarled, a low, throaty sound. His fur rippled and shimmered as he shifted his shoulders. "So do I," he spoke in a halting, feral tone. "For your sake as much as ours."

Duncan watched the leader join his tribe. The words filled him with a sensation that he could not identify, one that dulled the edge of the outrage and horror he still felt and stoked the hope for the future that smoldered inside him.

* * *

When he reached the town square, he found nearly the entire populace of New Dodge circled around a pair of picnic tables on which his son and his two friends stood.

They were entertaining the crowd with the story of how they lit the fireworks that had saved the day; how they tested the wind, measured the fuses, took careful aim, crossed their fingers, and watched the rockets burn. Doc Lieber had reported that Mick and Thom would pull through with some bed rest and careful medical care, and the settlers were already looking to find some humor in the night's events. When the boys finished their tale, Duncan waited for the laughter and cheers to subside before he stepped forward.

"Frankie, Grant, Colt," he said. "You boys played a bigger role in what happened here tonight than you know. Maybe one day you'll look back and understand it for what it was. As the sheriff of New Dodge, I want to extend the gratitude of the town to you for your fast thinking, your bold action, and your good humor through adversity. We might have been lost without it."

The boys beamed with pride, smiles creasing their mouths.

"But that doesn't change the fact that you broke the rules when you climbed the dew towers and that you broke them again, not an hour later, when you fooled around with Mick and Thom's fireworks. Starting tomorrow, you're all on three months duty digging trenches for the irrigation system," Duncan said. "And, dammit, I don't want to hear a word of complaint from any one of you the whole time."

Frank and Grant looked stunned. Their grins evaporated. Colt's shoulders slumped in resignation.

The people of New Dodge filled the square and the streets of their town with a typhoon of communal laughter.

"But tomorrow isn't here, yet, boys. So for now, get your butts off those tables and let's get on with the celebration!" Duncan boomed.

In response, a fiddle played and a horn blew, and the band picked up a jaunty beat as three young women dragged the boys into the center of the clearing and made them dance. Later that night, while the party wound to a close, the boys, tired and overexcited, puffed their cigars out behind the vehicle shed and grew dizzy on the potent smoke.

THE DRIVE

Robert E. Waters

PART 1

THE DUN-COLORED BRONCO BUCKED AND BOUNCED ACROSS THE corral. The young man in the saddle felt the rope dig deep into his hand. He'd refused to wear the gloves like his older brother had advised. Who needed gloves? He was old enough, strong enough to handle the pain. Gloves were for boys. But now this boy regretted his stubbornness. The horse swung its rump violently to the left, kicked and arched its powerful back. The rope bit deep again. The boy screamed and flew through the air.

The next thing Stewart Matson felt was dirt in his mouth, dust in his eyes, and laughter in his ears.

"You are the sorriest rider I've ever seen, Stew," said Joseph Matson as he bounded off the fence and used his younger brother's sore back as a footstool. "There's not a horse on Byanntia that likes you."

Stewart pulled himself up, spit dirt from his mouth, and rubbed his bloody hand on his canvas jeans. "Shut up, Joe. You could do no better with this one."

The real rider of the family was their father, Jacob Matson. But he was held up in bed, fending off fever and nursing wounds from an ancient beast known as the Gr'nar. It had almost killed the old man, but somehow he'd survived. Jacob Matson had survived all right, but not well enough to run the Matson ranch. Not for awhile, at least. That task now fell to his sons.

Joseph opened the gate to the corral and they walked out together. "Well, you better find a horse today, little brother," he said. "The drive starts tomorrow."

Stewart suddenly got a bad taste in his mouth. It's not that he didn't like riding horses; he just preferred something a little more high-tech, a little easier to control. "Why can't I just ride a hovercycle? We ride them all the time around the ranch."

Joseph sighed. "You know they'll spook the kison. The trail boss won't allow them, and we can't afford a misstep."

"It's our run," Stewart said, "and it's our kison."

Joseph shook his head. "You aren't the boss on this one, Stewart. Alvin Trainer is."

Stewart grunted and spit in the dirt. "Then why the hell do I have to go?"

"We've been through this already. A Matson must be present to lend legality and credibility to it. And to ensure that the kison arrive safely. You are the family representative. You *have* to be there."

Stewart pursed his lips. "You should do it. You have more drive experience than I do."

The young man, all of sixteen years, couldn't believe his own words. Was he growing up? God, he hoped not. Not yet, anyway. Growing up meant more duties, more responsibility. He wanted that, but now that their oldest brother Chad had been recently killed by the very same Gr'nar that had attacked their father, responsibility came on quickly like a thunderclap. And how in blazes was he, Stewart Matson, supposed to keep a thousand head of kison safe? He'd have his bolt gun and his foot-long knife made from a Kuzzi purjung blade. He was reasonably skilled in both, but how could one man hold off predators or a crew if that crew decided on mischief? How?

"The Vellong Trade commissioner insists on dealing with an elder representative of the family if the patriarch can't do it," Joseph said. "I don't like it anymore than you do, little brother, but we've no choice. I've got to go and play the business man."

Stewart couldn't imagine himself as a business man. He didn't have the mind or the patience for it. He preferred to be among the kison, out on the ranch, the hot Byanntia sun baking his skin and the tough ground beneath the hum of his cycle, the warm wind cutting through his clothing, the endless stretch of grassland all around. He loved that more than anything. But to be the family "representative" on a kison drive... it was too soon.

Their mother, Shelby Matson, met them on the porch of their ranch house. She was a strong, hearty woman, but Stewart could see the withering her face had taken over the past several weeks. Losing her first born tragically, then almost losing her husband in the same manner, was more than any woman should bear. She covered up her pain with a thin smile. She looked right at her baby boy. "Clean up, Stewart," she said. "Your crew is here."

Stewart's heart sank. He nodded. "I'll be in directly, mama."

Shelby Matson disappeared inside. Joseph turned to his brother and said, with that award-winning smirk, "Cheer up, boy." He patted Stewart's back and a cloud of dust billowed up. "It's just a five day run. Easy as drok. What could possibly go wrong?"

As Stewart watched his brother walk away, he began counting the ways. He stopped counting when he ran out of fingers and toes.

***

Trail Boss Alvin Trainer had that chiseled-stone look, as if he'd been beaten with thick iron hammers. His face was pock-marked with rabid acne and criss-crossed with scars from a dozen brawls. His skin was burnt leather, his clothing a throw-back to ancient earth myth when "cowboys" ruled the American Wild West. Stetson hat. Kison-skin chaps and vest. Canvas jeans. Silver buttons imported from earth. Double-holstered bolt guns with white handles wrought from kison bones. Thick leather boots with steel spurs. Despite his guns, he despised technology of any kind, and although Byanntia was not known for many high-tech gadgets, what little there was, Alvin Trainer despised them. He had deep, inset eyes that glared over huge, dark bags. He made Stewart Matson nervous. He couldn't trust a man who chewed a green stinger plant stick incessantly.

The fact that he talked softly was another reason not to trust him. "If it please you, Mr. Matson," Trainer said, bowing slightly to Stewart, "allow me to introduce our drive leads."

Assembled around them was a host of characters decked in trail finery. Stewart recognized some of them from New Dodge City. Some of them had worked with the Matsons before.

Stewart nodded. "Very well."

Trainer cleared his throat. It sounded like stones grinding meal. He placed his hand on the shoulder of a black man to his right. "This is Reiner Johns, our Chuckwagon Boss." He then pointed to others. Stewart shook hands with each as names were called. "Drover Captain, Prestor Jack. Outrider Boss, Michele Hughs. Hover-Wagon Master, Marshall Peete. Kison Boss, Remy Kay. Camp Boss, Lucia Belle."

Stewart was about to speak, then a hooded figure, crouched quietly behind Trainer, stood up and removed the hood. It wasn't a man. It wasn't human either. The figure towered over everyone, including Trainer. It tossed its cloak open and moved forward. On its furry chest were three pairs of small, firm breasts. Stewart's eyes widened.

"Kuzzi!"

He hadn't even realized he'd said the word out loud. Trainer nodded. "Yes, indeed. And my personal assistant." He stepped aside to give the female Kuzzi more room. He motioned to her and said, "This is Bainta, daughter of Sinaku, late Kuzzi warrior of the Red Desert Band. She'll be attending this drive."

Stewart didn't know what to say, his eyes fixed on the tall, sleek and muscular Kuzzi female. She was not as tall as a male of her species nor did she possess the thick black mane that cupped a male's face, but she shared the same blue and black striping that helped keep her camouflaged

against the harsh Byanntia environment. Her more subtle face was also speckled with grey and white dots that gave her visage a warm and pleasant appearance, contrary to the long, sharp teeth that Stewart could see clearly as he stared up into her rigid jaw. She was quite a magnificent specimen. Her eyes glowed like black coals.

"I—," Stewart said, the words catching in his mouth. He swallowed and tried again. "I didn't realize Kuzzi females drove kison. I didn't—"

"Bainta is not your typical Kuzzi female, Mr. Matson," Trainer said. "And she's been off-world for awhile. But she's a fine scout, and part of our route will take us over the Gordon Pass. It's a narrow and treacherous mountain gap and we'll need skilled guidance. I have every faith in Bainta."

"Did my father approve this?"

Trainer shook his head, the craters of his face glowing red like fire. "Your brother did."

Joe! Stewart bit his lip. He should have known. His brother was always pulling stuff like this. *Very funny, brother. Just you wait...*

It wasn't like the Matsons had personal problems with the Kuzzi. When Chad had gone missing, their mother had taken them to see Chief Bollatu in the Valley of the Twelve Peaks. There, they had discovered the nature of the Gr'nar. The Kuzzi had treated them well enough. But having one on a drive (and a female to boot) was unprecedented. What would people think? How would this affect future business?

All the crew leads were staring at him. This was his first challenge of authority, and Joseph had led him right to the abyss. *He expects me to fall over the edge,* Stewart thought to himself, *to overreact and cause a scene. But I won't jump.*

Stewart nodded and smiled. "Yes, indeed. No problem. We'll need all the help we can get. Thank you for offering your services, Bainta. I look forward to it."

With that fire quashed, Trainer turned to a chalkboard and began scribbling lines and dots. When he was finished, he turned and said, "Now, if you'll allow me, I'll explain our route and how I plan to win this competition."

***

The competition was simple, at least on paper. Three Byanntia ranch families – the Cools, the Bensons, and the Matsons – would drive a thousand head of kison each to Vellong Trade Federation slaughter tugs situated sixty-five kilometers north-northeast of New Dodge City. Across grasslands, parts of the Junsuka desert and through the Gordon Pass. Why the Vellong didn't simply fly their tugs to each ranch and pick up the herds was the question of the hour: It was the question of the galaxy, in fact. But that wasn't the Vellong way. They thrived on competition, and reveled in making their prospective clients jump through hoops to get their lucrative trade agreement. The family who won would reap great benefits so long as the meat flowed and Byanntia remained on its axis. The losers... well, the Vellong would buy their herds for their troubles, but no future considerations. That was why the Vellong demanded a competition, Stewart Matson figured. If a rancher went the extra mile for the Vellong, the Vellong would return the favor. At least he *hoped* that was the reason. He'd hate to think that the reason was because the Vellong were nothing but corporate jackasses.

But this competition had come at the worst time, and although the trail boss had an effective plan of attack, Stewart was worried. Looking out over the sea of kison below him, that meat tug seemed a million miles away.

Shelby Matson could feel her son's apprehension. She put her arm around his shoulders and hugged gently. "It'll be all right, Stew," she said, placing a light kiss on his cheek. "You can do this. Your father has faith in you. I have faith in you. And Alvin Trainer is a good man."

"I've never worked with him before, mama."

"He drove for us before you were born, Stew. He's been off-world for a long time. But your father believes in him, and so do I."

Stewart laid his head on her shoulder. "I wish Chad were here."

He felt her stiffen. Then she relaxed and said, "We all do, son. But he isn't. Just remember that a Matson never gives in, never compromises.

Your brother died because of it. Your father clings to life because of it. The matter is in yours and Joe's hands. No more doubt. Get it *done.*"

"Yes, Mama."

Shelby Matson held the reins while Stewart climbed his horse. He'd settled on a beautiful red roan. He took the reins from his mother, blew her a kiss, and spurred his horse into motion.

He cupped his hand over his mouth, "Move 'em out!" he yelled.

Albert Trainer repeated the call, and down the line the words were echoed from drover to drover, outrider to outrider, until the mighty wall of kison began to move.

The drive was on.

***

Kison were a curious beast. Big and cumbersome always. Docile grazers more often than not, yet unpredictable at the drop of a hat. A thousand head was only a small portion of the entire herd on the Matson's *Twin Feathers* ranch, but getting them all moving in the same direction was a difficult task indeed.

Kison bulls stood on average seven feet tall at the shoulders. Like their earthen counterparts, the ancient American bison, they were much taller in the front than in the back. Like the bison, they too had dark, thick fur covering their shoulders – sometimes black, sometimes tan, sometimes grey – which they shed in the summer. Underneath that fur, however, was a carapace of tough skin that spread from their broad necks and down their spines like body armor. Along their spines grew tiny spikes that started small near the tail, but grew progressively larger until they ended at the top of their heads in two horns that could penetrate a foot of ironwood at full charge. Such a nasty looking creature whose meat was so tender, it could drop off the bone with a mere hour of skilled seasoning and cooking. Amazing contrasts indeed.

The females were similar in stature but stood roughly a foot and a half shorter at the shoulders, and they sported fewer and shorter spikes up their spines.

In addition to the kison, there were team leads and many additional staff to keep the mountain of flesh moving.

There were eight drovers alone, all circling the kison and keeping them moving forward, tracking down independents and herding them back into the fold. Four outriders worked the flanks to spot any potential dangers ahead. Cooking support staff, camp staff, hover-wagon riders, three assistant veterinarians and one skilled calf berther. All of their support equipment and supplies were carried inside the three hover-wagons that Trainer insisted be held in the rear to ensure that the kison were not spooked by their engines. He'd wanted real covered wagons, but that was not possible, and frankly, impractical. Hover-wagons were thirty meter flat-bed vessels that could carry more cargo than regular wagons and run virtually non-stop on batteries powered by removable solar canopies. They did not require wainrights or teams to pull them. Virtually maintenance-free. Stewart checked the full drive manifest for a third time, counting bedrolls, tents, sacks of meal, beans and dried stinger leaves, potable water, smoked kison meat, and on and on. It made his head spin.

"Don't worry, young man," Trainer said, shifting a stick left and right in his mouth, "Everything's in place. Sit back and enjoy the ride."

It was difficult to hear over the rumble of kison hooves, their constant baying and bawling, shifting and shuffling, but Stewart shook his head. "It's a massive undertaking. If things go wrong—"

The trail boss leaned over in his saddle and stared into Stewart's eyes. "I'm aware of the risks, son. I've been on a drive or two in my time."

Stewart nodded. "I'm sure you have, Mr. Trainer, but your plan requires us to make a minimum of thirteen miles daily. Not impossible, but it doesn't leave much room for error."

Trainor's face grew red. "I plan on making fifteen miles per day. And I don't need you to be telling me—"

Trainer's rant was interrupted by a commotion up the line. The kison around them began to shift left and right, as if they were circling around an outcropping of rock or a large tree. But no such obstacle existed,

Stewart knew. Only soft, rolling grassland lay ahead for several more miles.

Stewart strained in the saddle for a better view. "What is it?" he asked. "What do you see?"

Trainer lifted in the stirrups. He spit his stick out and cursed. "Damn it all!"

"What's wrong?"

"We've got trouble. Big trouble."

The boss was gone before Stewart even spurred his horse.

The big trouble was four bull kison locked in battle, pounding their armored heads together, circling each other, scraping the ground. Kison were, for the most part, very docile creatures, but it was not uncommon for bulls to pit off against each other during rut. Struggle for dominance in a cow klatch was expected, with the loser often dying of its wounds. But a brawl of four or more could be deadly indeed. If not brought under control, the battle could spread to other bulls, a stampede ensue, multiple deaths.

Stewart brought his roan into full view of the battle and pulled the reins tightly before he slid into the thick of the kison. Already four drovers were attempting to circle around the battle, working desperately to keep the fight contained. Kison Boss Remy Kay screamed orders as his men tightened the noose: "Watch it now. Not too close!" Stewart had seen many a man get gored through the leg or shoulder. One had even been pierced through the heart. With so much weight behind it, a kison bull with its blood up was a dangerous beast indeed.

A drover pulled an electrical prod and stabbed it into the flank of one of the bulls. An arc of blue lightning spread across the kison's body. It jumped three meters, but did not stop. It thrust its head into the air and twisted its body around until it faced its assailant. The drover tried to stab the beast again, but the bull's horns caught the prod and ripped it from the man's grip. The drover's horse reared up. The man fought to keep his balance but he went over hard, his head hitting the ground. The bull was on him instantly, trampling his back and rolling him forward with his

horns. The man's screams could be heard over the roar of a herd that was quickly becoming uncontrollable.

The other drovers thrust their prods into the side of the beast. The electrical current rushing through the bull was enough to cook its insides, and Stewart could smell its fur and flesh bake. His stomach churned. He leaned over to release his breakfast into the high grass below.

Then he was flying through the air, like he had done just two mornings ago. This time, however, it was not the horse that had kicked him free. A rogue bull, in panic from all the blue light and stench of burnt fur, slammed into the side of the roan and hurled them backwards. Stewart hit the ground hard, rolling through the grass. He grit his teeth as his left wrist twisted. He bit back the pain and rolled to keep from getting trampled.

He rolled out of the path of the stampede and came up on weak legs. The roan had been gouged through the belly. It lay dying in a sea of crumpled grass and blood. The bull that had struck them was now pitched against another bull, their horns locked in a death roll.

Stewart tried to run to his horse, but a hand pulled him up and out of the fray. Before he knew it, he was sitting behind the trial boss. "Are you some damned fool, boy?" Trainer yelled as they turned and galloped away. "You trying to get yourself killed? Let the professionals handle it!"

Stewart looked back as they fled. From nowhere, Bainta, the Kuzzi scout, fell on the bull's back. She was a streak of fur, all claws and purjung spear. She thrust the weapon through the neck of the bull and it went down. As it fell, she jumped up, spun in the air then dropped alongside another bull whose panic had gouged a cow and her calf. She ducked its horns, kicked it in the head, then thrust her spear into its side.

The speed of the attack and the jet of blood pouring from the wound were too much. Stewart's eyes rolled into the back of his head and he slid off the saddle.

***

Six hours later, the herd was brought under control. A third of it had broken off from the main body, stampeding east for about five kilometers.

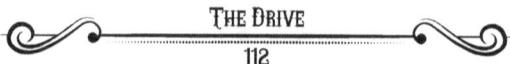

In total, six bulls and two cows were euthanized due to wounds. Another two died of sheer exhaustion and fright. A mere pittance in ratio to the full herd, but a loss nonetheless. The rules of the competition required that at least ninety-eight percent of the herd make the drive. They were a long way from falling below that number, but a crimp was now in the chain. The drover was so badly mauled that he had to be evacuated immediately by horseback at full speed, and they had lost hours of drive time, which would have to be recovered over the next couple days. And tomorrow, they would cross out of the grassland and into the hot waste of the Junsuka. Anything could happen there.

Stewart rubbed his sprained wrist and watched the setting sun paint the horizon in beautiful red and blue.

Stewart had never seen any other sunset. He'd never been off-world. Byanntia was his birth home, and it looked like that would never change. Joe was off hobnobbing with important traders, sipping beer no doubt, having a big old steak, laughing, clasping hands in bargain. *And here I am,* Stewart said to himself as he rubbed sweaty dirt off his sore neck, *getting myself half killed while* he *lives it up.* Stewart was beginning to reconsider the role of businessman.

"She's amazing, isn't she?"

Stewart jumped to his feet, chest pounding. He turned and saw the trail boss standing there, as big as life, smiling and chewing the end of a dirty stick. It was hard seeing his face, though the bright red sky gave him a glow of fire. The shape of his shadow suggested a man twice his size. Stewart backed off and took his kisonboy hat off instinctively.

"Who?"

"Bainta."

Indeed she was. The image of her lithe and powerful body flying through the air was hard to forget. He'd never seen anything like it. Humans tended to shoot from a distance, using boltguns or other kinds of ranged weapons, to bring down a foe. Bainta just tore into them like they were butter. Amazing.

Trainer smiled as he saw Stewart's beaming face in the growing moonlight. "Don't get any ideas, young man. She's mine."

Stewart shook his head, blinked his eyes. "No, I didn't, that is, I –"

Trainer waved him off and pushed past the young man to get a better look at the sky. "Don't sweat it, boy. I'm just playing with you. Besides, it doesn't work. We're too big, and they're too small." Trainer laughed. "And they're far too violent for us tenderfoots."

Stewart's face turned beet red; he couldn't help but snicker. He didn't know what to say, so they stood there for awhile, listening to the night creatures sing their songs. A Byanntia Grim Wolf howled in the distance. Turquoise Rock Crickets chirped loudly. A warm desert wind blew past them, carrying smoke from the crew's campfires below. Despite a difficult day, some of the crew found the strength to sing. Voices rose up in the wind, and the strum of a guitar filled the dead space. Stewart breathed deeply and took it all in. Finally he said,

"How did you meet her?"

Trainer pulled the stick from his mouth and rolled it between index and thumb as if it were a cigar. He stared at the stick for a long moment, then said, "It was about ten years ago. I was working as a land surveyor for the Hardy Ranch at the time. They hired me to scout out a patch of the Junsuka oh, maybe, two hundred kilometers from here. Watering holes, mountain gaps, underground streams, what have you.

"I came across this one pool up in the mountains. At least two dozen Kuzzi lay massacred on the ground. They'd obviously been hit by a rival band, and if you recall, that was around the time when the Kuzzi were at war with each other. I was picking around the bodies, you know, looking for trinkets, weapons, anything I could find, when something pokes me in the calf. I screamed and fell to the ground. Suddenly, there was this little Kuzzi girl standing over me, waving a bloody purjung spear at my throat. She lunges for me. I grab the spear, break it, and lock her in a bear hug. She struggles for about fifteen minutes or so before giving out. Neither one of us could understand each other much; a word here or there, but nothing substantial. But what I did know was that, despite her pluck, she wouldn't survive long in the desert alone. I figured her to be about ten or so, but I couldn't tell. Sometimes it's hard with the Kuzzi. They grow faster than humans.

"Anyway, I finally got her to calm down and she agreed to go with me. I tried leaving her in the care of a nearby Kuzzi band, but they rejected her."

"Why?" Stewart asked.

Trainer shook his head. "The Kuzzi are a strange lot. She was from a rival band, and thus if they had accepted her, she would have lived her life as a slave. But more importantly, they rejected her because they feared her."

Stewart furrowed his brow. "Feared her?"

"She had survived a massacre. To them, that's a kind of prophesy, as if the gods had let her live to carry the spirits of those murdered until their deaths were avenged. I know, it sounds strange to you and me, but that's the Kuzzi way."

"So what did you do?"

"At first, I didn't know what to do. I considered bashing her head against the rocks. Why let her die a slow, painful death of starvation and exposure? Killing her would be the right, ethical thing to do. But then I suddenly realized that this creature, this little alien girl, had indeed survived, all alone, in the sweltering heat of the day and in the freezing cold of the night. It didn't seem right that I would pass judgment on whether she lived or died. Some force greater than me – hell, maybe it was the gods – had already decided to give her a second chance. So I kept her."

The young Matson stood slack-jawed. "And you raised her yourself? I don't recall ever hearing about –"

"Off-world, son. You think I'd risk staying here on Byanntia with a Kuzzi pup in my home? Remember, we hadn't been on the planet for long at that point. We had no clue about who, or what, the Kuzzi were. Friend? Foe? Hell, we don't even know now. You think she'd have survived under those conditions? Best thing to do was leave. FTL travel had just come to Byanntia, and so I resigned my commission with the Hardys and left immediately. It wasn't until a couple years ago that I returned."

"And she came back with you?"

"Of course. By that time, she was old enough to be on her own. She rejoined her people, but time and distance had made her alien to them. She was accepted, but grudgingly. She's never felt very comfortable around them. So she comes and goes. In their language, the name 'Bainta' means bright soul, but the Kuzzi call her Wi'shak'alun, Wind Without End, a restless spirit, one that cannot find a home."

Stewart listened in wonder. In the midst of this tale, he felt small, insignificant. It seemed as if he hadn't lived a day in his short life. So many people were doing important things, going to important places, experiencing far more important things than he.

"We aren't doing very well, are we?" he asked, his mind returning to the matter at hand.

Trainer looked him straight in the eye. "We had a bad day, but it'll be better tomorrow. And you're alive. That has to amount to something, right?"

Stewart nodded and placed his hat back on his head. He was about to say something else, when they were interrupted by a voice echoing through the darkness. "Trainer!"

Bainta appeared before them. She was winded, but seemingly in fine shape despite any wounds she might have incurred during the stampede. Stewart looked her over; he could find no markings. "Come quickly."

"What is it, Bright?"

"They have found something you need to see."

The crew leads had assembled around the rear of a hover-wagon. Kison Boss Remy Kay was there with two of his veterinarians. On a platform that jutted out from the wagon was a silver box, and emanating from that box was a hologram of, what looked like to Stewart, the rotating skull of a kison bull, segmented and labeled with call-out lines in bright green. Stewart sidled up beside Chuck Boss Reiner Johns, who did not look pleased with the interruption. "This better be good," Johns said, a two-pronged skewer in his right hand, "I've got a lot of hungry people to feed."

Kay motioned Stewart and Trainer forward. "Sirs, look at this."

They stared into the rotating skull, and one of the veterinarians began, "As you know, when a kison is put down, its DNA is scanned and logged into the ranch database to ensure that it can, if necessary, be reintroduced into the herd when its genetic integrity needs a revival."

Trainer nodded. "Yes, I'm aware. What of it?"

"Well, we took the scan of this bull," the vet said, pointing at the glowing skull, "per the normal procedure. However, during the scan, I kept getting unusual brain wave activity."

"Not uncommon," said Drover Captain Prestor Jack. "Random synapse can fire for a little while after death."

"An hour later?"

The silence among them was deafening. "How can that be possible?" Stewart asked.

The vet shook his head. "It isn't. Within five minutes of death, all brainwave activity should have stopped cold. So we took a scan of the brain, and this is what we found."

The vet tapped his fingers along the edge of the box and the skull dissolved, leaving only the image of the kison's brain. The green glob shifted from red to black, to red then green, over and over, multiple times. Stewart watched silently, his eyes swimming in the light show.

"The only way this kind of hyper activity is possible, sir," the vet continued, "is through the introduction of some kind of psycho-somatic or psycho-tropic substance so powerful that it continues to run the brain long after death."

"Did you find anything in its blood?" Camp Boss Lucia Belle asked.

"No," Remy Kay said, "nothing at all. But that doesn't mean anything. There are scores of substances virtually impossible to detect. It could have been Bilosotyx, Caminostrope, Psyofough, or –"

"Dent'li!"

All heads turned toward Bainta. The Kuzzi stood there, staring down at the image with wide, dark eyes.

"What's that?" Stewart asked.

"It is a root from a cactus that the Kuzzi use in burial ceremonies. But it is only found deep in the Junsuka. Not here."

"What does it do, Bright?" Trainer said.

"They call it 'The Dance of the Dead', and it is used most often when a chief or an important Kuzzi dies. The Dent'li root is ground up and brewed in a tea, or chewed raw. Its most potent form is raw. These honored dead are too proud, too dignified to allow themselves to be carried to their graves. They meet the ancestors on their own. Their bodies are laid out and the tea is poured into their mouths. In a few minutes, the body begins to dance the final dance, and if the Kuzzi is truly an honorable soul, he will dance all the way to his own grave. Some have claimed to see the body bury itself, but I have never witnessed that."

"You said that the root can be chewed," Reiner Johns said, "but dead men can't chew."

"Young Kuzzi warriors will sometimes chew it before battle," said Bainta. "It gives them great strength and courage, but sometimes they chew too much. They go mad. Often die."

"That explains it," said Remy Kay.

Stewart looked at him and furrowed his brow. "Explains what?"

"It explains why the bulls went mad this morning," said Kay. "It explains why my drovers couldn't bring them down with five thousand volts of electricity. It means –"

"It means," said Trainer interrupting, his voice quite agitated, "that we have a saboteur in our midst."

**

The dust cloud that the herd kicked up in its rumble across the Junsuka covered the sky. It looked as if some desert spirit, or devil, had whipped itself into a thundercloud and now threatened rain. It would be nice to have some rain, Stewart thought as he wiped sweat from his brow. The sun was hot and incessant, the sand coarse and relentless at

his neck. He'd been beneath the Junsuka sun many times, but it seemed different today, more aggressive, more deadly. As if he alone were the only one beneath it, and all its raging fire trained on his back. He felt that if he closed his eyes, he'd burn away and no one would notice.

Saboteur!

The word stuck in his throat like a toothpick. He swallowed and mouthed the word again. *Saboteur.* But who? And why?

The 'who' was difficult to determine. Someone with access to the herd no doubt. That eliminated no one except himself. Michele Hughs? Marshall Peete? Unlikely, for they had worked with the Matsons for years, and he had handpicked them personally for the drive. The Drover Captain? Prestor Jack was indeed a newcomer. He'd never worked for the family, but Trainer swore by him. What about Trainer? Mama said that Father trusted him completely. Would the trail boss betray such a long and dedicated service? Stewart did not know, but Father always said that every man had his price.

Stewart looked over the herd, and through the wall of dust found Bainta walking alongside a klatch of cows. When they stopped or trailed off in another direction, she gently guided them back into line. Her motions were ethereal through the hazy heat, the precise lines of her long arms almost swimming through the air. Stewart couldn't take his eyes off of her.

One thing was clear, however. Many in camp suspected the Kuzzi. Not only had she never participated on a Matson drive, she was a 'damned alien', as the Chuck Boss put it this morning while he ladled out watery grits. "I don't trust her," Johns had whispered into Stewart's ear. "She's a damned alien, and good-for-nothing by my accounts. What's she here for, I ask ya? What?" The cook clammed up quickly when Trainer stepped into the line and gave one of his patented glares.

But this sentiment wasn't unique among the crew. Even though Stewart had not taken a survey of their minds, he could see it in their eyes and in the way they quietly moved aside when she walked by. They did not trust her.

The Kuzzi were indeed a puzzling species. They were native to Byanntia and had, quite surprisingly, allowed humans to settle this god-forsaken shit hole with little or no disruption. Why, was anyone's guess. Perhaps they found humans interesting, a curiosity to be admired from afar. More likely than not, they simply didn't realize what it would mean to them and their planet if they allowed humans to climb aboard. Now humans, like the pesky Ming Beetle, were everywhere. Hunting, trapping, killing, poaching, skinning, raising kison, doing all sorts of *human* things. How did the Kuzzi feel about this? Stewart did not know, and his trip to Chief Bollatu's valley had not given him any deeper insight into their psychology. They would remain a mystery, perhaps, forever.

Was Bainta the saboteur? And if so, why? Stewart did not know, and in the broiling heat of the late morning, he did not care.

The trail boss was nervous and angry all morning. His one show of generosity was loaning his horse to Stewart. It was a good sturdy horse, but one that fitfully swished his tail and conducted little stamping hops that threatened to throw the young Matson from his perch.

Atop a spare outrider mount, Trainer barked orders, keeping everyone on a short leash. When one of the drovers accidentally allowed a bull to stray too far from the herd, Trainer accused the young boy of being weak and wanting; they nearly came to blows. Bainta had to intervene to end the argument.

But by noon, tempers calmed as they reached a watering hole. Stewart could hear laughter coming from the staff. Even Trainer had taken off his hat and was jawing with the camp boss about the evening's plans. Another eight hours driving would take them to the base of the Gordon Pass.

Stewart took this moment to relax, lean against a hover-wagon, and drink kison milk from a jug. He looked out across the Junsuka and marveled at the landscape. Sand dunes as far as the eye could see; rocks and tufts of stinger and sage brush; tiny blue dust clouds. But the most amazing formations were the stacks of pancake-like rocks that hugged the edge of the watering hole. They were a cross between mineral and vegetable life. Stewart didn't really understand the science behind them, but they were beautiful. They gave the Byanntia desert a unique look, like something one might see in a dream. Stewart closed his eyes, breathed deeply, and let the images wander in his mind.

"Stewart!"

He finished his milk and set the jug in the back of a hover-wagon. He then climbed an outcropping of rock where Trainer, Hughs, and Bainta stood waiting for him. There, Hughs was looking westward through a pair of high-powered binoculars. Trainer looked disgusted, his face redder than usual. "What is it?" Stewart asked.

Hughs handed him the binoculars. "See for yourself."

Stewart adjusted the lenses. The digital display in front of him placed cross-hairs on the horizon, and on that horizon was a dust cloud moving fast.

"The Cools have arrived," Trainer said.

Stewart blinked and checked again. He zoomed in further and caught the fuzzy images of kison and drovers on the edge of the dust cloud. "What's going on? Why are they here?"

"They're trying to cut us off at the pass," Trainer said.

"But that's cheating. That's against the rules," Stewart said, handing the binocs back to Hughs. "We all agreed on designated paths. Why are they doing this?"

"Well obviously, they're changing the rules of the game!" Trainer said, snatching the binocs away from Hughs. "I bet they figure that if they reach the pass before us with their thousand head, we won't be able to get through until they do. They'll be a day's drive ahead of us before we clear it. Goddamn them!" He spit his stick away and started down the rock.

"Wait!" Stewart said.

"We've no time to delay, boy," Trainer said, "We've got to get the herd moving. We'll have to press on hard through the afternoon. No more stopping."

Stewart jumped down and blocked Trainer's path. "Hold a moment. If we push the herd that hard, we'll lose too many. We can't afford it."

Trainer turned, his eyes glowing with anger. "If we lose the pass, we lose the race, and I ain't going to let Branson Cool beat me to the punch."

"But—" Stewart tried to place his hand on Trainer's shoulder.

Trainer knocked it away, grabbed the front of the young boy's shirt and pulled him close. Stewart could smell stale coffee on the trail boss's breath. "Don't you begin to tell me what I must do, boy. I'm in charge here!"

Trainer was strong, but Stewart managed to break the hold. Their hands were on their bolt guns. Bainta stepped between them. "Peace, damn you both! We cannot afford to fight among ourselves."

"You're forgetting yourself, Trainer." Stewart stared straight into the trail boss's eyes. "You forget who you're working for. This is not your herd. It's mine. It's my father's!"

They stood there for long moments staring at each other. The Kuzzi's hand was tight on Stewart's shoulder. Painful, in fact, but he dare not move, nor break his stare first. Trainer may indeed be in charge, but this time he had gone too far.

It was Trainer that blinked first. He removed his hand from his gun. He breathed deeply, then folded his arms across his chest. "Very well. What are your orders, Mr. *Matson?*"

Bainta released his shoulder and Stewart took a step back. He turned and looked across the Junsuka, towards the dust cloud coming on strong. Even from here, he could see it. There was no denying the Cools were making an aggressive move. The rules were the rules, but such a move would no doubt be looked upon by the Vellong Trade Federation as clever, ingenious. Trainer was right. If the Cools reached the Gordon Pass before them, all was lost. The right thing to do was to press on through the day, risk kison losses and make it there first. But to reaffirm what Trainer had already said, after making such a scene, would be too humiliating to bear. Oh, how he wished Joe or his father was here. He wished he could call them on radio and get their advice. But no radios had been brought; that was against the rules. *What rules?* Stewart wondered. First a saboteur and now this. The rules were the rules... but the rules be damned.

He removed his kisonboy hat and scratched his messy hair. Boy, could he use a bath! To lay in water, to be submerged, to be—

A broad smile spread across his face. He looked at Bainta, then at Hughs, then Trainer, that same broad smile greeting each in turn.

Trainer blinked, "What have you decided?"

Stewart cleared his throat, then said, "We turn east and cross the Ku'sac'allak."

His confident smile was greeted with looks of horror.

PART 2

The crew's enthusiasm for his idea didn't improve over time. As he laid out his plan, they stared at him as if he were mad. Veterans who had seen many a drive wavered in place. They gave each other nervous looks, and peered around as if searching for an excuse to be somewhere else. And the more they fidgeted, the better Stewart felt. Finally, he was the center of attention. They were listening to him. They might not like what he was saying, but by God, they were listening. "This time of year," he said, pointing to the holomap, drawing their route with a light pen, "the water shouldn't be too high. I know it'll be dangerous, but it's the last, best plan we have.

"We turn the herd now and head ten miles straight east. We'll get there by nightfall. We camp on the bank, then cross in the morning. Even if the Cools make the Gordon Pass, they'll be driving over hard rock, narrow, hazardous ground. Once we cross, it's flat grassland all the way to the Vellong ships. Hell, with any luck, we'll get there a day early. The Cools will be left in our dust."

He stopped talking and waited for comment. No one spoke.

Then Bainta stepped up, her purjung spear in hand as if she were ready for battle. "The Ku'sac'allak is a sacred river, young human. It is not to be taken lightly, nor should it be soiled with kison."

"Hogwash!" said Remy Kay. "You can't tell me, Kuzzi, that wild kison do not drink from that river."

Bainta turned carefully, thoughtfully, towards her challenger. Her face was solid rock. "For my part, I do not care either way, but there may be others of my people who are watching. And if they see such beasts step in that river, they may bring down a war party that will put an end to this drive. Do not underestimate my people's beliefs... human."

The literal translation of Ku'sac'allak was 'River of Death', and the Kuzzi believed it with all their hearts. It was a foolish superstition, Stewart knew, but tell that to a seven foot cat-like alien with a weapon that could skewer a kison bull. He was not about to make that claim.

"All superstitions aside," said Prestor Jack, taking the bait, "the undertow of that river is savage, Mr. Matson, even in the dry season. We try to drive the herd through that, and we'll take a hit."

"How many?" Trainer asked.

The drover captain shook his head. "Don't know for sure. Six, maybe, seven percent. Maybe more. Kison aren't very good swimmers. They tend to panic when they can't feel anything below their hooves."

"That'll take us below the required percentage," said Remy Kay.

That opened the floor for argument, as everyone began talking loudly, debating the feasibility of the plan. Stewart watched as they paired off in shouting matches, Bainta and Remy Kay going toe to toe on the merits of the Kuzzi myth. Stewart felt a sinking feeling in his chest as his plan unraveled before him.

"Everyone, shut up!"

One by one they turned and looked at Stewart. He stood there quietly, waiting for their bickering to stop, his chest pounding like a drum. When they settled, he took the light pen and scribbled on the holomap. "To circumvent the undertow, how about we do this..." he drew three rectangles over the river, one after the other in a long line "...we latch the wagons together and run the kison over them like a pontoon bridge. This keeps them out of the undertow and keeps the Kuzzi off our backs."

Trainer stepped up and ran his finger through the holomap. "The river is wider than our three wagons, son. It'll never work. Besides, the engines will terrify them."

Stewart shook his head. "It's not that wide everywhere. And even if it is, we can rotate them like a rolling stack. Once the last kison clears the last wagon, we move it to the front of the queue and shift the others back. As far as the engines go, if we keep them focused and moving, they won't have time to notice. We just have to be vigilant."

Remy Kay laughed. "You're going to shift hovers with kison bulls on them? Boy, are you nuts?"

"I didn't say we would," Stewart answered. "I said if necessary. It may not be necessary."

"Can the hovers even hold that much weight?" Prestor Jack asked. "Peete?"

The hover-wagon master stepped up and looked at the map. He rubbed his face, then said, "Yes, they can. But only in a narrow line down the center. One or two at a time and keep them moving quickly. Any more than that, and –"

"Enough," Trainer said, erasing the holomap by running his hand through it. "We've no more time to discuss it. The Cools are on our backs. We either do it, or we don't. What is your decision, Stewart?"

Get it done. His mother's words rang through his mind. *Get it done.*

Stewart nodded. "Let's do it."

***

They spent the rest of the day driving the herd east towards the River of Death. They stopped once more before reaching the bank to let the kison rest and refresh. Keeping the herd fresh and lively, on a drive or at any time, was a constant battle. Stewart wondered why his father ever decided to become a kison rancher. Of course, on Byanntia, there was little else to do, save for some kind of desk or mill job in New Dodge. But that kind of lifestyle did not suit the Matsons. They were ranchers, and despite the hardships, it was the best life in the world. The freedom to do what you wanted to do, and the space to do it in. What a life.

Trainer did not speak for the rest of the day, and whenever Stewart tried to make eye contact, the trail boss always looked the other way. Stewart could not decide if Trainer was angry because the young Matson

had usurped his authority, or if it was because the river plan was bolder than anything Trainer could have come up with himself. Surely, crossing the Ku'sac'allak must have been something the older man had considered. Why did he discount it so readily? Had he reached that point in his life where a controlled risk was the only option? Or did he reject the idea out of deference to Bainta's beliefs? Whatever the reason, it was clear he did not like the idea, and his lack of faith was evident in his demeanor. This in turn made everyone else nervous and kept the drive quiet. But there was no turning back now.

They reached their evening camp. Around-the-clock shifts for all drovers and outriders were put in place. The last thing they needed now was to lose kison from straying too close to the bank and falling in. Prestor Jack had been right. Even before they reached it, the roar of the river's current could be heard loudly. One false step, and you would never be seen again. Stewart understood now why the Kuzzi respected, and feared, the Ku'sac'allak. He was beginning to feel a little of that fear himself.

That evening he personally oversaw the hover-wagon preparations. Their solar canopies and supplies had to be removed. Then they were latched together with rope, every last length available. The one problem that proved the most difficult was how they were going to get the kison to actually climb onto the first wagon. They found a crossing that could accommodate the three wagons without rotation, but there was a one meter gap at both ends. A kison could easily jump that space, but any miss-jumps would send the beast into the river, and likely knock the entire train out of order, which would take time and manpower to straighten. Manpower they had; time they did not.

They settled on strapping the wagon to the shore by cutting poles from a nearby bed of Calkuska Reeds. These green, but strong plants stood five to six meters tall with a very smelly yellow flower at the tip. The Kuzzi used the pollen from the flower in medicines, and sometimes used the red gel inside the reeds to color their weapons and themselves before battle. With Camp Boss Lucia Belle's assistance, Bainta instructed the staff in making two sturdy ramps which were put at both ends of the train. Then dirt and rocks were piled underneath them for support.

Everything was in place for the morning.

After supper, Stewart went looking for the trail boss. He found Trainer alone by the bank sitting on a petrified stump, chewing a stick and staring across the river.

"Am I disturbing you?" Stewart asked.

Trainer stopped chewing and shook his head. "No. What can I do for you tonight?"

Stewart swallowed his nerves. "I – I want to apologize. I didn't mean to step on your toes. You are in charge, and I'm sorry that we don't agree on this plan, but I think it's the best we can do given the circum—"

"It's a fine plan, son," Trainer said, standing up and flicking his stick into the raging water below. "A fine plan. Better than mine. If we had gone on to challenge the Cools, who knows what might have happened?"

"Then why are you so angry?"

"Because I hate this goddamned river!"

Stewart waited, letting Trainer collect himself. He'd never seen the man's face so red, so distraught, so full of emotion. This had nothing to do with being outclassed by an inexperienced teenager. This was pure revulsion.

"My brother died in this river," Trainer finally said. "I was about your age; he was a couple years younger. My family worked for the Winstons at the time."

"I remember the Winstons. They went bankrupt and left the planet a few years ago. My father bought their land."

Trainer nodded. "Yes. They were a good family, but not business people. Anyway, when he drove kison, my father would always take us along, sometimes as drovers, sometimes as outriders. One day we camped here along this river. The Winstons were driving a small herd to slaughter, only a couple hundred head. The river was pretty high that day, but we found a place – much like this one – where the gap was narrow. My brother wanted to gig for lizards. At first I said no. We'd been warned about not going too close to the water. But he persisted, and I gave in.

"It was night and the bank was steep. We were catching good ones. We were having a good time. Then my brother saw this big, plump bastard on a rock. It was a pretty long jump. I warned him not to do it, but he ignored me. He made the jump, but when he stood up to gloat, his foot slipped, and he fell in. I tried to get him. I followed him downstream as far as I could. I screamed for help. We all tried to get him. But then he went under and was gone. We never found him."

He stopped for a moment, then said, "Bainta's right. This *is* the river of death."

Stewart stood there. There was nothing he could say or do to make this better.

Trainer shook his head, wiped his face, then turned to Stewart. "Tomorrow is a big day, son. Try to get some sleep."

Stewart watched him leave, the roar of the river strong below his feet.

***

The first wave cleared the bridge with little trouble. Drovers and outriders funneled the herd to the Calkuska ramp and guided them carefully up and onto the wagon. Stationed along the way were others with electric prods keeping the beasts moving quickly. If the line stopped for too long, the herd would build up in the back and cause breakouts. One such occurrence happened shortly after the first wave cleared the ramp. Two bulls began sparing. Others panicked and started breaking the line. It took Bainta and three others to gather them up. One lost its footing and fell into the river. Prestor Jack lassoed it and they managed to pull it to safety before it drowned. They lost a cow and her calf during the third wave; two more during the fourth wave. On the seventh wave, the ramp on the far side broke. It took them an hour to repair it and start again. But overall, the morning progressed smoothly.

The weight of the kison made the wagons bob up and down like keys on a piano as each stepped on and off. It was hard for Stewart to keep

his footing. He was battling motion sickness, but he had tethered himself to the wagon. If he slipped, he'd at least not fall into the water.

Marshall Peete smiled from ear to ear. *His* wagons were doing splendidly, and he was not too proud to show it on his face.

Wave after wave came on, and by early afternoon, the last one was assembled and beginning its move. Trainer had stayed with the herd, assisting Remy Kay. Now they came into view as the last kison was corralled into the funnel. Stewart turned to the trail boss and saluted him. Trainer, seeing the last bulls fall in line, allowed himself to relax.

Remy Kay got off his horse and began walking to the last grav-wagon. His movements were shielded from view, and Stewart paid little attention to them as he turned once more to the kison moving quickly in front of him. His mind drifted for a moment; the relentless shift of kison bodies made his thoughts waver. He had not realized just how tired he was; all the adrenaline of the past couple days was keeping him sharp, alert, active beyond physical endurance. Now that the crossing was nearly finished, he took a moment to let all the stress bleed away. For the first time in days, he felt happy and peaceful.

Loud voices behind him shattered the serenity.

It was Trainer and Kay, nose to nose near the end of the last grav-wagon. Trainer's face was a crimson scowl, the veins on the old man's forehead popping madly across the rough skin. The trail boss held Kay's right wrist: something was in his right hand. Stewart squinted to make out what it was: a flat oval object of some kind, metallic perhaps. A weapon? Stewart could not tell. But the two men struggled over it, shouting at one another through flying spit. Kay pulled, Trainer resisted. They shifted back and forth along the muddy bank. Others were beginning to notice the scuffle and were moving to intervene.

Suddenly there was a bolt pistol in Kay's hand. Trainer grabbed for it but he slipped on a wet rock and lost his footing for a moment. Kay trained the gun on the trail boss's chest. Trainer's arm flailed upward. The arm sweep did not dislodge the gun, but it forced Kay to redress his aim and put a slug through Trainer's arm. The trail boss rocked backwards,

but he kept his hold and both men went down hard into the Calkuska ramp.

Stewart tried to pull his own gun, but something slammed into his leg. At first he thought it was a spooked kison, but it hit again, taking him to his knees. Through the pain he looked up and saw the face of a drover, a boy he had seen on the drive, but could not remember the name. The boy towered over Stewart, his expression desperate and dangerous. He waved a bolt gun in front of Stewart's face, then turned the gun to the bottom of the wagon. He fired, and a burst of water sprang up, dousing them both and a kison bull a few feet away. The sides of the wagon flickered and its engines sputtered and stopped. Then the wagon's engines shut off and hit the water.

The kison lurched to the side, lost its footing and fell overboard. Its flank grazed Stewart and he went over too. The rope on his foot bit deep into his ankle and kept his face mere inches from the water. For a moment, he thought of the rope that cut his hand just a few days ago in the corral on the ranch. *Funny the things one thinks about in times of stress*, Stewart thought, then cleared his mind as the two wagons tethered to Stewart's buckled and snapped their bindings. Another wagon hit the river. Its engines roared as water sprayed from its propellers. Electrical currents leeched up its sides and ran over the kison who were wailing and falling all around. Stewart grabbed his rope and tried to pull himself up.

The drover appeared, leaning over the side and aiming his gun at Stewart's chest. Stewart waved his arm and tried knocking the gun out of the boy's hand. The drover took a desperate shot that missed Stewart but tore into the back of a kison desperately trying to right itself in the river. Blood poured from the wound and spread down the current.

Then the wagon snapped free and fell deeper into the water. Stewart's head bobbed in and out of the current. He held his breath but water seeped into his mouth. He gulped, trying to clear his throat. *I'm going to die*, he thought as his head hit a rock.

The wagon slipped down the river and rotated as it hit rock after rock. Stewart's head came up and he grabbed his rope. He shook his head,

clearing his eyes of blood and muck. The drover was still on the wagon, but he clung frantically to the side with one hand as his other took shots at something moving along the bank.

It was Bainta, running with the current, purjung spear raised, waiting for the right time to throw. "Stewart," she said, her voice like a whisper above the roar of the water. "Cut the rope!"

She had to mouth it several times before he understood what she was saying. Of course. His purjung-bladed knife was on his hip. He held himself to the side of the wagon and reached for his blade. He reached too low and cut himself on its sharp edge. He ground his teeth and ripped away the leather bindings holding the knife in place. He pulled it free. It was big and bulky; not the kind of knife for quick slashing. But he didn't care. He raised it up, waited for the wagon to crest, then struck the rope.

One, two, three cuts and he was free. The wagon pulled away and Stewart watched as Bainta's spear pierced the drover's chest. The boy fell dead into the water, disappearing into foam under floating kison bodies.

The current was strong. Stewart paddled his arms and feet as hard as he could to reach the bank, but it was no use. He could not break against the current. A kison bull floated by, still alive, still working its tired legs. Stewart grabbed hold of a horn on its back and held tightly. How long this would last was hard to say. Not for long.

The saboteurs had struck. The damage was done. What exactly had happened behind him he did not know. It did not matter, really. All was lost, and he would die here in this river of death.

I've failed.

But as the bull went under for the last time and Stewart released him, he felt the clutch of a rope around his neck. He gasped for air and pushed his hands beneath the fibers to keep from choking to death. He rolled around and saw Trainer on the bank, on his horse, the right side of his body covered in blood. The other end of the rope was tied around the saddle horn, and the trail boss was pulling as hard as he could. Stewart pulled too, one hand over the other, working toward the shore.

Trainer's horse slipped on the slippery bank, his front legs digging into the mud. It stumbled back but Trainer kept him steady by jumping off and pulling on the reins. The horse braced his hind legs and pulled slowly. Trainer guided him back, back, back, until Stewart could feel ground beneath his feet. He pulled himself up, took three steps and fell onto the bank. Trainer rushed to his side, grabbed Stewart's belt and pulled him to safety.

Stewart lay there, coughing up water and mud. Trainer pounded on his back. A few more coughs and it was over. Trainer rolled him over and Stewart rested his head on the man's bloody arm. They both stared at the river, terror in their eyes.

"You're safe," Trainer said, blood flowing down his chin. "I've saved you."

The Ku'sac'allak had exacted its pound of flesh.

PART 3

Two hours later, Alvin Trainer lay dead. A tourniquet had been applied to his arm, then a brand with the Matson capitol "M" had cauterized the wound, but it was too late. The bolt from Remy Kay's gun had cut through the arm, breaking ribs, and puncturing the lung. He drowned in his own blood despite the veterinarians doing everything they could to keep him alive. He passed away in Bainta's arms.

Stewart had heard crying before. The night after they had been told that their father was dying from organ deterioration caused by wave distortions suffered on the trip from Earth, and then again after the attack by the Gr'nar, his mother had cried fearful tears, and moaned as if her soul had lost its way. Perhaps she did not know that her sobs could be heard. When she emerged from her room, however, her face was clean and stoic, masked in that unshakable courage that defined Shelby Matson. A courage that had always defined the Matsons in fact. But seeing the Kuzzi on the ground, her step-father's limp body in the crook of her arms,

Stewart did not feel courage. He felt sorrow, a deep soulful sorrow that made his chest hurt.

He shook from a chill in his bones. The river had been cold, and even an hour later, his clothing was soaked through. His ankle was swollen and his head wrapped in gauze. Prestor Jack and Michele Hughs had also suffered injuries, but theirs were minor and confined to arms and hands.

The traitor Remy Kay and his accomplices had scuttled away with fifty head of kison, bulls, cows and calves. The attack was swift and deliberate. Kay had strategically placed men on all the teams: one drover, one outrider, one wagon handler, one cook. After being shot, Trainer had seized Kay and they had fought on the ground, but the trail boss's arm was badly wounded. He lost his grip and Kay pulled away, gathered his men and rode off. Were they rustlers, working for one of the other families? That was the most likely explanation, but rummaging through Kay's bed roll and personals left behind, they found no clues to his motive or patronage. Now, with the stampede, the drowning, and the theft, they were well below the percentage required by the Vellong Trade Federation.

The race was over.

"Do we let them stay like that all night?" Lucia Belle asked, pointing to Bainta. For hours the Kuzzi held Trainer in her arms, rocking back and forth, chanting words nobody could understand. *Na'tashekala'e. Na'tashekala'o.* Over and over, keeping in rhythm with her rocking, until the sun fell and the moon took its place in the sky. Stewart shook his head. "Leave them alone," he said, "it's not our place."

One wagon was destroyed outright, having fallen into the river and its air-skirts smashed against the rocks. Another wagon's air-skirts were damaged but repairable. The third was banged up but still fully functional. It would take Marshall Peete and his crew all night to repair the damaged one.

"This is what Kay had in mind," Marshall Peete said, handing over a piece of oval-shaped metal. "We found this by the river."

Stewart turned it in his hand. It was the item Kay was holding in the fight. "What is it?"

"It's an energy leech," Peete said. "Dissolvable alloy. It's placed on an engine and drains it of power. It dissolves itself as it drains, thus there's no evidence of where the failure came from. Anyone looking would simply conclude some internal manufacture deficiency. A clever saboteur's weapon... and very expensive. Trainer must have caught Kay trying to put it on the last grav-wagon. Their timetable was disrupted. Kay panicked and pulled his gun."

Stewart smashed the device in his hand, cursed, and threw it into the weeds.

It took the rest of the day to gather up the stray kison. Outriders had to be refitted for drover duty. By nightfall the herd was comfortably grazing while Reiner Johns and his remaining cooks prepared supper. It was a quiet, somber meal. Stewart sat on his bed roll near the fire, eating slowly and staring into the flames.

It was the drover captain who spoke first. "Surely the Vellong will take Kay's treachery into consideration. We can't be faulted for that."

"They're businessmen, Prestor," said Michele Hughs, "not saints. I've dealt with them before. All they care about are the horns. The numbers."

"Yes, but we can't be blamed for this!"

"I agree, but at the end of the day, we won't have enough. We're going to lose."

That last point sank in hard. They sat there around the fire, not speaking, not wanting to admit what they all knew to be the truth.

"Damn you, Remy!" Prestor Jack spit into the fire. "If I ever catch you—"

"We should go after them," said Marshall Peete. "I want to string his sorry ass up for what he did to my wagons."

"Go after him with what?" Lucia Belle took a seat next to the fire, a plate of beans and cornbread in her hand. "We don't have enough men to drive the herd and play posse as well."

"We can't let this stand!" The drover captain slammed down his plate and knocked over his coffee. He stood up, stamped his feet. "I'm gonna kill that son of a bitch!"

"Quiet!" Stewart said, his face stretched in the firelight. He'd heard just about enough of their talk. What good would talking do anyway? Lucia Belle was right in a sense: with the loss of Trainer and Remy's gang, there were too few hands to make the run efficiently. But logic be damned. Justice, too, had to play a part in this matter.

Stewart chuckled inwardly. *Justice indeed!* That's something his mother, his *father*, would have said. Jacob Matson would not have stood for this insult to the pride and dignity of his family, to the Matson name and its brand. To simply limp forward and deliver a herd for sympathy money... *never!* But to go after them; that too was farcical.

Get it done. His mother's words rang in his mind. *Get it done.*

Stewart's eyes lit up as he stood, checked his purjung blade and bolt gun, and gathered his bed roll. "Lucia's right," he said. "We don't have enough to do both. I'll go after them."

There was a rustle of activity as those gathered around the fire stood and began to make their case against his decision.

"This is madness, Stew," Lucia said. "You're just a–"

"A boy?" Stewart turned and stared into the camp boss's face. "That's what you were going to say, wasn't it, Lucia?"

Lucia opened her mouth to protest, but Stewart put up his hand and silenced her. "And you'd be right. I'm just a boy. I've been a *boy* during this whole damned show. But this is my drive, Lucia. This is my family's herd and my responsibility. Besides, I'm no good to you all." He turned and looked at all of them, assembled around, their nervous expressions flickering in sweat and trail dust through the firelight. "You people are the experts, the professionals, and I can think of no other group to entrust the herd to than you all."

"But you can't go alone," Marshall Peete said. "It's too dangerous. You'll be outnumbered and –"

"He will not be alone!"

Bainta stepped out of the shadow and into the firelight. In her arms lay Trainer, wrapped in a white shawl, his entire body covered save for his pale, stiff face.

The fur around the Kuzzi's eyes was matted and crusty. The eyes themselves were bloodshot and angry. She wasn't crying anymore.

Stewart walked to her and raised his hands. "Thank you Bainta," he said, "but I think it'd be best if I went alone."

The Kuzzi laid the dead trail boss down by the fire, ran her hand across his face, nuzzled her snout against his cheek, then stood. Her expression was even more enraged; her cheek muscled worked incessantly beneath her dull fur. She stood tall before Stewart, just like she had done when they first met. "You are going to refuse my offer?"

All Stewart could think of was that flash of fur he had seen during the kison bull rumble, how magnificently she had moved through the air, and how swiftly she had dispatched them with her spear. He swallowed deeply and said, "No, no, I didn't mean to—"

"My *father* died trying to save this herd, trying to protect this venture," she said interrupting. "He died to protect your family's honor. This is not a matter for negotiation, young human. I am going."

Stewart cleared his throat and nodded quickly. The matter was concluded.

In the darkness they found their horses. As if it understood the magnitude of the situation, Stewart's horse neither moved nor protested his mounting. That was a good sign; but the night was young and many, many miles lay ahead in the darkness with only the instincts of a Kuzzi to lead them. Stewart breathed deeply and looked at Bainta. She looked back calmly, adjusting herself in the saddle and grabbing the reins tightly. She winked, or something that looked like winking to Stewart. "No fear, young man. No fear."

Stewart nodded and gripped his own reins to keep his hand from shaking. He looked down at Prestor Jack. "You and Marshall are in charge," he said. "In the morning, drive the herd. Keep driving it until you reach the Vellong. Get it done."

"But what if you don't return in time?" The drover captain asked.

"If I don't return in time," Stewart said, biting back a tear. "If I don't return at all... tell my mother I love her."

***

The blazing Byanntia sun peeked over the horizon. It was morning, and they had ridden hard through the night. Stewart could barely see the entire way, save for the flashes of moonlight that spread a blue tint across the grasslands and the sands of the Junsuka. It was Bainta that led them forward, stopping momentarily to measure the wind, her sleek head thrust into the dull light like a cat sniffing prey. All Stewart could smell was dust, heat, and the occasional waft of decaying brush. Bainta, however, seemed to smell something much more, and when she caught it, she would nod and point in the direction they needed to go. It went on like that for hours, until finally they found a lay of land that had been battered by a large herd of kison. The sand was pocked with hundreds of hoof marks; kison dung lay everywhere, scattered in long lines as if dropped on a run; and a wall of dust, even hours after their passing, still hung in the air. Stewart had to cover his face with the kerchief around his neck just to breathe.

In time they slowed, dismounted, and walked slowly up a small mound of rock and sand. Stewart favored his ankle, still swollen from the fight in the river, but the wound on his head no longer throbbed and a headache that he had been nursing for hours had disappeared. They hitched their horses to a large stinger bush, then crawled forward until they looked down into a tight ravine. There, four men sat beside a small fire, talking loudly, drinking morning coffee, laughing at stupid jokes. They seemed quite pleased with themselves. That, more than anything else, angered Stewart the most. "Bastards!" He hissed. He pulled a stinger branch, cleaned it of its leaves and brambles, then tucked it between cheek and gum. He worked it back and forth with his teeth. "Damn bastards. Look at them, all smug and confident, laughing, whistling!"

"They will change their tune in a few minutes," Bainta whispered.

He looked off into the horizon to his right. Not far from the camp stood a mass of black and brown and gray fur, horns catching the glint of the morning sunlight. Back and forth, the echo of kison voices rang out as they picked at the scarce shrubs and grass on the hard, rocky ground.

Stewart breathed relief. The herd was okay at least, and within a short enough distance to be rounded up once the fight was over.

He looked back at the traitors' camp. "They don't even seem concerned about who might be coming after them."

"A weakness of the race," Bainta said, shifting her purjung spear from right to left hand. "Humans are so foolish."

Stewart ignored her remark. "Well, we better get started. Dawn is approaching, and they'll be trying to move the herd again." The thought of it boiled his blood. He spit the stick from his mouth. He pointed to a patch of rock on the other side of the camp. "How about you get back on your horse and get over to that side? We'll pick them off one at a time. With your spear, my gun, we should —"

"No," Bainta said, shaking her head. "You can do what you want, but I am going right at them."

She moved to get up, but Stewart blocked her path. "Don't be foolish, Bainta. They may look like they aren't ready for a fight, but I guarantee you, the guns'll come out fast if they're cornered."

Bainta pushed him aside and continued walking down the hill. "I will say again, I am going down there now, with or without you."

Stewart gnashed his teeth. Sweat beaded on his brow. He wanted to wipe it away, but he refused to move. Bainta looked back up at him fiercely, the muscles in her jaw working overtime. Finally, Stewart blinked. "Okay, we'll do this your way, Bainta. But I reckon Trainer would not be so reckless."

"My *father* would be the first one down the hill, human, and you know it."

With help from Bainta, Stewart climbed into his saddle, grabbed the reins, and turned his horse up the hill. He pressed his legs tightly into the sides of the horse, leaned over and gave the beast a little pat. "I know you don't like me," he whispered, "but cut me some slack for a bit, okay?"

The horse blew steam through its flaring nostrils, gave a little kick, and seemed to nod its head in agreement. Stewart smiled, pulled his bolt gun, and turned to Bainta who sat nearby with her spear pointed sharply

up the slope. Despite his misgivings at her plan, he was not about to let her steal all the glory. He winked. "Race you to the bottom."

He took off, spurring the horse up the hill. The beast strained to keep its footing, dust and small rocks being kicked up in clouds as they ascended. Stewart caught himself trying to yell, forgetting for a moment that silence was best in these situations. He had little experience with fighting, only stories that he had heard from his late brother and father. They knew what fighting was all about. They knew how to take a fight to someone. His father had almost died because of it. And now, here he was, the youngest Matson, driving headlong into... *What am I doing?* He thought to himself, cresting the top of the hill. There was only one answer that came to mind.

Being a man.

Down the hill they half slid, half galloped, the horse's weight pushing him forward through a cloud of blue dust. There was no hiding the attack now, as the rustlers around the fire jumped up quickly, nervous and confused at first, but then hearing the echoes of Stewart's descent and reaching for their guns.

Bainta appeared beside him, her steed straining to keep from toppling, its powerful legs churning up the ground with a fierceness that matched only the Kuzzi's expression. Her spear looked alive as well, as if it could smell human blood and was just waiting for the right distance to strike. Bainta did not look at him, her eyes fixed on their prey below.

A shot rang out. Stewart heard the buzz of a bolt fly through the space between him and Bainta. Another shot, then another. Stewart's heart leaped into his throat. *Damn! They're shooting!* But what did he expect? These were criminals, men who would sell out their patrons, men who had already proven that they would kill for what they wanted. They would keep firing until he and Bainta were dead. *But they won't get that chance*, Stewart thought as he squeezed off a bolt.

They blew into the camp. Stewart pulled his reins tightly to bring his horse under control. The pressure of the sudden stop nearly threw him off, but his legs reacted instinctively and squeezed to keep his saddle. He cocked his gun and tried to point it at a traitor outrider he recognized from the drive, but something hit him in the side, knocking him hard to the ground.

Pain knifed through his ankle as his foot hit a rock. Stewart cried out and almost dropped his gun. It flailed momentarily in his hand, but he grit through the pain and kept his hold.

In the chaos, Stewart could see Bainta moving. She sparred with two of the other rustlers. It was almost as if she were playing with them, letting them get a jab in from time to time to give them false hope. But her spear moved effortlessly, gracefully deflecting one punch or desperate charge again and again. Even in his dizzying state, Stewart could see that they were losing, their faces streaked with blue dust, sweat and fear. Finally, Bainta grew tired of playing. She stepped away from a round house, turned her spear over in her hand, and drove the tip through the shoulder of the nearest rustler. The man screamed and clutched his bleeding wound. She pulled the spear free, spun it sideways and cracked it over the nose of the other rustler. A spray of blood and a snap of bone sent the man to his knees.

Stewart tried getting up, but a fist slammed into his face.

He blacked out. How long, he did not know. But when he came to, his hands were empty, his jaw throbbed in pain, and an angry, yet terrified, face hovered just inches before him.

Remy Kay spit his words. "You made a mistake, boy, coming after me. You're as stupid as your father!"

"You've ruined the drive, son of a bitch!" Stewart heard himself say the words, but they seemed to drift from his mouth, through a cheek swelled up fat and purple. "You've ruined my family's good name. You'll pay for that."

Kay's laugh hurt Stewart's ears. A rough, open hand struck his face. Stewart felt blood drip from his nose. "I don't think so," Kay said. "I'm going to finish the job I started with Trainer." A bolt gun was drawn and held to Stewart's temple. "Goodbye, *boy.*"

The gun sounded, but no bullet ripped through Stewart's brain. He fell down, whole, the roar of the blast sounding off the rocks around him. He focused and saw Bainta in the distance, her spear working against a more effective defense than he would have imagined. Remy Kay was no weakling. He blocked blow after blow from Bainta's spear, a mad grin smeared across his face. Her sharp teeth were barred in response. She screamed Kuzzi words, obscenities perhaps, as her spear twisted and turned through the smoky air. A jab here, a stab there, but Kay kept moving backwards, backwards, keeping Bainta off her mark. Why was she so erratic, so indecisive in her moves? Is she tired? Stewart wondered. Probably so. But it was something more, something worse. He could tell in her face, her motions. She was wild, insane with rage. They had not been together for long, but he could tell. The fur along her spine was up and splayed sharp like quills, her face flushed pink, her ears perked, stiff like iron. She was not herself, and though he could understand why, he could also see the danger in it. Her anger, her sorrow for the loss of her father, Albert Trainer, was making her irrational and sloppy.

Stewart scrambled across the ground on weak knees, found his gun and rose up tenderly. His head, his jaw, his ankle, all throbbed in pain. But he breathed deeply, set his arm forward, cocked the hammer of his gun, and stumbled towards the fight... towards the campfire.

The fire!

Now he knew why Kay had kept falling backwards. "Bainta, stop!" Stewart screamed, but the Kuzzi did not hear his plea or was ignoring it. She kept fighting.

Stewart moved to the side and tried to aim through the jumble of human flesh and clothing and the dry, fire-prone fur of the Kuzzi. If she got too close to the fire and if Kay did what Stewart thought he might...

"Bainta, the fire!"

Suddenly a light ignited in Bainta's mind. She halted and Kay, in desperation, kicked forwards, plowing through a pile of burning ash and sending it swirling into the air. Bainta vaulted backwards, using her spear as a brace. Most of the red-hot embers fell harmlessly to the ground, but

Stewart could see a few of them hit the Kuzzi and singe her fur right to the skin. Kuzzi skin was tough, he knew, but not so tough as to deaden the effects of fire.

Though she tried to hide the pain, Stewart could see it on her face, and for a moment, he forgot where he was. He wanted to go to her, to help her through it, to put it right. He forgot his own pain, his throbbing head and ankle. A colleague (a friend?) was injured and she needed help. That's what his father would have done, he knew. It's what a Matson would do.

But his mind was suddenly turned again to the matter at hand. Out of the corner of his eye, he caught Kay moving away from the camp and towards a frantic horse hitched nearby. Stewart leveled his gun at the moving figure. *I've never shot anyone*, he thought as his finger fell to the trigger. Could he do it?

Before he answered, the gun went off, but Kay did not stop. *Miss!* Stewart re-cocked. "Stop!" he yelled, but Kay neither turned nor stopped. He reached the horse and tried to mount. Stewart fired again, low and steady.

The bullet tore through Kay's leg. He screamed and fell to the ground. Stewart re-cocked and moved forwards carefully.

Kay moaned and clutched his leg. Blood trickled through his fingers. He tried to crawl away, but Stewart fired again, purposely missing but hitting just close enough to discourage Kay from moving any further. "Give it up, Kay," he said, "it's over."

Kay scooped up a handful of pebbles and sand and flung it towards Stewart. "Go to hell!"

"There is no hell on Byanntia, don't you know that?" Stewart stood beside the traitor. He managed a sly smile. "You're going to pay for what you've done."

"He will indeed."

From nowhere, Bainta appeared. Before Stewart could resist, she ripped his purjung blade from its sheath. The Kuzzi leaped onto Kay's chest, grabbed the top of his head, pulled tightly, and set the knife against

his throat. A small line of blood dripped from the gleaming edge. "You are going to die for what you did to my father."

Bainta lifted the knife into the sky, screamed Kuzzi words, then tried to bring it down quickly across Kay's throat.

Stewart grabbed her arm before she could strike. It was all he could to keep his balance against her strength. "No!"

Bainta, surprised and indignant, tried to pull free. "Let me go! You have no rights here. I demand my father's revenge."

"No!" he said again, keeping his grip firm. "He must live. If he dies, we've no proof of his crime. If he dies, we've no way of knowing who's behind the sabotage."

"It does not matter anymore, human!" Bainta rose up and pulled Stewart close. Their faces were inches away from each other. Stewart could smell her rage, like stale sweat. "We are going to lose anyway, even if we return the missing kison in time. We get our revenge now!"

"I said no!" Stewart could not believe it himself, but he set his pistol against her chest. He was tired of playing games. He was tired, period. Tired of it all: the grass, the sand, the sweltering heat, the fighting. Plain tired. "We do this my way, Bainta. My way! Or turn yourself around and leave."

They stood like that for a long moment. It was Bainta who blinked first. She turned, and Stewart suddenly regretted what he had said. But she did not walk away. Instead, she stepped over Kay's weak, twitching body. She lorded over him. The traitor tried to rise and spit obscenities at her. She silenced him with a swift kick to the head. Kay rocked backwards and was out cold.

She turned back to Stewart and calmly returned his knife. She then fixed herself, rubbed back the mussed fur on her face, redressed her spear, and headed in the direction of the herd. "Get him roped up," she said. "I will take care of the kison. And Stewart," She turned and looked him square in the eye, "never, *ever* threaten me again."

But there was no real anger in her voice; it was more of surprise perhaps, shock that he had actually had the courage to even try it. Stewart nodded and watched her move away.

He took a deep breath, redressed his own weapons, then got to work.

***

Below them in the valley sat the three Vellong slaughter tugs. Stewart had seen space ships before, but never ones as large as these. Surely the ship that had brought the First families to Byanntia had been this large: its hull had been used to construct New Dodge itself. But these ships were huge. Looking at them, Stewart almost forgot where he was and what he was doing, but the roar of kison hooves around him brought him back. He spurred his horse forward and flew down the hill.

They had pressed on hard through the next day, and had camped for only four hours before rousing the herd again. Driving fifty was much easier than driving a thousand, and he and Bainta kept the kison going at a steady pace, despite the obscenities and screams from the bundle behind Bainta's saddle. The Kuzzi had wrapped the package well; he would not escape, hadn't even tried in fact. Looking at Kay all rolled up tight in burlap, Stewart couldn't help but feel a throbbing in the back of his mind, and it wasn't from the injuries to his head or ankle. *It shouldn't have happened this way,* he thought as they drove the kison into the valley. *I should have been better, stronger.* Too many had suffered in this drive, and for what? A bunch of aliens that did not give a whit for humans or for Byanntia? Looking down into the valley at the three large corrals being filled with kison, Stewart's face ran hot.

Vellong representatives stood in front of each corral, holding communication equipment and waving large feathered banners. The red-and-gold banners represented the Matson's corral, and the last of their herd was being secured. Stewart nodded to Bainta and she shifted the herd. Shifting kison in mid-stampede was a difficult task, even with so few, but Stewart was not afraid anymore. He shifted his horse, slammed into a kison bull and snapped his whip. The kison turned and all the heads around it followed suit.

The Bensons and the Cools were moving fast to fill their respective corrals. "Come on!" he shouted over the roar of the herd. "Let's go!" He cracked his whip again.

As he and Bainta raced towards their corral, Stewart could see other figures standing by the gate. His brother Joe was there, waving a banner proudly above his head. For the first time in several days, Stewart smiled. It was good to see family. And then, from behind his brother came another figure, a lady in a smart blue dress, her left hand on her hip, her right shielding her eyes from the sun.

Mama!

Stewart's smile grew larger as he spurred his horse forward. He pulled the reins to the right and took the lead. Onward they raced, all fifty head beating a path across the valley, their weight shaking the ground. It was the most amazing sight Stewart had ever seen: nearly three thousand kison in one valley. Was there anything better in all the world than being a kison rancher? In Stewart's mind, the answer was clear.

He pulled up just short of the gate, jumped off, and hitched his horse to a post. He winced as his sore ankle met the ground, but he grit his teeth and bore it well. His head and jaw too were still sore from the beating he had taken from Kay, but both were healing nicely.

Stewart waved his hand as the last of the Kison poured through the gate. Stewart watched them fly past. A weight lifted from his shoulders; he breathed a sigh of relief. They'd made it. The race was over.

But not quite. As the last kison passed and the gate closed, Stewart turned and began limping across the field where the Cool's herd was being corralled.

Joseph Matson came up behind his brother and slapped his shoulder. "Welcome back, little brother!"

Stewart shrugged the hand away. "Not now, Joe. I've got to take care of a little business."

"What are you talking about? What's going on?" Joe suddenly noticed his brother's injuries. "And why are you banged up so badly?"

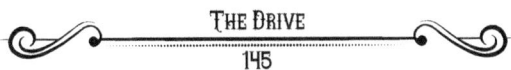

Stewart ignored him and walked on, his eyes fixed on an old man with a dusty grey felt bolo, a leather vest, and a plain white shirt.

When Branson Cool saw the young Matson, he walked up and said, "Boy, we need to talk."

But Stewart wasn't interested in talking. Instead, he balled up his fist, and with all his strength, drove it into the jaw of the old man, sending him reeling backward, a line of spit and blood and grey hat arching through the air. Branson Cool hit the ground hard.

"That's for cutting me off at the Gordon Pass!" Stewart said standing over the man, fists ready for more.

Joseph wrapped his arms around his brother and pulled him away. "Whoa, Stew. Hold on there. What's he done?"

Stewart laid out the entire situation, from the drugging and bull fight, the Cools shifting their route to close off the Gordon Pass, the sabotage at the River of Death, and the murder of Alvin Trainer. By the time he finished, a crowd had assembled. Cool's twin sons Sammy and Chester had helped their father to his feet. Cool's crew had assembled behind them as had Stewart's. Both sides glared at each other, their hands inching towards electric prods and bolt guns.

"Alvin is dead?" Shelby Matson clung to her young son's arm, tears in her eyes.

"Yes, Mama," he said, rubbing her shoulder. "Killed by saboteurs."

"It wasn't us!" Chester Cool snapped back. "We didn't do any of those things you say."

"You deny blocking us from the Gordon Pass?"

Branson Cool pushed his sons away and stood on his own strength, a streak of blood down his chin. He wiped it away, cleared his throat, and said, "Yes, that we did. I won't deny it. But that's all. I did not sabotage your herd, or kill anyone."

Members of the Vellong Trade Federation moved into the fray. Their thin, elongated bodies, warped and genetically altered to handle a life in zero-g, were covered in body-tight moldable alloy that protected their brittle bones from snapping in Byanntia gravity. They looked like

armored thugs, but they were as gentle as lambs; that is, their *bodies* were gentle. Their minds and tongues were sharp and fast.

"Stop this fighting now! We demand it!" said one of the members. "The matter is concluded. The herds are gathered. It is time to declare a winner."

"Not until this matter of sabotage is resolved!" Stewart said, straining against his brother's hold.

"I tell you we only shifted the herd," Branson reaffirmed. "We had to."

"Why?"

"Because we were attacked also."

Stewart stopped struggling. "Explain."

Branson rubbed his swelling lip. "Shortly after leaving the ranch, some of our kison grew mad with rage. We lost a good deal. Then several of our horses were poisoned. We lost nearly eight hours on the first day. We had no other choice but to pivot and make for the pass."

"Even though you knew that was the Matson's designated route?" One of the trade commissioners asked.

Branson looked at his sons, sighed and said, "Yes. Actually, we were hoping to run into your herd, young man. We thought perhaps... well, perhaps we could drive our herds together."

"Together?" Shelby Matson moved forward and offered a kerchief to Branson. He took it humbly and pressed it to his mouth. "To what end, Bran?"

"Strength, and safety, in numbers," Branson said. "We figured if it had happened to us, maybe it had happened to you. But then you didn't show. We started thinking that perhaps it was *you* who had sabotaged us. It made sense: Force our delay, then shift your herd in another direction."

"That's nonsense," said Shelby Matson. "We don't cheat. Besides, our families have been friends for years, Bran. Why would we do such a thing?"

Branson Cool motioned to the Vellong trade commissioner. "This is a sweet deal, Shelby, and don't tell me your husband isn't above doing what he has to do to ensure his family's survival."

Branson and his mother went on arguing for awhile, but Stewart tuned them out. He thought back to his challenge of Trainer's authority. If he had only stuck to the original plan, Trainer's plan, none of this would have happened. They would have met up with the Cools and things would have been resolved. *Damn this competition! Damn the Vellong!* He gave the commissioner a dirty look. How dare these bastards come to their planet and pit them against one another, friend against friend? The more he thought about it, the more this "lucrative" deal chapped his hide.

The Bensons waded in on horseback. Their patriarch, Yuri, dismounted and adjusted his leather holster and belt. "Let's get this thing over with, please. It's been a hard, dangerous ride. I'm hungry and in need of a stiff drink."

Sammy Cool stepped up and pointed a stiff finger at Benson's chest. "It was you, wasn't it?"

Benson stepped back, shock on his face. He smacked the finger away and two of his crew behind him pulled pistols and pointed them forward. "You better step back, boy," Benson said, confidence spread across his face. "We don't want this to get ugly. What exactly are you accusing me of?"

"Sabotage," said Stewart, moving in between, his hand resting on the hilt of his purjung blade.

Benson leaned back and laughed, his large, toothy mouth open wide. "Don't be ridiculous, boy. A Benson never cheats." He pushed past and opened his hands in a kind gesture to the Vellong commissioner. "Sir, I implore you. Let's end this now. Time is up."

The commissioner nodded, his neck hydraulics working smoothly. "Agreed. The competition has ended. Put your accusations aside, or I swear, there will be no agreement today."

Everyone backed off and stood down. A long ten minutes passed, then a tiny man whisked in on a small hover-cube. Obviously, his bones were too old and weak to withstand even the body armor. In his hand lay a small tablet which he handed to the commissioner, nodded politely, then floated away.

The commissioner looked at the tablet. When he was finished, he tucked it into his belt and said, "The herds have been counted, and their tallies officially recorded into the Vellong Trade database. The Matson herd was the first to corral, beating out the Cools by two point three seconds. The Benson herd corralled last."

Joseph patted his little brother on the shoulder. "Congratulations, Stew."

Stewart shook his head. "Wait for it, brother."

"However, neither the Matson herd nor the Cool herd corralled with the requisite integrity. Thus, despite their third place arrival, the Bensons win the competition."

A cheer went up among Benson's family and crew. A hiss of disgust and anger spread through the Matsons and Cools. Joseph Matson cursed and Shelby Matson protested. "This is an outrage," she said, her hand in a fist. "We demand an investigation. Sabotage has been accused, and you're going to do nothing?"

The commissioner waved her words away. "The competition is over, Lady Matson, and you have produced no clear evidence to your claim. Therefore, the results stand. The rules are the rules."

Stewart Matson turned to the commissioner. "You want proof, eh? Very well." He motioned Bainta forward.

In the midst of their squabble, few had noticed the Kuzzi. Now all eyes were on her as she rode up slowly on her horse. She stopped in front of the commissioner, dismounted, and unhooked the bundle behind her saddle. The man inside tried to break free, but Bainta's grip was too strong.

She walked up to the Vellong commissioner, dragging the bundle behind her. The commissioner was tall, but Bainta dwarfed him. He seemed weak and tiny in her shadow. "I am Bainta," she said forcefully, "daughter of Sinaku of the Red Desert Tribe and of the human Alvin Trainer, who died bringing the Matson herd to your corral. I am here to present proof of Benson treachery." She stepped aside to show the bundle.

Yuri Benson's face boiled. "This is ridiculous!" he screamed. "The competition is over. I've won fair and square."

"Fair, you say?" Bainta drew her spear from her back, turned its blade down, and cut away the bindings of the bundle. She then cut a line in the burlap and ripped it open.

Remy Kay lay within, bruised and battered, his clothing tattered, his hands and feet bound. He was conscious, but he shivered, and when the sunlight hit his face, he cowered and curled up like a baby. "This is the man who brought shame and dishonor to the Matsons. This is the man who killed my father." She pulled a bolt gun from the belt at her waist and offered it up. "This is the gun he used to kill him."

Bainta kicked the bound man. Remy grunted and curled even tighter. "Tell them the truth. Tell them who you work for."

Slowly, Remy Kay crawled out from the bundle. Bainta threatened to kick him again. He put up his hand, coughed and spit blood, then said, "Mr. Benson hired me and my men to stop the Matsons and the Cools... any way we could."

"Liar!" Yuri Benson pushed forward and grabbed the gun from the Kuzzi's hand. "I've never seen him before in my life. She's a lying Kuzzi bitch!"

Benson raised Kay's pistol. Bainta knocked it out of his hand, and swept his legs with her spear. The old rancher went down hard. His son tried to pull his gun, but Stewart had him covered immediately.

"Enough!" The trade commissioner said. "I said the competition is over. Our decision is made, and it is final."

Stewart turned and glared at the Vellong. He wanted to reach out and snap the little pecker's head off, but he held his anger. "So even after this man's confession, you still do not believe? Then how's about checking in the back of my wagon? Alvin Trainer's body is in there. There's a bullet lodged in his lung. I'm sure if you check the markings on the bullet casing with the barrel of his pistol, you'll find a match. Go ahead and check. Do it!"

The commissioner stepped forward. "And if I don't?"

Matson's and Cool's alike moved forward. They did not stop until they had encircled the entire commission. Though they did not draw pistols, it was clear from their faces that it would take little to bring this

matter to blows. The commissioner and his staff twisted and turned their augmented heads, looking for escape. There was none.

The commissioner's voice sounded higher than usual. "We come here in peace to sign a fair trade agreement, and this is how we are treated?"

"No better than how you've treated us," said Stewart. "Making us jump through your hoops. Treating us like rodents. We won't stand for your games anymore, commissioner. You will reconsider your decision, or you'll have a hell of a time getting off this planet."

The circle loosened, giving the commissioner and his staff room to back away and huddle. Long minutes passed. Finally, the commissioner emerged from the huddle, cleared his throat, and said, "in light of the evidence, we have decided to give the contract to the Matsons. With their first place finish, they have won fair and –"

"No!" said Stewart. "This is unacceptable."

"Stew," Joseph said, "what are you doing? They're giving us the contract."

"The Cools will share the contract, or no deal. Fifty-fifty split. They too were affected by Benson's deceit. Down the middle split, or no deal."

The motor in the commissioner's jaw ground his teeth tightly. Finally he nodded. "Very well."

Benson pushed away Bainta's spear. He jumped up, his face burning red. "I won't stand for this!" He turned on Stewart and waved his fist. "This isn't over. I'll have satisfaction. I swear it!"

Benson climbed on his horse and drove his spurs into its sides. When all the Bensons were gone, a resounding cheer went up and hands were shaken, backs were slapped, friendly insults were bantered back and forth.

Shelby Matson grabbed her son and hugged him tightly. "Your father would be proud of you today, son." She said, giving him a kiss on the cheek. "Very proud."

Stewart nodded. "Thanks, Mama."

He accepted more congratulations, and smiled and joked as best he could. In time, the Vellong departed along with Joseph and a Cool

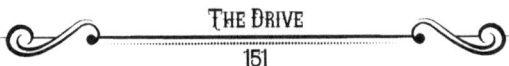

delegation to discuss the details of the agreement. When the crowd dispersed, Stewart and Bainta faced one another alone.

This time, he looked her straight in the eye. "Thank you, Bainta," he said. "I owe you one."

The Kuzzi nodded. "You are welcome. But tell me one thing. Why did you hit the old man? You knew he wasn't guilty."

Stewart smiled. "I had to get it all out in the open, didn't I? I had to show the commissioner I meant business. Sometimes, that's the only language people like them understand. Besides, the old man deserved it for cutting us off."

Bainta smiled. "You are a brave, smart little warrior, human," She placed her hand on his shoulder. "In time, you will do great things for your people."

"No," Stewart said, shaking his head. "I'm just a kison rancher... and a Matson."

Bainta smiled "Indeed you are. Goodbye, young Matson," Bainta stepped back and bowing politely. "I've enjoyed our time together. Bury my father in honor and someday our paths will cross again."

She turned to leave. "Wait," Stewart said. "Where are you going, Wi'shak'alun?"

She did not turn, but she stopped, shrugged her shoulders, and said, "As you say... wherever the wind takes me."

Stewart stood there, in the hot Byanntia sun, and watched her disappear.

THE HARDEST GLORY

C.J. Henderson and Bruce Gehwelier

"**T**YRANNY, LIKE HELL, IS NOT EASILY CONQUERED; YET WE HAVE this consolation with us, that the harder the conflict, the more glorious the triumph." – Thomas Paine

"You know," started the doctor, holding his glass aloft, not knowing tragedy was but five minutes off, "I figure there has to be at least one son'va bitch harder to kill than you somewhere in this universe. Problem is, I'll be damned if I ever met him!"

Laughter and cheers rose up from around the Matson family table. A flurry of glasses went skyward, were knocked one against the other, drunk from and set down so hands could applaud. It was a good party and as at all good parties people were determined to celebrate. And, of course, they had a reason—Jacob Matson was still alive.

"That's my dad," said Joseph Matson, wiping a stray lock of dirty blonde hair from off his forehead. "The one man on Byanntia just too stubborn to die."

The assembly cheered again. Two years earlier the doctor, now toasting Matson's health along with the rest, had given him a few weeks to live. His tests and the resultant facts they surrendered had told him the patriarch possessed absolutely no more than a month of remaining life. To soften the blow he had indicated to Matson that he might have as much as a year. Might. If he was lucky, and did everything he was told. But that was it—no more. Absolutely no more than a year. The old man had then immediately gone out and gotten into an altercation which had broken six of his ribs, shattered two more.

"I understand," said Matson, his voice stretching to find a tone that at least resembled humility, "that I should be long dead. I know that would've made this birthday of mine a lot more festive for a lot more people, but I, well, I fault Doc Lieber here with keepin' me around to plague the rest of you."

A chorus of good-natured boos and catcalls were heard around the table, now but four minutes from disaster. Matson nodded in appreciation. Others began lifting their glasses and making their own toasts. As they did, the old rancher sat back, feeling the efforts of having made the short speech a moment earlier. He was a man living on borrowed time who fully understood how cautious a banker the Grim Reaper really was. That he had survived long enough to train up his surviving sons to take over Twin Feathers, the family spread, he considered a blessing.

Not the only blessing you've had in your time, old man, a voice from the back of his mind told him. As he listened to those around the table, he knew the words were true. Decades earlier, he had landed on the world now known as Byanntia with most of the rest of its population. A number of new arrivals, like his sons, had followed naturally, and a few off-worlders had found their way there, it was true. But, for the most part, the majority of the planet's human citizens had made the same trip, 875 people crossing the light years in a slumberocket taking them to a new life.

Tired of Earth and its myriad regulations, taboos and restrictions, they had thrown the dice on carving something out of a wilderness for themselves. The only thing the long range scans could tell them was that the planet had a breathable atmosphere and no competing sentient beings. The scans had been right about the air, at least.

They had been wrong about Byanntia's other citizens, however, the Kuzzi. When the humans' one-way ship had touched down, never to lift off again, the colonists had discovered the feline nomads, the smallest of them taller than any human—or been discovered by them, depending on one's point of view—and tensions had immediately jumped to the breaking point. The humans, of course, were in the worst position. They could not leave. But, the Kuzzi were also in a bad position. They were more numerous than the humans, true, but the humans' weapons were far more terrible than theirs.

"Hey, Jacob," called out Troy Duncan, the planet's sheriff, "ever tell these kids how you made the deal that got us to Byanntia in the first place?"

Before anything hostile could happen, however, the Kuzzi leader Bollatu had welcomed the humans. Boundaries had been drawn up, and some tensions had ensued, but for the most part the towering feline creatures decided to act the perfect hosts. Of course, that decision had more to do with a certain piece of knowledge the natives chose to keep from the humans than it did etiquette. The Kuzzi knew that a creature their ancestors had named the Gr'nar would return when its cycle was due. Every time it had come, it had killed hundreds of Kuzzi. This time, they knew, smirking inwardly, it would kill humans. Bollatu had left Byanntia in disgrace when the humans had repulsed their god-thing with a minimum of effort.

"Oh," drawled Matson, glad he had stayed in bed the day before, pleased he was rested enough to party as if he were not rapping on Death's door, "I may have mentioned it once or twice—in passin'."

Joe Matson rolled his eyes and groaned. Stew Matson gave out with an exaggerated "heehaw" laugh that drew more merriment from around the table. Their mother merely smiled. Those keeping score could have noted that there remained only two minutes before their world would collapse.

Matson looked to his own glass at that moment. Actually, it was not really a tumbler of any kind, but more of a chalice, one made of pure Byanntian clay, fired and glazed right there on the planet. It was a grand and beautiful object, made by foundry owner Josh Mosheberg with

his own two hands. Thirty-five years ago, Josh had followed Matson to Byanntia. He had come out into the darkness and stars for his own reasons as had they all. The husband and father had worked eighteen, twenty and twenty-two hour days, constructing his ovens so that when the rest of the expedition was ready to start building, they would have the bricks with which to do it.

And, when work was done for the day Josh Mosheberg would put aside all facets of himself except that part of him which had been his motivation to go to a new world and experiment with the native clay. The artist he felt within himself worked with the potter's wheel he had brought from Earth, and as the years went on, he learned how to move his thumbs just so, when to pour water of what temperature in which quantities until he had discovered all the secrets needed to make bowls and cups and plates and mugs, vases and ashtrays and all manner of artifacts which would survive his death. Pieces which would become family heirlooms—the treasures of Byanntian families—his family and his neighbors' families.

Thirty seconds from horror, Matson lifted the blue-glazed goblet to his mouth again, once more thinking on how lucky he was. Lucky to have had the opportunity to come to Byanntia in the first place. Lucky to have two strong sons, his beautiful wife, Shelby. Lucky to have stumbled onto a natural beef product on the planet the taste of which appealed to most every carnivore in the galaxy. Lucky enough to have made the journey to Byanntia before the building of the gates.

While the travelers had slept, Earth technology had harnessed the power of the stars and found a way to throw ships and people through other dimensions. Matson learned to herd and slaughter Kison beef just as Earth figured out how to reach his doorstep in days rather than the decades it had taken him and the others. The day they found his doorstep, they came with orders for all the beef he could ship, and suddenly he was the head of a dynasty.

"Okay, okay, if everyone's finished with their tomfoolery," said Shelby, filling the fifteen seconds of ignorant bliss the assemblage had remaining, "there's a lot of food waiting to be eaten in the kitchen ... that is if anyone is hungry."

Sheriff Duncan was just about to respond to her invitation when the first great explosion jarred the house.

As an event it was not that spectacular. Bookcases did not tumble; the ceiling did not collapse. But the tenor of the party changed instantly. Peoples' heads turned, ears marking the direction, eyes searching for windows. Instinctively all knew the tremor they had felt had come from the direction of New Dodge. The town was some twenty miles away, nothing of it visible to those at the ranch except for light reflections cast off from the town hall building's main radio tower.

When the ship which had brought the first settlers to Byanntia had landed, it served two purposes. Much of it was stripped away to facilitate the building of private residences and businesses. The great shell of it, however, was their first home, later maturing into the business and political center of New Dodge. It would do so no longer.

"Do you see that?"

"I ain't blind, you know."

A great plume of smoke could be seen in the distance, rising from the spot everyone knew was New Dodge.

"What the Hell ..." Matson mused quietly. Louder, he asked, "Can anyone get a signal from town?"

Personal comms were tabbed. No one could generate a response. The comms were all charged and operational. There simply was no out-going signal to be picked up.

"Somethin's gone sideways and back ag'in in town," declared Stewart. His brother nodded in response as the second great explosion was felt. This one much closer. Much closer.

This time the party-goers were given all the drama they could handle. These shock waves threw people to their knees, on their faces. Chairs were thrown over, depositing more of them onto their backs, across each other. Women screamed. The bassinets set up in the side room crashed to the floor, babies tossed out across the hand-made rugs, lungs and bowels exploding. Great clouds of blue-gray dust threw themselves against the house, through the windows, rock fragments shredding the screens.

"What was it?" asked Shelby. "What's happening?"

Jacob Matson had no answer for his wife. He had no answers, period. Lying on his side, gasping for air, the pain of a score of old injuries flaring immediately, the old man could barely breathe, let along think. Slowly, painfully, he calmed his racing heart while younger hands helped him to his feet, slid an undamaged chair beneath him.

Just a helpless, crippled-up fool now, ain't ya?

The thought washed its way through Matson's brain, sneering as it traveled throughout every corner of it slowly, taunting the old man. All about him, the confused screaming continued for another full minute and a few random seconds. Then, the new masters of Byanntia made their first demands known.

***

A small dart of a warship had hovered over the main house of Twin Feathers long enough to make an announcement. All household heads were to report, unarmed, to the center of New Dodge immediately. The ship had whirled about in the air and then snapped off in the direction of Twin Feather's nearest neighbors. The party-goers stumbled from the Matson home, barely whispering goodbyes, staggered at the way their secure world had changed in a handful of heartbeats.

"Drokin' bastards, they blew out the comm tower," yelled Stewart. "Figure that must be what they did in town, too."

Jacob Matson agreed with his son. While most everyone else milled about directionless, staring at either the black plume rising from town, or the one billowing there before them, Joe began to round up those workmen that were at the ranch proper at that moment, putting them to the task of extinguishing the flames remaining from the attack. As he did, Stewart reached his father's side.

"Who were they," he demanded. "Who the Hell would do this to us?"

"Think that's what the nonsense about going into town is all about," answered Matson. "Probably they want to introduce themselves."

"What do you think they want?" asked the doctor of his old friend.

"What do these types always want?" answered Matson. The growl in his voice left no doubt in anyone's mind as to what he meant.

Joe and two ranch hands got the minor blaze under control quickly. The attack had been quick, efficient and surgical. Little damage had been done outside of that which had been intended. Matson did not find that detail encouraging.

"These are professionals," he told Duncan quietly. "They know what they're doin' and they know what they want. And us, we don't know neither."

"What're you sayin', Jacob?"

"I'm sayin' they have all the cards right now. I'm sayin' that they have air power and explosives and combat knowledge. I'm sayin' that whatever the Hell they want they've got a good chance of getting it."

The sheriff bristled at Matson's anger, but Doc Lieber interfered. Cutting off their growing shouting match, he reminded them both of the older man's condition, then lambasted the pair for snapping at each other when they had a completely unknown force blowing up their buildings. The doctor was right. Both men knew it and cooled off at once.

With Lieber leading the way toward sensibility, it was soon decided that they should probably start for town. Twenty miles was a ways to travel, especially on horseback and in wagons. When Matson suggested to the others that they abandon their gliders and other powered vehicles, the patriarch explained;

"Look, we don't know how much these bastards know about us. Let 'em think we all ride around on horses. Why not? We may need an advantage soon. They blow up much more around here, the charges and the fuel our rides have right now may be all they ever have again." People nodded in agreement. Matson kept talking. Forcing his voice loud enough to be heard over all the minor bits of background chaos, he told them;

"I don't know what you people think is goin' on here, but I'm tellin' you right now, we're in a war. Maybe it's a war we done already lost and we just don't know it yet. But, it's a war, nonetheless, and the quicker we start acting like it is, the quicker we might start having a chance of livin' through whatever the hell it is that's come our way."

***

Several hours later the party from Twin Feathers reached the outskirts of New Dodge. They were neither the first nor the last to arrive. The sheriff went to his office at once, as did Doc Lieber. The Matson boys and their mother went with the others to where the main body of Byanntians had congregated, outside the ruins of their town hall. They had not gathered there merely because the smoldering debris occupied the center of town. They did so because a ship had landed there—a ship like one none of them had seen before.

Gray it was, long and bulky, covered with arrays of odd antennas and bristling with weapons. Cannons of various sorts protruded from every surface. No one felt the need to touch the ship. After the first few minutes, most did not even keep looking at it. They simply waited near it to find out what its owners wanted of them.

Jacob Matson had remained at the ranch, claiming tremendous fatigue. When his wife had gone out of hearing range, he had instructed Joseph to take a talkie with him, and to keep it open so he could monitor all that went on in town.

Joe had taken the antiques out of their case in the tech shed, marveling at the old-fashioned workmanship of the portable comm devices. A quick test showed that their batteries were still working, another fact that impressed the young man greatly. Joe slipped one to his father as he and the others were leaving. Matson nodded slightly to acknowledge their clandestine maneuvering, then kissed his wife goodbye and went back into the house.

In town speculation ran wild as to what the invaders might want, who they might be, what it all was going to mean. After several additional hours had passed, a hatchway in the side of the dreadnought suddenly bent outward and down. In the end it formed a platform some fifteen feet above the ground. A humanoid figure completely masked by combat armor on a par with that worn by Rim Enforcement Officers stepped out onto the metal platform. He wore an old style pellet-flinger on his hip and was flanked by much more heavily armed men—one to each side. Then, as the central figure positioned himself on the end of the newly-formed balcony, one further figure stepped out, standing behind the others, a head and a half taller than any of them. As the crowd waited, the central figure removed his helmet.

The action revealed what looked from the ground to be a middle-aged Caucasian, clean-shaven, possessed of a full head of nondescript, close-cropped brown hair. As the figures to his sides kept their weapons trained on the crowd, the man spoke, his voice amplified by unseen technology.

"I'll take us directly to where everyone wants to be," he said, his tone harsh and condescending. "My name is Dorton. I'm your ruler now. Understand that simple fact and we'll have no trouble. My arrival signals a shift in power here. My men and I, we are now the lords of Byanntia. We are in control of the entire planet. We will not harm anyone who does not ask to be harmed. Now, of course, how, you might be wondering, does someone 'ask' to be harmed? Indeed, that's a good question. Such a good one in fact that I'll answer it at once." Dorton paused for a moment, then continued.

"Those who do what they are told will be left reasonably alone. Those who do not will be eliminated—without question—immediately." The black garbed figure leaned forward, his eyes scanning the crowd.

"Now, if there is anyone who would like to be made an example of, please—this would be a wonderful time to do so. Anyone, anyone who'd like to throw a rock, pull some kind of weapon, even just shout out some disparaging remark about my ancestry, by all means, feel free, for I would dearly love an excuse to show just how ruthless we can be."

"Why not just kill someone anyway?"

Scores of people moved away from Joe Matson. From his platform, Dorton called out;

"Good question. I like to see a man who thinks. Hopefully you'll appreciate my answer. The reason we're giving you all a chance to behave on your own is because to do otherwise would mark us as madmen. If we were that irrational, you'd have no choice other than to defy us. After all, what difference would a little risk make at that point?"

Smiling down at Joe, Dorton added, "But we're not mad, young man. Simply filled with avarice. We want what you have, and we don't plan on paying for it. This planet markets beef to a hungry galaxy. We'll be taking those profits from here on in while you do the work and keep the protein flowing."

And then, people screamed, running in confusion as the sound of gunfire broke out. Before he could react, two lead slugs crumpled against Dorton's chest. The man barely moved in reaction, however, thanks to his armor. Before a third shot could be fired, though, the marksman to Dorton's left used the motion tracker built into his helmet to sight the line-of-attack vector of the slugs which had bounced off his boss's armor. The computerized system locked in, raised the guard's arm and returned fire automatically. Sheriff Duncan disappeared in an explosion which vaporized his body as well as half the rooftop from which he had decided to stage his short-lived offensive.

On the ground, Byanntians trampled each other, shoving wildly, knocking one another about, neighbors trampling neighbors in their howling desperation to live. Staring downward in amusement, Dorton allowed his voice to boom forth once more.

"Thank you, citizen, for offering us the chance to present the preceding demonstration." As the people below him began to slow their frantic desperation, the man in black added, "I'd like at this time to point out that the only person our forces dealt with was the one foolish enough to use a mere projectile weapon against static armor."

All around the still smoldering town square, folks stopped running, swallowed their panic. Above them, Dorton smiled. Hands on his hips, he addressed them once more.

"Of course, he thought he had an opportunity to take me out of the picture, what with me taking my helmet off and all. He most likely had my skull square in his sights, but funny think about static armor, it sends out blur waves, throws off the human eye."

As folks turned, looking up once again, calmed by Dorton's tone, cowed by his words, he continued.

"It was a brave act, but a foolish one. I spent a long time planning this affair out. Trust me, my new vassals, all of the angles have been mapped, and any chance you might have had to repel us has been figured and eliminated. But, as long as you all can learn and profit from this first, all too graphic example, why, I'm certain we'll all get along just fine." With a chuckle in his voice, Dorton spread his arms wide, then added;

"I think you'll find that we came here to make a new life for ourselves, just as you did. So, all you ranch owners, I want you to assemble together where my men can find you. They'll escort you into our ship and then we'll all sit down and have a nice friendly meeting wherein I shall explain how this whole new king/serfs relationship is going to work."

***

Dorton did not like the fact that Jacob Matson was not with the other ranchers. He had somehow done his homework before coming to Byanntia. He knew Matson was the leader of the original expedition. Knew that he was well-respected. Knew that if he had Matson's cooperation that things might not only go ahead smoothly, but with a minimum of bloodshed.

"And why isn't Mr. Matson here," asked Dorton smoothly. "Did we not catch his attention when we, ah, adjusted the frequency, shall we say, of the comm tower at Twin Feathers?"

Not that Dorton had any problems with bloodshed. Quite to the contrary. He had put his force together and gathered the credunits to finance his plan with great quantities of bloodshed. But, as naturally disposed to washing the walls scarlet and black as he was, he also knew the mask he needed to wear for the good people of Byanntia at that moment.

"Oh, no," answered Shelby, "we noticed that all right. But you have to understand. My husband isn't well. Two years ago our doctor gave him a few weeks to live. A year at the most. That he is still alive is a miracle, but he's terribly frail."

"Yeah," added Joe. "And your 'adjustments' to our property threw him to the floor and almost did him in right then and there. So, you'll have to forgive us if we didn't feel like killing him by dragging him into town. Or would this be another one of those moments that's going to force you to prove how ruthless you are?"

Dorton's eyes narrowed, but he kept his jaw line firm. The mask he needed etched into his features at that moment was the firm but understanding visage of the tolerant despot. Cruel, but fair. Demanding, but tolerable.

"I was under the impression Mr. Matson was a much heartier individual," responded the black-garbed conqueror, showing his demanding side. "But no matter. What we need right now is to hash things over with the head of every ranching concern and that is something we need to do today."

"There won't be any problem with that," answered Joe Matson. "My dad trained me up for that job over this last year. I speak for Twin Feathers at the general store, at the space port and everywhere else. I can do it here, too."

Dorton sat unmoving—staring. Unblinking. He had learned the habit in childhood, learned it to protect himself from an abusive parent. It disconcerted most adults more than threats or curses. He let his silence keep the crowd at bay while he thought. He did not like variations, disruptions—changes in plans had never suited him.

Of course, he knew full well that anything could have happened between the time he had finished his investigation of the planet and their arrival there that day. Half the people in the room before him could have died in a landslide, or been paralyzed by a plague. It did him no good to worry about such changes. Indeed, Matson was described as a cantankerous, obstinate son of a bitch who did not give an inch on anything. Considering himself perhaps fortunate that the elder Matson was out of the picture, Dorton said finally;

"You probably can at that. So, let's not worry about it, shall we? Instead, let's just get down to business. I'll do the talking. You all listen."

The ranchers listened. None of them heard anything they liked. In short order Dorton explained that he and his men were taking over. Their terms were simple. As of that moment they were the lords of the planet. Every ranch would pay a tribute according to its size, a payment which would end up being the rough equivalent of eighty percent of its yearly income.

At this point one kisonboss, Rabe Gutherie, spoke up, saying that Dorton and his bunch were crazy if they thought they were going to get away with that kind of robbery. While Dorton stared at the man, one of the intruder's henchmen silently raised his hand laser and fired. Gutherie's head fizzled, then began to smoulder. He fell face forward to the table, skin rupturing, blood and other juices spattering on impact. People shouted, some of them screamed. One threw up. Most merely turned their heads away—staying silent. Beaten.

There was more to cover, however, and Gutherie's body smoldered where it had fallen while boundaries were drawn up, curfew times established, restrictions made on the size of gatherings, et cetera, but such minutia was all inconsequential. The invaders' point had been made with the death of Sheriff Duncan, let alone Gutherie's.

The ranchers were angry, of course. Furious. They also knew their anger was mostly directed at themselves. They had placed their faith in distance when they had left the Earth. They would be so far from any other human beings by the time they got to their new home that they need not fear outsiders. They had thought. They awoke and landed only to discover that Dispersion Cracks had been opened throughout the galaxy, and that travel between systems now took only hours rather than decades.

There were the Rim Patrol agents, of course. For what little good they might be. Yes, they would come if signaled, but the invaders had leveled Byanntia's off-world communications. The next agent to travel out their way might drop in to see why no one had heard from them. And any lone agent would have as much chance against the force which had landed in their town square as Duncan had had. Or Gutherie.

Then, when Dorton was just about to dismiss them, one last blow was struck. All eyes turned toward Joe Matson as a furious beeping emanated from his belt. Embarrassed, Joe took the talkie from his belt and shut down its incoming call signal. Always a man who enjoyed the discomfort of others, Dorton insisted Joe answer the communication. The young man did as instructed, only to react with shock as he listened to the message. When Dorton demanded to know what the news had been, Joe told him;

"That was the foreman out at Twin Feathers." The younger man's tone was clipped and brittle. Nasty. "Apparently the excitement of the day was too much for my father's heart." As everyone stared, Joe clarified;

"Jacob Matson is dead."

***

Joe thought on the expression on Dorton's face for much of the trip back home. The invader had been angry, confused, relieved, all at the same time. He had been suspicious for a moment as well. The man had stared at him for quite some time, his eyes studying—probing. Eventually they had stopped, however, satisfied with their inspection of the eldest Matson boy.

The ranchers had been dismissed then. The Matsons had headed for home as had the others. Once out of town Shelby Matson had immediately questioned her son, asking if he was trying to pull something. The look on his face was answer enough for the woman. Quietly she sat in her saddle, her hands barely capable of holding her reins. None of the others had much to say, either. That changed some hours later when they arrived at Twin Feathers.

"What do you mean, he's not here?" Shelby Matson was white hot with indignation. Slamming her finger into her foreman's chest, she rammed it against him repeatedly, driving it deeper into his flesh each time as she shouted, "You told us he was dead. You told us he was *dead*. If he died, then what did you do with him? Where's my husband?!"

"He's gone."

Jacob Matson had not died. He had instructed his foreman to make the call to his son after listening to the way the meeting with Dorton was going. While the foreman had done so, Matson had left the main house and gone to the barn. There he had saddled his horse, a grey and tan mare named Dancer, picked up the talkie from his foreman and then ridden off toward the West. A quick inspection of the house and barn gave them a partial list of what he had taken with him. It also gave them a note which Joe found in a place only he would have known to look in, which is why his father had left it there.

Figured you'd think of looking here. Didn't want any uninvited types to find this. Russ told you I was dead. You told those bastards the same thing. Keep it that way. I'm dead. Bury me.

Play the game. Do what they say, within reason. You don't know what I'm up to because I'm not telling you. We need an ace. Fast. Me on the outside is the only thing I can think of, so I'm going for it before it's too late. I have something like a plan. Obviously I'm going to go guerrilla on their asses.

I'm taking the talkie with me. Don't call me. No idea if they're monitoring the airwaves. I'll call if it's so damn important I absolutely have to.

Sad to think of Duncan dead. Gutherie was a good man, too. We'll fix them. This is our damn world.

Don't worry. I'll be home to kiss you once more, wife. That's a Matson promise.

Shelby wished for more. So did Joe. For a moment, anyway. Then they threw off their anger and their sorrow and pulled themselves and those around them together. After all, they had an empty coffin to bury.

***

Matson rode along through the foothills approaching the mountains. He had made good time. With luck, he might reach Kincaid before nightfall.

"Good thing Byanntia runs on a thirty hour day, eh Dancer?" The horse nodded its head with the enthusiasm of a colt. The mare had been born on Byanntia, was one of the oldest horses on the planet—the oldest one still considered a working animal and not merely a decoration or child's pet. "I think we ought to be able to find that old desert weevil before the sun runs out on us."

From what Matson had heard through the ranchers' meeting with Dorton, the invaders had come with more than a little knowledge of the planet. They knew spreads by name, knew their owners, knew where people were concentrated, how many of them were there, what kind of defenses Byanntia had ...

"Too damn much," Matson said to the wind. "They know too damn much. Gotta even up those odds."

The old rancher went silent then, conserving his strength, hanging onto each precious breath in the parched environment. If he dried out he would have to take a sip from his canteen. Too many sips and canteens go empty. Too long without water and old people die.

And I promise you one thing, Mr. Dorton, thought Matson, his eyes narrowing to slits, I will not be dying before you. That's another goddamned Matson promise. One I intend on keepin'.

A little over three hours later Matson found himself approaching the home of hermit Kincaid. It was a cleverly designed home, the old man had to admit. Anyone heading straight through the mountains would never notice the turn off from the main trail needed to find it. Indeed, even those looking for it would have difficulty.

Matson guided Dancer across the barren rock, searching his memory for the proper directions. Kincaid had come to Byanntia for only one reason—to get away from people. He was not sick of life, had no interest in dying. He simply wanted no further truck with the human race. As soon as the settler's ship had landed, Kincaid had taken his meager weight allotment and had marched straight away into the desert. Nowadays most Byanntians knew nothing of his existence. Matson knew about him only because of a freak coincidence.

Traveling through the mountains once, he had spotted the man stuck on a cliff face far above him. Reaching a spot where he could help, he found Kincaid reluctant to accept his aide. Again, the hermit did not want to die, but the thought of being beholden to another so incensed him that it took him hours before he would consent to being rescued. Matson had gotten him up onto the trail, set his broken leg, and taken him to his home. It had been the only time since the landing that any earthling had seen him.

Could be dead for all any of us knows, thought Matson.

The old rancher leaned hard to the left, playing the reins slowly, giving Dancer her head. One wrong step on the treacherous path could send them both screaming to the desert below. Coming around the last bend, Matson breathed a sigh of relief as the rock floor began to level out once more. In minutes horse and rider were moving through the scrub pines natural for that level. Not Earthly pines, of course, but a breed close enough for the transplanted Christians of the group to chop down and drag home every December.

Matson thought on the planet's jury-rigged calendar, created ahead of time to give the settlers some sense of continuity.

"Forty days, hath September," he said, "April, June, and November. All the rest have fifty-three, except February, which has twelve, and December, which has thirty-one."

So many ways it could have been simpler, Matson thought. But, no—people had to have their damn holidays fall like back home. Good God, but people make me tired.

And then, at the closest he had ever come to understanding exactly what hermit Kincaid thought of the human race, a voice called out, "That's far enough."

Matson reined in Dancer, then responded;

"Kincaid, I need to talk to you."

"Well I don't need to talk to you. Just turn yourself around and head back the way you came or I'll put a round in your horse's head and send you both on the big tumble."

"You can't do that," answered Matson. "Not to me. You owe me one. And I've come to collect it."

A long pause followed. The old rancher sat his saddle, waiting in the cooling breeze. Far off, Byanntia's sun began to set behind the edge of the world. The sky filled with orange streaks, the clouds flaming to pink. Matson admired the view as the seconds ticked off one after another.

"You took your time collecting," came the voice again.

"Might never've bothered," the rancher shouted back. "But things are bad and I need your help. Everyone needs your help."

"And," the voice came clearer, no longer muffled by the trees as its owner stepped into view, "just who the Hell would *everyone* be?"

"All the people you came here with," answered Matson. "And all their children. And, if things get really ugly ... possibly you, too."

"That's a lot of people," Kincaid answered.

"Yeah."

"One of 'em I even care about somewhat."

"Why, sir," replied Matson, purposely misunderstanding the hermit's joke, "you'll turn my head."

Kincaid snorted, then turned, heading back to his home. Matson gave Dancer's reins a slight flick, signal enough to the old mare to move forward. As the two entered the trees, fat ground underneath them once more, Matson thought;

Well, here goes nuthin'.

***

"Who the hell is behind this?" Dorton was scowling, his anger twisting his face into a frightening mask. Behind him stood one of his armored men, the massive, helmeted figure that had stood behind him the first day on the platform. The ranchers before them stood immobile—frightened. Silent. Not certain of which figure they were more afraid.

"We don't know," pleaded the man to the front, an Asian in his forties. "We have no idea."

Joe Matson stood to the back. He remained as quiet as the others, but not because he had no answers. He knew who the current thorn was in Dorton's side, but he dare not let such knowledge show on his face or in his manner.

"Bullshit," snarled Dorton. "You *have* to have some idea."

"But," offered another ranch boss, barely able to keep from stammering, "you've got your fliers watching us, tabbed everyone with a tracking chip, how could any of us do anything?"

"Listen, Mr. Dorton," interrupted Pete Dawson, former deputy of New Dodge, "everybody's scared to death. Nobody here is gonna go against you. I'm not goin' to lie to you. No one's happy about you takin' over. But there just ain't anything we can do about it. You pretty much proved that the first day."

"Obviously not to everyone," replied Dorton. "Unless you think my pilot shot himself out of the sky, or that I'd see some advantage in blowing up my own ground tractors. Or maybe you think the two men of mine shot down last night killed each other."

"I don't even see how any of us *could* kill one of you," offered Joe. "You know the level of weapons we've got on this world. Ain't none of us on Byanntia has anything powerful enough to scramble your armor."

"Nobody on Byanntia has anything powerful enough to scramble our armor," repeated the warlord in a mincing voice. He let the question hang in the air for a moment, then slammed his fist to the table, roaring, "Then who the Hell is killing my men?!"

All in front of Dorton remained quiet. Most hung their heads in fear. None of them was ready to play the hero. They had families to think about, children to protect. They also knew that a man like Dorton might decide to blame one of them anyway. Or to use one of them as some sort of example. Joe could tell from the tension he could feel in the air that if most any of those present knew his father was still alive, they would give him up immediately. He kept his head lowest of all.

"Maybe I should just join forces with the Kuzzi," said Dorton to the silent room. "Just wipe you shitheels out and work a deal with them. What do you think of that idea?"

"I don't think it would work," answered Joe. When Dorton called for an explanation, the young man told him, "the Kuzzi don't like any humans, but they've started to realize that we're not out to do them wrong."

"Convenient theory," responded Dorton. "What makes you think we couldn't convince them we're as noble as you? Why wouldn't they work for us if we rewarded them right?"

"A while back," piped in one of the other ranchers, "some vermin landed in secret. They came to hunt the Kuzzi, to skin them, so's they could sell the pelts for coats. Apparently there are some pretty twisted rich bastards out there. Anyway, we fought alongside the Kuzzi to stop them. We turned the survivors over to them to do with as they saw fit. Since then we've been gettin' along pretty good."

The man wiped at his forehead with his sleeve, adding, "I don't mean no disrespect, Mr. Dorton, it's just the truth. You couple that with the fact the Kuzzi ain't really the kind to be bought off, and I think Joe's right. We ain't got no heroes in this room, sir, least of all me. We just want to stay alive."

Dorton stared his unblinking stare for a long moment. After a handful of seconds he turned in his chair and looked up at his massive guard. Joe watched the man's eyes, wondering if he were somehow asking the sentry a question. When the guard's helmet moved a fraction of an inch, Joe was certain he was nodding to Dorton.

But, wondered the young rancher, what was he nodding about?

After another few seconds, Dorton dismissed the ranchers. He told them to go back to their spreads and to stay there. The invader made it quite clear that he and his men would be looking quite strenuously for those individuals who had been playing havoc with his operation.

"We're going to be tearing up your precious planet, so you'd all better stay close to home, because anything we see moving anywhere outside the designated safe areas is going to be fair game." No one spoke; they merely turned and headed for the door. Then, just as they reached the door at the back of the room, Dorton called out;

"Oh, and we'll be seeing just how how well you and the Kuzzi are getting along these days."

As the ranchers filed out into the street, those to the rear of the group heard him mutter;

"We'll be seeing about that real soon."

***

Kincaid and Matson rode through the darkness along a trail just below the mountains to the west of New Dodge. In the weeks they had lived together, scouting the enemy, hiding, waiting, planning, it was amazing how little they had actually said to each other. Matson was not completely surprised that Kincaid had no questions as to what had happened to this or that person. The hermit cared nothing for humanity, that part of it he had left behind on Earth, or those who had traveled the stars with him. Indeed, every conversation the two had had thus far Matson had initiated. Thus the old rancher was caught completely by surprise when Kincaid asked him;

"So, we killed some of 'em. How long you gonna hold me to my word—'til I'm dead?"

"If that's what it takes." When the hermit did not respond, Matson reminded him, "you'da been dead years back if it weren't for me, so what's the problem?"

"No problem. Just curious."

Matson nodded—satisfied. He did not add any unnecessary words to their conversation. Kincaid was not a talker, and besides, words carried a long distance on the night air in the open desert. Especially with the mountains behind them to act as an amplifier. Their foes could be anywhere in the darkness, listening for them. The old man thought it unlikely, but he was not one for pressing any amount of luck unnecessarily.

After another hour the pair reached the spot to which they had been headed. As Kincaid began to pull together a shelter for their horses, Matson began to climb the rock wall behind them. The going was slow

for the old man. He was tired and he was dying. His breath came in short gasps and his fingers hurt as he dug their bony lengths into whatever cracks he could find and then used them to haul his body upward. The weapon slung over his back weighed like as anchor does on a sinking ship.

Just a few more weeks, Lord, he thought, refusing to look down, refusing to quit. Just a few weeks. I ain't been one to ask much, you know that's fact. But, I don't think I can do this one on my own. But, you give me the way out of this one, let me deliver my wife and boys outta this, and believe me, Lord, I am more than ready to join you.

Matson's hand found a pocket of dust and loose shale shards. His hand struggled to find purchase, fingers stung by the keen stone edges, slipping in the dust. Grinding his teeth together, he ignored the pain and continued upward. By the time he reached the ledge he needed, his weary heart was pounding madly, blood throbbing loudly in his ears.

Matson shrugged his way out of his weapon's harness, falling onto his back as soon as it was safely beside him. Air rushed out of his lungs as fast as he could drag it in. For several long minutes the old man lay helplessly on the outcropping, panting and wheezing and praying to not die—not just yet, anyway.

Finally, once Matson had calmed his nerves and heart, once the throbbing pounding had left his ears, he held his hat out over the edge of his sanctuary and then clicked his pocketlight on and off within it several times. Down on the ground below, Kincaid did the same. Although the hats did not completely hide their signals, the pair judged the idea safer than shouting. At this point the men began phase two of their plan.

Breaking off a small piece of rock with a small hammer, he then tied an end of fishing line around the rock and threw it over the edge, holding onto the end of the line. When he felt a tug he began hauling the line back up the cliff. After a moment, Matson's efforts were rewarded when a length of dark nylon rope came sliding over the outcropping's edge.

Securing the rope through the neck loop of one of the two pitons he had brought up the side of the mountain with him, Matson then took his hammer and, using his hat as a mute, he hammered the securing rod into the ledge. He ruined the brim of his worn Stetson, the last article of Earth-made clothing he still owned doing so, but the sacrifice had been made to muffle the noise of his efforts. After a few minutes tense waiting brought no enemy patrol ships, the old man lay back, placing the damaged hat over his face as he muttered;

"And now, we wait."

***

It was three days before Matson was able to put his plan into operation. Three days waiting on his ledge. Three days alone. In the baking sun. Thinking on why he was doing what he was doing. Because no one was going to take Twin Feathers away from him. Because no one threatened his family and got away with it. Because he goddamned well felt like it.

Because he was dying.

Jacob Matson had clung to his ledge, hour after hour, the sights of his weapon aimed toward New Dodge. At night Kincaid sent him up food, refilled his canteen, all transfers made via their length of rope. During the daylight hours, Matson lay stretched out, enduring the relentless heat, his eyes shaded by the brim of his hat constantly scanning the horizon, watching for the enemy's small attack fliers.

After observing the opposition's forces for a while, Matson and Kincaid had determined that the enemy's main ship had disgorged only four of the smaller assault vehicles. The old rancher knew if he could take out those fliers, he would have gone far in evening the odds between the invaders and the rest of Byanntia.

Dorton knew a lot about their planet, about its people and their ways. He knew their communications systems, their transportation routes and their weapons capacities. At least, he thought he did. Luckily for Jacob Matson, he did not know everything. When the Kuzzi's god-thing, the Gr'nar, had begun its rampage, it had been stalked by a big game hunter who had believed he had an ace in the hole—a Hoffman Brother's Wide Bore. The hunter had perished, but Matson had quietly appropriated his rifle and stored it away for ..., well, the rancher did not know for what exactly he might use it when he took it, but he was now glad he had done so.

The Wide Bore came with explosive rounds so powerful they could topple any creature the Earth had ever seen. If Matson could place a round just so, he could bring down the fliers. He knew he could; he had already done so. Now, with the invader's makeshift staging area on the edge of town in sight, he waited for the fighters to return to homebase.

After three days, they did.

Dorton had only four fliers when he arrived on the planet. Now he had three. Not knowing if he could count on ever getting another opportunity to take out the aircraft, Matson had waited day after day for all of them to return to base at the same time. Often he had found two of them parked there on the outskirts of New Dodge. There had almost always been one of them there in his sights. But, it was well into his third day stretched out on the ledge, his body aching from constant contact with the sometimes burning, sometimes freezing granite, that all three of the fighters were at their landing strip, on the ground—all in the same place at the same moment.

"Well, praise Jesus," muttered Matson, stiff and tired and aching all over, "and pass the humpin' ammunition."

Quickly the old rancher stretched his arms, his legs, forcing the pain and knots and all the other little crippling annoyances from his body. Reaching into a vest pocket, he pulled out one of the stims he had been holding for an important moment. Opening the small metal box, he frowned at the sight he knew would greet him.

Two.

He had only two of the pills left. Doc Lieber had given him thirty of them less than a month ago, just before his birthday. Lieber had been strict in his instructions. The stims were only to be taken on extremely bad days, when he needed the energy and relief they could flood one with far more than he needed the days they would cut off from his life. Matson had been taking them recklessly since leaving home to find Kincaid.

Indeed, they were the only reason he had made it so far. The last one he had taken just before making the climb to the ledge. He could have never made the assent without one.

Couldn'ta done any of this without 'em, he thought, disgusted with his weakness. Picking one of the pills out of the tin, he slid the box back into his vest and tabbed the pocket secure. Then, he stared at the pill.

He had to take it; he knew he did. He could not risk making his next shot without a steady arm, without a body free from the agony his was feeling at that moment. A thousand times over the preceding days he had thought of taking one of the stims, dreamed of it. He had barred such dreams from his consciousness, however, forbidden himself such thoughts.

What was the use, he told himself, to be alert and ready if there was nothing to be alert and ready for? What did he think he was going to do for energy when the moment came if he gave into his petty weakness and gobbled up his only chance? The only chance his wife and sons and everyone he knew had?

That was over now, though. For the moment the abuse he had endured was banished from his body. Smiling, he reached out and pulled on the rope—two short, two long, two short. Kincaid understood the signal and began tying off the end to his saddle horn. Then, he moved his mare along slowly until the rope grew taunt. After that he waited.

Above, Matson kept his eye glued to the Wide Bore's sight, waiting for the right moment. He knew it would come soon. Dorton had been clever so far, keeping the fliers separated. Something must have gone wrong with one for all three of them to be on the ground at the same time.

Com'on, he thought. Pop the lid on one'a 'em. Any one of 'em. Just gimme my shot, goddamnit.

After another eighteen minutes, a small team approached the fliers at a rapid clip. As they drew close, they split into two teams, each heading for a different ship. Grinning with anticipation, Matson followed their movements, waiting for what he needed. He had used scores of explosive rounds on the flier he and Kincaid had brought down, slamming away at

its tremendous hide until he had ruptured it and toppled it from the sky.
He no longer had that luxury.

With less than a dozen rounds left, he had to be careful, had to think
about what he was doing. Not believing his good fortune, two of the fliers
being opened up at the same time, he dried his clammy hands off on
his pants and then gripped the Wide Bore, studying the scenario below
him. The view through the weapon's sight revealed that the men were
opening the one flier to tinker with its engine. The other, Matson blinked,
astounded to have Lady Luck showering him with such an opportunity,
they were making ready to fuel. The old rancher chuckled. He could not
help himself.

Well, go on, get to it, he told himself, adding, or were you thinkin' they
were going to make it even easier for you?

Deciding such a thing was barely possible, he began to plot his
attack. He had his angles ready, when suddenly one of the workers stepped
directly in front of the fuel chamber. For a second, Matson cursed his luck.
Then he remembered just what kind of ammunition he was using, shut
one eye, and squeezed the trigger.

The first round tore through the mechanic as if it had not noticed the
man's presence, not exploding until it hit the solid resistance of the flier's
chemical converter. Before the first round had struck the man, however,
a second had already been squeezed off. As it struck the converter, a
third was sent directly after it. Instantly the area exploded in confusion
as the flier being refueled tore itself to pieces. Hot metal and sputtering
chemicals flashed in every direction. Flames green and black and orange
flashed into existence, then winked out just as quickly, replaced by an
ominous gray cloud of mushrooming dust that billowed upward.

Even as the first explosion was just beginning to erupt, however,
Matson was cooling squeezing off his fourth shot. The explosive shell
tore into the flier with the open engine. The force of its explosion had
just begun to lift the machine from the ground when a second round
hit the same exposed area. The second flier exploded then, not quite as

spectacularly as the first, but the force of its demise added enough power to the holocaust to tear open the third vehicle.

As more smoke poured into the open sky, the rancher was already making his way down the cliff. He had his hands tight on the rope and was skidding down the wall at top speed. On the ground, Kincaid was moving his horse back toward the mountain, allowing Matson to descend without having to work hard. Both men made a silent prayer that the single piton would hold.

It did.

"What took you so long?" Kincaid's wisecrack gave Matson pause. The rancher merely smiled, however, and answered;

"Stopped for lunch. You ready to ride?"

"Ask me at dinner," answered the hermit. Throwing off the line from his saddle horn, the two men abandoned everything not packed in their saddlebags. Throwing himself up into the saddle with relative ease, Matson silently thanked Doc Lieber's unintentional aid, and then fell into place behind Kincaid as the two worked at putting as much distance as possible between themselves and the nightmare of fire and explosions which was still working at destroying the north end of New Dodge.

***

"Well, I sure in hell don't like this."

Matson lowered his binoculars to turn and look at Kincaid. The hermit moved his head and face in a way that indicated he was not pleased with the sight before them, either. Both men turned back to the sight that had drawn forth Matson's comment.

Down below them was stretched out the winter campground of the first Kuzzi tribe the original human settlers had ever met. Although normally nomadic through the spring, summer and fall, the Kuzzi had gone to their winter retreat when Dorton and his troops had first arrived. Their plan had been to simply wait out the violence they knew would have to follow. Their hopes had been to wait out the tide of Earther aggression, hopefully to pick up the pieces when the two sides had destroyed one another.

Their hopes had been shattered as Dorton had chosen that morning to move on the clan's winter home with all his remaining forces. Though Matson and Kincaid had indeed deprived the invaders of their air support, they still had three heavily armed and armored vehicles along with those ground skitters they had taken from the Byanntian humans.

Seeing Dorton and his people arrive at the winter campground was not what disturbed Matson so, however. Although that would have been a curiosity for the rancher, what was unfolding before him was not something so much curious as it was frightening. The Kuzzi Matson had known and dealt with since his arrival on the planet were all there, but they were not alone. Something had brought other Kuzzi tribes there as well. Dozens of them. Scores of them.

Hundreds of Kuzzi firespots dotted the early evening scene. Matson knew that translated to literally thousands of the feline creatures being in the area.

But, disturbing as the idea of Dorton meeting with such a massive amount of the Kuzzi was, it was not that fact which had bothered the old rancher, either. The thing that had him swallowing hard was the fact that Dorton's forces had at least a hundred Byanntian humans captive with him. And an equal number of Kuzzi women and children as well. Whether his wife or sons were among the prisoners he could not tell in the failing light. But he meant to find out. Moving down out of the hills as quickly, yet carefully, as they could, Matson and Kincaid headed for sea level to find out what was going on.

When they had reached the plains and were about to start for the center of the activity, Matson suddenly turned to Kincaid and told the man;

"Hey, no sense in both of us gettin' fried. Go on, take off. You done enough."

"What?" Kincaid simply stared.

"You asked me before if I was goin' to guilt you to death, and I guess the answer is 'no,' after all. I appreciate your help, but you done all a man can do. Ain't no reason you dyin' with me. You paid your debt in spades. I'll finish this hand."

The hermit continued to stare for a moment, then said quietly, "Invite a man to supper, make him cook the meal, then send him home before the main course gets served ..."

Kincaid let the words hang in the air, then spat out a sticky wad of phlegm that glued itself to the inter-laced branches of a nearby spiner bush. As the thick wad oozed slowly through the plant's thorns and tiny leaves, he added;

"You don't mind, Mr. Matson, I'll be tagging along a while longer."

The old rancher stared in surprise as the hermit gently snapped his horse's reins and continued on toward the event unfolding before them. Then, Matson got over his surprise, accepted that Kincaid had as much right to throw away his life as anyone else, and cued Dancer to start moving as well. Silently, the two men moved toward the massive gathering still growing before them.

***

"The humans who came in the before time are not the friends of the Kuzzi."

The speaker was Dorton's over-sized personal guard. The big soldier spoke to the felines in their own language, his voice amplified by his helmet's electronics to the point where all could hear him across the vast plain where the new arrivals had camped. Matson took in the scene as they approached.

"You all know what they are capable of."

The guard had chosen a most horrific of podiums. He stood on a boulder situated near the center of a chilling sight. Roughly six months before Dorton had arrived, another group bent on exploiting Byanntia had invaded the planet. These men had been hunting Kuzzi, however, killing them for their pelts to satisfy a monstrous off-world taste for wraps and jackets made from the skin or fur of aliens. The local humans had stopped the interlopers, then turned them over to the Kuzzi along with the several hundred pelts the murderers had procured.

"Look around you if you have forgotten."

The felines had hung the skins on sticks planted in the ground surrounding the boulder. The monuments had been decided upon as a way to not only honor the dead, but to remind the living of what humans thought of the Kuzzi. Any who looked closely would note that a number of the sticks did not hold a feline pelt, but a flapping flag of human skin and hair, sign posts which made it quite clear what had been done with the hunters. And what Kuzzi thought of the human race.

"We came to this world to bring permanent order, to bring an end to human exploitation. But the humans who came to steal your land, to shove you off your own planet, they resist. They destroy. You saw what happened in New Dodge two days ago."

Matson and Kincaid kept their heads down as they dismounted their steeds, tieing them off at the scrub forest's edge. Slowly they made their way forward, listening to Dorton's bodyguard as his voice continued to boom.

"Explosions that tore open the sky, that rained filth and acids down upon you, the crops you harvest, the seas you fish." His hand pointing toward the captive humans, he bellowed, "If they push us back, you will be their next targets. And yet, you help them against us."

"You speak wrong," answered an elder Kuzzi near the front. Speaking in English so Dorton and all the others could understand, he said; "We no interfere with you. Why would we? Want you to destroy each other. Want you gone. Help one side over the other ... for what reason?"

"I don't know," answered the towering guard. "But it has to be. We knew where every human being on the planet was, and yet there has been sabotage since we arrived. Who has done this if not the Kuzzi?"

The crowd stood silent. None had an answer. After a moment, however, a different Kuzzi elder shouted in response;

"Enough talk of human this and that. Forget human. Mean nothing to us. Tell us why you take Kuzzi slave. What you think? What you mean?"

"We hold your people for two reasons," answered the bodyguard. "First, to make all tribes in this area come to this place. Second, to prove that we will not stand for your turning your hands against us."

As the large armored figure waved its arm, another of Dorton's soldiers moved two bound figures forward—one human and one Kuzzi. As the pair were driven to their knees, the guard shouted;

"One from each race will be slain until you give up those who have fought against us. We have no grievance against the Kuzzi peoples except in this thing."

Matson strained his eyes, then felt his stomach churn violently. The Kuzzi male on his knees he did not know. The human woman was another matter, however. It was his wife, Shelby. As he calmed the rage boiling his mind, rage that could only harm his chances of doing anyone any good, the bodyguard's voice boomed out once more.

"Give us those who have tried to aid the humans and we shall not only free all Kuzzi, but we shall give you these other humans as your playthings, to dispose of as you see fit."

The dried hairy skins flapping on their monument sticks rustled ominously. Then, before any more could be said, Matson stepped boldly out into the light and began making his way toward the boulder and the speaker perched atop it.

"Oh, hell," he shouted. "What're you botherin' these good people for, ya moron? I'm the one's been griefin' ya."

Shelby screamed out an indecipherable string of syllables, then burst into tears. Atop his boulder, an abnormal amount of shock seemed to rock the towering guard. Pointing at the advancing rancher, he bellowed;

"Jacob Matson."

All heads turned. The old man continued to stride with as much confidence as he could muster as the Kuzzi ranks parted to grant him passage, their eyes going wide with the sight of him. Their reaction was understandable, of course, for as far as any of them knew, Jacob Matson had died and been buried. As the rancher moved forward, however, he wondered;

Now how in hell did that bastard know who I was?

Not wanting to give his opponents a moment to think, he shoved his personal thoughts aside and shouted to those around him;

"Remember this moment. Think on it long and hard. These men are thieves and murderers. Without the slightest proof, they would have killed your women and children, because they were simply too stupid to figure out what was going on."

From inside one of the armored vehicles, Dorton ordered Matson shot down immediately. But, despite the path the Kuzzi had opened for the rancher, none of the invaders had a clear shot. After foolishly threatening the felines, no one thought it wise to stir them up by accidentally killing one now. While they continued to flounder, Matson made the only move he had left. Yanking one of the monument sticks from the ground, he pulled the human remains from it and flung them down, spitting on them where they fell. Then, hefting the sharpened stick in both hands, he shouted;

"Well, I say it's time to clear these deathers out of here. I call for one-on-one."

"Old weak thing," the bodyguard growled, "I will kill you with the ease of dispatching a pinga beetle."

Who was this guy, wondered Matson once more. He speaks Kuzzi, he recognizes me without a second glance ...

The towering figure leaped down from atop his boulder, hitting the ground with an easy grace. Grabbing up another of the human-draped sticks, he tore the skin from it and flung it behind him, coming forth to meet Matson in the clearing between the monuments and the massed Kuzzi. Off to the side, the prisoners pressed forward to see what was happening, blocking Dorton and his men from interfering. Waiting for him, the old rancher moved his hand to his face. He had slipped his last stim into his hand before he had left the shadows. Now he moved it into his mouth surreptitiously, tearing it with his teeth and swallowing it dry as best he could.

The drugs found welcome in every corner of the old man's body. His nerves praised their relief as did his muscles, his spine, his churning stomach and burning eyes, his raw legs and hands. Matson tested his grip on the stick, loosening and tightening his fingers. He felt his heart racing, could feel the ice sweats springing from hundreds of pores, letting him know he had finally pushed his luck one time to often. Knowing his window of effectiveness could be monumentally short, Matson cursed;

"You gonna fight or you just gonna play around all day?" Dorton's bodyguard stared down at Matson, then made a noise of disgust.

"You think not being dead is a surprise," answered the towering figure. Reaching upward, as he snapped open the catches which held his helmet fast, he added;

"You be not the only one with surprises to reveal."

And suddenly, the rancher understood how Dorton had known so much about all their ranches, all their operations, so much about Byanntia itself ...

"Great hoppin' weevils ..."

So much about the Kuzzi ...

"I don't believe it ..."

And how he had recognized Jacob Matson instantly ...

"Bollatu!"

The massive guard was a Kuzzi, the one who had made the decision to allow the first humans to stay, confident the Gr'nar would destroy them. The only Kuzzi chief ever thrown out by his own people and one of the only felines to go off-world, with a ticket paid for at the spaceport by Matson himself out of the Twin Feathers account.

"So," spoke Bollatu, grinning down at his opponent, "you are as surprised to see me as I was to see you. Fine. You do realize, calling one-on-one means nothing. Even if you could beat me, Dorton would not honor any victory demands you might make. You have killed yourself, old human."

"Did you hear him," shouted out the rancher. "They will not honor the ways of the Kuzzi."

Matson stopped talking and rushed his stick above his head, blocking Bollatu's opening attack seconds before it could crush his skull.

The effort strained the old man's recently renewed strength, forced the breath from him. The Kuzzi whirled his stick about, bringing it around and in toward the rancher's side. Matson ducked down and let the length sail over his head. He also managed to stab forward as he did so, but Bollatu easily stepped back out of the way.

"Do you see this coward's face?" Matson cried out to the warriors all about him, "Do you see this one who hides behind human armor, who wears pants? Pants?"

The rancher smiled as he heard the harsh titter of Kuzzi laughter all about him. He fought desperately to keep his teeth showing as he blocked another of Bollatu's shattering blows, feeling the hit through his shoulders, down his back, in both hips. The Kuzzi whirled his stick again, forcing Matson backward into the circle of monuments.

The action gave the old rancher a moment's rest for the larger Kuzzi could not maneuver as easily through the sea of fur-wrapped poles as could the human. Angered at the accidental refuge Matson had found, Bollatu swung wildly, knocking down monuments left and right, sending the skinned remains of the slain felines crashing to the dirt.

"Do you see his actions," cried out Matson, voice panting, veins throbbing, vision blurring. "Is this a creature you can trust?"

And then, a false step caught the rancher's heel in between two rocks. Down he went, ankle twisting badly, spine cracking against the ground, head slamming into one of the monuments. Pain filled every corner of his body. Blood flung itself up his throat, over his lips, splashing down his chest. The stim was already wearing off—far earlier than it should. Matson knew what that meant.

In a rush, Bollatu moved forward, bringing the pointed end of his stick to bear just over Matson's throat. The Kuzzi savored the moment, years of torment vaporizing as he tasted the sweetness of his triumph. Matson, who had brought the humans, who had beaten the Gr'nar, who had survived and prospered while he had been forced out of his tribe— now all was reversed. It was the human who would be thrown away, useless. Finished.

The old rancher released his grip on his own stick, grabbing instead at the one aimed for his throat. The Kuzzi only smiled. Let the puny human try and turn his hand. He would show them all that humans were no match for the Kuzzi. Which, of course, had been his intention all along.

Earlier, he had convinced Dorton that coming out of town and grabbing feline hostages would be the best way to get their cooperation. Of course he had known better than that. Since the beginning, since he had met the mercenary far off-world, Bollatu's plan had been simple. He would use the fool Dorton to his own ends, to return to his home, to rout the humans, and then he would trick him into angering the tribes so that he might step forward and grab control, not just of his own tribe, but of a hundred tribes. A thousand. Seconds from his triumph, he asked;

"Would you like to beg for mercy before the mighty Kuzzi nation?"

"Yeah," answered Matson in a tired but loud voice, "I got somethin' to say to the Kuzzi about mercy."

Testing his failing grip on Bollatu's weapon, flexing his fingers, the old rancher sucked down a deep breath, then shouted as loudly as he could;

"As far as mercy is concerned, I hope you furry son'sa bitches have got the good sense not to show this bastard any."

And then, Matson pulled with all his failing might, jerking Bollatu's stick down and through his body, pinning himself to the ground.

Shelby screamed, then struggled to her feet. As she ran forward, hands tied behind her back, Bollatu stared in horror for endless seconds. The miserable human Matson had cheated him again—*again*. Then, suddenly, he looked about himself. First he noticed the Kuzzi pelts knocked to the ground by his attack. Then he noticed his former tribespeoples closing in on him.

The Kuzzi bounded for the bolt thrower he had left behind on the boulder. At the same time several of Dorton's troops started gunning down hostages—human and Kuzzi. Screams shattered the night and the world erupted into a nightmare of struggle at that moment, Kuzzi armed with spears, humans with rocks, all united in their singular desire to slaughter the invaders.

As Shelby Matson collected the kiss she had been promised in her husband's final note, the gathered humans and Kuzzi charged the armored cars recklessly, and they died by the hundreds. But one by one, they peeled their hated enemies out of their cans and punished them for their perfidy long into the night.

In the morning, the survivors counted the dead. The number was not reported as so many Kuzzi murdered, or so many humans slain. The number was reported as 472 Byanntians lost.

Byanntians.

From that day forward.

KINCAID'S LAST STAND

Jack Dolphin

1

WHEN KINCAID LOWERED HIMSELF OVER THE RIM, THE Kuzzie came out of hiding and knelt beside the boulder where the rope was anchored. The Kuzzie was a young one named Haavoth, long and lean like all his people, bluish-gray fur bristling in the erratic winds of the canyon. Although he was consumed with the curiosity of youth, his father's warnings and the warnings of his tribe's leader *were* fresh in his mind.

Avoid the newcomers.

It couldn't be more simple or direct.

But resisting the chance to observe one of the strangers was impossible. He didn't fear discovery; he'd been careful and, while these alien creatures were interesting, they couldn't possibly pose any threat. They were, to his eyes, at odds with the environment – ill at ease and clumsy – and remarkably unobservant.

This long thing tied around the boulder fascinated him. What might it be? Made of something unfamiliar to the youngster, it must be something they'd brought with them from wherever it was they called

home. This region of Byanntia had no plant-life that produced vines, so the concept of a rope was unfamiliar to the Kuzzie. Besides, getting down from the ridge to the ledge – almost certainly the newcomer's aim – was a matter of a short leap or an easy climb for any of Haavoth's people. That was part of Haavoth's fascination with the newcomers – their lack of physical ability and the methods they'd found to compensate for their weaknesses.

The thing around the boulder, for example. Though he'd never seen its like, Haavoth quickly grasped its purpose. He felt pity for the newcomer, reduced to trickery for so simple a task. But he could see where such an object might prove useful.

He reached out his paw and, after rubbing his pads against the rope's rough surface, flicked a talon across its surface. The razor-like point of the claw sliced easily through the rope and nearly severed it. He watched in horror as the few strands that still held the rope snapped one by one until the separation was complete and, in a flash, the ends whipped around the sides of the boulder and vanished. Haavoth heard a cry from below, then a muffled thump.

Oh, no! If his father learned of this, he would punish Haavoth severely! With no thought to the old man whose lifeline he'd just cut, the young Kuzzie melted into the hills and was gone.

2

Kincaid came to on his back, clear sky above him and the fierce light of the afternoon baking his leathery skin. His shoulders ached. There was a throbbing at the back of his head and sharp pain in his left leg.

He cursed quietly as he tried to move. Seemed okay. Nothing broken, hopefully. But the leg hurt too much for just bumps or bruises. Twisted an ankle, maybe. Or wrenched the knee. The pain was pulsing through the lower leg. Only way to figure the problem would be to try standing up.

How the hell had he fallen? He was a better than average climber. He was in decent shape for his age and he was stone cold sober. What had gone wrong?

He rolled over and saw the ends of the loop lying beside him. Pretty clean cut. Sliced through most of it with a single blow. A sword? An axe? Even a sharp knife could have done the deed. But the method wasn't really important, was it? The real mystery was who would do such a thing? And why?

Kincaid had no illusions about his place in the world. He knew he was considered a cantankerous coot. He had no use for other people and wasn't at all shy about letting them know it. Hell, that was his whole purpose in getting to Byanntia – the chance to kiss off so-called civilization, for good and all.

It wasn't perfect; after all, hundreds of folks had signed on for the journey. But the planet was big and it proved easy enough to separate himself from the group; move to the outskirts of their chosen territory. Still, as disagreeable as he could be, he couldn't remember annoying anyone enough for them to try killing him.

The planet's natives, the Kuzzie, weren't exactly friendly, but they weren't exactly hostile, either. At least not the way Kincaid defined the word. He came from a long line of pioneers, folks who'd always turned their backs on whatever society they were born into. Nearly a thousand years earlier, they'd crossed an ocean to a new world. Soon after, they'd crossed a continent to escape the crowded settlements. They'd taken up residence in every God-forsaken outpost the Earth had to offer and, in every case, they'd faced real hostility – from native tribes, unforgiving landscapes and the evil of human predators who sought out the pioneer, the pilgrim, the explorer. And they had prevailed. Finally, Kincaid himself had fled the planet altogether.

He wasn't sure what caused this penchant for flight in his ancestors, but he knew what it was in himself.

People.

Incompetent boobs traipsing through life with an astonishing sense of entitlement, sure someone else would happen along any minute to clean up whatever mess they'd made. Hands always out, hearts always locked away. Wanting, wanting, wanting, never giving. And it wasn't the material things they wanted that Kincaid begrudged them. He had little, needed less, desired nothing. Their grasping for money had no effect on him and their pursuit of power he overlooked, long as they kept their distance.

No, the thing they wanted, the thing that Kincaid would never be prepared to give, was time.

Time.

The only thing you had that you couldn't get more of and couldn't ever know for sure how much you had left.

Kincaid valued his time. He spent it carefully, doling it out as sparingly as he could, seeking ways to maximize efficiency in daily tasks. He savored the free moments, few as they were, looking down on those who wasted their time but saving his true contempt for those who tried to waste his.

He'd grown ever more impatient with them until impatience had turned to anger and then blossomed into rage. Kincaid knew the next step would be violence, so he'd signed up to leave Earth and its disappointing denizens behind. Well, most of them, anyway. And so far, that had been good enough.

Now, except for a monthly trip to the settlement for supplies, he remained in and around his cabin in the foothills – raising what produce the poor soil could sustain, hunting and trapping for meat and supplementing his meager diet with the occasional Glueur egg. Which was the reason he'd been climbing down to the ledge, having spotted a nest with two eggs from the ridgeline opposite.

The Glueur eggs were larger than the chicken eggs he'd enjoyed on Earth and they had a slightly sour taste that took some getting used to, but they were better than no eggs at all. The scientists had tested them, found them not only safe to eat but an excellent source of protein in the bargain.

The Glueur were plentiful and Kincaid was smart enough to only take one egg at a time and only from nests that had two, since sustaining a species that provided food made sense. Besides, eggs were only obtainable while both the parents were out of the nest and that was a rare occurrence. No one in his right mind wanted to come face to face with an adult Glueur – immense predators with beaks and talons that would shred a man into a bloody heap if they got hold of him.

Which reminded Kincaid of how perilous his position was. He had two hours, tops, before the Glueurs returned. And he still wasn't sure what was wrong with his leg.

It took effort and no small degree of pain to get up on one knee, the damaged leg splayed out and pounding. Not a good sign. And that damn rope wasn't going to help. A quick glance over the side confirmed it; the drop to the canyon floor was double the length of the rope, easy, maybe more.

Well, one way or another, he'd have to get himself out of this scrape. But how? And, scanning the skies for the expected return of the Glueurs, he started thinking.

3

Jacob Matson wheeled his young filly, Dancer, around a string of boulders and urged her up the trail towards the ridgeline. Only a couple hours left until sunset and he wanted to get some samples of the greenish-gray rock he'd spotted from below. Most of the rock in this area shared the same bluish cast as the native Kuzzie, so the anomaly was intriguing.

Matson was no geologist; he was a rancher. He had a large spread, Twin Feathers, in the valley to the east where he raised kison, a herd animal native to Byanntia with a taste and texture not unlike beef. Originally, the Matson clan, Jacob, his wife Shelly, and their three sons, had gathered up a small herd of kison, intending to provide meat for themselves and the inhabitants of New Dodge, the settlement of 875 souls that had accompanied them to Byanntia. But soon after their arrival on a sleepship (a thirty year journey) the people of Earth had solved the problem of interdimensional travel and ships could now reach Byanntia in hours rather than years.

With the shortage of cattle on Earth and the prevalence of kison on Byanntia, Matson found himself in the right place at the right time to create an empire.

Partly from curiosity and partly because he believed in contributing to his community, Matson had volunteered to do some exploring and mapping of the colonists' new world. It made a nice break from herding kison – stupid creatures with accommodating natures, but possessed of a rude odor that made herding them a nasty job in the scorching Byanntian summer. His sons could handle an afternoon of work on their own just fine.

He reached the strata of greenish rocks and chipped away at them with a small rock hammer, storing the pieces in his saddlebag. Then he paused to take in the vista before him. Earth had possessed such scenic wonders once, but that was many centuries ago, before the corporations bought up the National Parks and turned them into massive landfills and nuclear waste dumps. Sitting there gazing out over miles of rugged country, Matson felt as though he could understand what his ancestors might have experienced when they had crossed America in wagon trains nearly a millennium earlier.

He raised the *Powernocs* to his eyes and focused on a distant mountain. Black clouds poured over the western horizon but they were too far off to be a concern – he'd be home with Shelly in front of the fire with a mugful of grog before the rains came.

In truth, it was an accident he spotted Kincaid. He'd lowered the 'nocs and was putting them in their saddle-mounted case when a movement across the canyon and slightly below the ridge caught his eye. He pulled the 'nocs out again and powered them up as he strained to identify what he could barely see in the shimmering heat. When the 'nocs were ready, he aimed them and was able to make out the shape of a man on the ledge, several hundred yards to the south. The fellow looked injured, up on one knee with his other leg at a queer angle. Although he couldn't see clearly, he knew it was Kincaid. Had to be. Who else but that half-crazed desert rat would be out here?

Besides, just about any regular fellow, finding himself in such a tight bind, would automatically call out for help. Didn't matter he was way the hell and gone from any populated area. A man would just naturally give a couple yells to see. But Matson hadn't heard anything and he didn't doubt for a second that the thought of crying out never crossed Kincaid's mind. He knew the old man was as independent a cuss as any he'd ever met.

When he saw the nest, that sealed it. Even though Gleuer eggs had been found safe for consumption, Kincaid was the only one he knew who ate them. Several ranchers had brought small flocks of chickens from earth and while eggs were not plentiful, they could be had. But that required face-to-face contact with the owner of the birds.

Well, Kincaid looked to be in trouble and time was short before nightfall or the returning Gleuers would make assistance pointless, so Matson scanned the area for the easiest route to the spot above the ledge. Then he urged Dancer down to the base of the canyon.

It took him twenty minutes to reach the summit above Kincaid. He carefully tied Dancer to a bit of scrub sprouting from a crevice, then strode over to the edge. Dropping down to his belly, he inched forward until he could see Kincaid, struggling to move about.

"Hey, Kincaid," Matson called. "Hang on a minute and I'll toss a rope down to you."

The injured man, startled by Matson's voice, reared back and fell over. Must have been painful, because Kincaid loosed a colorful outburst. Matson did his best not to chuckle as the old man ranted.

"Who in the bright red inner ring of hell is up here spoiling a fine summer day with their blasted caterwauling?" Kincaid demanded in his used-up rasp.

"It's me, you old fool, Jacob Matson. Got yourself in a bit of a spot, I see, but no matter, I'll help you get out."

"Like hell ya will," sneered Kincaid. "I've been in worse trouble at a Sunday School picnic and ain't never needed no meddlin' buttinski to save my back pay. Now get outta here before I climb up there and clap yer ears for ya."

Most folks would have been horrified or, at least, surprised by Kincaid's eruption, but Matson had expected it. He didn't generally put up with people barking at him, mostly because he preferred to do the barking himself. But he had a sneaking admiration for Kincaid's pioneer spirit that kept him in check. And regardless of insult, he'd never abandon someone in such a spot. So he said, "You couldn't climb up here if you had a whole day to do it, you cockeyed crackpot. Even I can see that leg's broke."

"Like hell it is. I just wrenched it some. It'll be fine in a day or so and when it is, I'll come by and give ya a swift kick for pokin' yer schnozzle into my affairs. Now move along and leave me to it."

"Leave you to what?!? You got some notion you'd like to end up as dinner for them Gleuers? I figure you got maybe ten, fifteen minutes till it's dark enough, they give up the hunt and come home to the kiddies. Good thing you didn't already have one of the brats in your shirt. Prob'ly woulda broke when you fell. That'd go over big with Ma and Pa."

"I ain't worried about any damn birds. They come back, I'll wring their necks and cook 'em for supper. Now, hit the trail, ya interfering jackalope."

"Kincaid, for glory's sake, get offa your high horse and talk sense. Your leg's broke and you ain't clearin' off that ledge on your own less'n you jump and save the Gleuers the trouble of slicin' you up."

"So what?" demanded the old man. "It's my own damn business. Just cos yer a big shot 'round here all of a sudden, don't mean us peons got to prostrate ourselves for your lordship. I got down here on my own and I'll get back up on my own."

"How?"

"Never mind how. Got more important things to do right now than give you lessons in self-reliance. Just get outta here so's I can hear myself think."

Matson was reaching the end of his meager supply of patience and while he muttered his response it came out louder than intended. "Yeah, I can see where you'd need it quiet to hear a voice that small."

"Oh, sure," yelled Kincaid. "Insult a man when he's in no position to defend hisself. 'Bout what I'd expect from the likes of you. Just the sort of feller can't wait to take advantage of a situation – force a man into a debt of obligation when options are limited and..."

"What in hell are you bleating about now?"

"I'm saying I'd rather die right here than be in any man's debt and that goes double for you!"

Matson was mad now. "Damn you, you dried up sack of misery! Do I have to remind you about the contract you signed when you joined our little party? It's my duty to extend a helping hand and you are duty-bound to accept it. You want your last act to be a willful breaking of your word?"

Silence.

"That's what I thought. I'm tossing a rope down to you and you best get it 'round you right quick."

Matson shoved himself back toward where Dancer was tied and started to get up but he waited for whatever line of bluster Kincaid would offer as a response. Surprisingly, Kincaid remained silent.

Had Matson hit home with him at last? Kincaid was the sort of old timer who'd put a lot of stock in keeping his word. Maybe he was trying to find a way to give in without losing face. But he sure was slow about it.

Finally, knowing he was running out of time to get home before the storm hit, he yelled in exasperation, "Damn it all, Kincaid, don't you know pride is supposed to come *before* a fall?"

Matson listened as the echoes of his words rattled around the canyon, finally fading away. Then he heard something he could scarcely believe, so he shifted forward to look over the canyon's rim to the ledge and it was

Kincaid alright, rolling on his belly, pounding the ground with his fists and laughing his damn fool head off.

"Fine," Matson muttered. "I'll get the rope."

SURVIVAL

C.J. Henderson

"**O**NCE ONE DETERMINES THAT HE OR SHE HAS A MISSION IN life, that it's not going to be accomplished without a great deal of pain, and that the rewards in the end may not outweigh the pain—if you recognize historically that always happens, then when it comes, you survive it."–Richard Nixon

Shelby Matson watched the research vehicle in the distance carefully. Or, more specifically, she watched the men and women working near it carefully. She, of course, had every right to do so. Not merely because the people doing the work were off-worlders and thus worthy of suspicion, but because they were doing their work on her property. They had arrived on the United Planets Vessel Argo and, so far, had been fairly tight-lipped about why they had traveled to her world.

Oh, they had what sounded like a cover story well in place, and in truth Matson appreciated the simplicity of it. Now that the planet had well established itself as part of the U.P. business community—supplying protein to the galactic markets board in sufficient weights on a tight schedule—it was due some of the benefits warranted by that association.

Those that had migrated to the world they would designate as Byanntia had done so simply to escape what they felt was the stifling yoke of U.P. restraint and regulation. They had known only that the world for which their slumberocket had been aimed contained a breathable atmosphere and water. For all they knew, they might have found a land so hostile they might have all perished within a few months. That they found one teeming with a natural resource which would make them all wildly comfortable had been what all involved felt was a well-deserved bonus for the sacrifices they had made and the risk they had taken.

The U.P. team claimed to be researching the viability of installing a weather control station. As a blanket excuse to do as they pleased while on-planet, it was a good one. Any homesteaded world that not only survived the thirty year colonization period, but found a way to be a benefit to the U.P. system as well—as had Byanntia through its massive protein exports—often came under the umbrella of the loose protectorate. When they did, one of the first things agrarian worlds were checked for was the need for climate regulation.

"And," thought Matson, sipping at the cactus tea with which she had filled her canteen, "if that's why you're really here I'll fold my legs behind my head and spin like a top."

Shelby Matson had been blessed with the outrageous fortune of having reached her sixties possessed of figure and features that allowed others to still describe her as a handsome woman. Her straight silver hair had lost none of its sheen, her warm brown eyes none of their intensity.

They had hardened some, certainly, and the tight lines that had set in after the death of first Chad, her oldest son, and then her husband, had in some ways marred the innocence of her beauty. On the other hand, those same lines had emboldened the intelligence to be found within her eyes' burnt mahogany, a factor many had missed in her younger days.

But there were none on Byanntia who, if they had doubted her abilities in the past, did so anymore. Years earlier, when her eldest had been taken by the nightmarish monster the indigenous tribesfolk called the Gr'nar, she had been forced to take on more responsibility. Mainly in the training of her two younger sons, Stewart and Joseph, helping her husband catch them up to where they would need to be—to take over the running of the family spread when the time came.

"Even hurrying, though," the woman thought sadly, "we didn't have enough time, did we, Jacob?"

Matson pursed her lips at the memory, a flash of images, their world invaded, her husband Jacob dying in the final moments of expelling those who would have stolen Byanntia from them. The two had not been close in a romantic sense any longer. Such adolescent notions had been set aside when they had left Earth with the others to make their own way out among the stars. For years they had been more partners in an enterprise than anything else, but it had been a rich and fulfilling partnership, and it had been good enough for them both.

"But now, someone's here nosing around again," she said to herself. "And I just have to wonder, what is it you bunch want? Are you here to try and steal the whole damn place out from under us, or just some sizeable chunk you think we might not miss? How many people are going to die this time?"

Shelby Matson had no legitimate reason to be suspicious of the group from U.P. Yes, it was true, off-worlders had caused more than a touch of trouble for the Earth-born residents of Byanntia and their off-spring. But, not every person from another planet to set foot on her adopted world had come to cause trouble.

As many as twenty times a year shuttles from major transport ships landed at the Byanntian spaceport. Transactions would be completed via electronic communications and then the ferry ships would deliver whatever goods were due. Mostly the Byanntians paid in protein futures, collected by the travelling salesmen on some United Planets world with a banking arm.

Sometimes other goods were bartered for instead. One team that had come out from Earth in the old days had gambled on finding minerals, gemstones or other elements still valuable in a galaxy of worlds. Amazingly, gold had proved to be even rarer off the old homeworld than it was on it. It had taken seventeen years, but the group had found gold, and far more.

Then there were the ships that stopped simply to stop. They were the range world's far more frequent visitors—military ships looking for fresh food and the possibility of R&R, traders, construction teams, scout ships—many found reasons to drop in-atmosphere. Byanntia had gained somewhat of a reputation across the known galaxy after its citizens managed to stop the Dortons, the name given to the para-military group that had attempted to steal the planet from its owners. After that story had circulated, the place took on a romantic charm—for those who had never been there.

Suddenly reconstruct images of the Byanntian deserts and mountains were everywhere. Word spread throughout the privileged communities that this was the world to head for to spend time in unspoiled wilderness, one with plenty of social amenities and all the expected standard comforts no more than a requestcall away. No, Byanntia was no longer isolated. People came to it for its seemingly unending rivers of protein, its hiking, its climbing, its rich oxygen atmosphere, its slightly lower gravity, its friendly recreation centers—all manner of reasons the original founders had never envisioned.

"But," thought Matson, staring across the harsh plain at the uniformed figures in the distance, "you're not here for any of that, are you?"

Sipping at her tea once more, she wiped her mouth on her sleeve, then corked her canteen and stood up out of the shade of the rock formation under which she had been resting. Slipping the container into its customary slot in one of her saddle bags, she slid one booted foot into a stirrup, then threw herself atop her stallion, thinking;

"Well, I'm sick to death of waiting to find out what you mealworms are up to. Maybe it's just time someone asked."

An experienced rider, the woman nudged her mount gently, sending it forward across the desert toward the research vehicle. Or, more specifically, toward the researchers. Shelby Matson had, in her mind, waited long enough for these intruders to reveal their true purpose. Oh, she was willing to believe that Byanntia might actually end up with a climate control station out of the affair. U.P. never lied to its client worlds outright.

However, the rancher knew—could feel in her bones—that something else was going on. Yes, the crews spotted around the planet were indeed releasing weather balloons, taking atmospheric readings, measuring moisture levels in the various strata and so forth. But, some of what they were doing did not add up to Matson, and she was determined to uncover the real reason for their visit. Reining her steed in as she approached one of the white-uniformed workers, she asked who was in charge.

"In charge of just this detail," asked the man, "or the whole bloody she-bang?"

"How about just this detail for starters?"

"Depending on how you weigh things, it's your lucky day," answered the man, wiping at his brow. "I'm in charge of this dig."

"And," asked Matson, watching the man's eyes in particular, "if I wanted to know about the whole 'bloody' she-bang?"

"Why, interesting coincidence ... that would be me, too." Matson stared unblinking, gauging the tone of the man's voice, the width of his smile—watching to see how long it would take for him to notice she had not been amused by his answer. In only a matter of seconds, the fellow added;

"Sorry, someone once told me I was funny and I've been trying to live up to it ever since." Wiping several layers of soil and sand from his hand onto his pant leg, he continued, saying;

"I'm Dave, ah ... David, David Renni. My mother would still like it if I were to make that 'Dr. David Renni,' but she's enough light years away from here that I'm going to risk being myself. And if I might ask, you are ...?"

Matson pursed her lips for a moment, staring at the doctor's out-stretched hand. Having found nothing in his manner or his gaze that set off any of her internal radars, she finally took his hand in hers, answering;

"I'm Shelby Matson. This is my land you're on right now. Considering our location, it's pretty much my land in every directions as far as you can see."

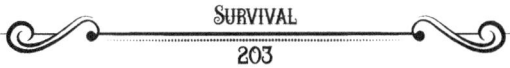

"It was your husband that killed the creature, the Gr'nar, you called it. Correct?"

"No, actually," answered Matson. "He didn't kill it. He stopped it, but he let it go."

Renni turned his head slightly from side to side, considering the woman's words. Nodding unconsciously, he told her;

"Yeah, that's right. Sorry. I've heard the story told several different ways since we arrived."

"What does it matter?"

"Pardon?"

Pulling herself back slightly, settling her carriage more erect within her saddle, Matson held her reins in both hands, her fingers resting on her saddle horn as she explained;

"What I'm asking you is, what does that damn monster, or what it did here, or what we did to it, matter to you? You are simply here to put in a weather station." And then, her voice dropped to a harsher, accusatory tone as she added;

"Aren't you?"

"Actually, no," answered Renni, his smile leveling off into a simple thin line. "I'm not. Most everyone else is here for that. But they sent me to make the final decision." When Matson merely stared, the doctor continued, saying;

"My degrees are in zoology and animal husbandry. I was sent to find out what happened to this Gr'nar of yours, and to determine what it is that makes you people think there's only one of them."

* * *

It was several hours later when dinner had finally been served and finished at the Matson ranch. While the servants cleared the main dining table, Shelby Matson and her sons retired to the comfort of their living room along with their guests. When the dual invitation had been made to the U.P. representative to come to dinner, so he might also explain himself, Renni had suggested the inclusion of the scientist heading the weather research.

Dr. Catherine Welsh proved to be much younger than Renni, but old enough to have been given the amount of authority she held. Her pleasant manner and unbridled enthusiasm over each and every dish served had endeared her to Matson's staff, if not the rancher herself. Her wavy, ebony hair, strong cheekbones, devilish green eyes and well-maintained figure endeared her to the male Matsons. As they took their seats, Stewart offered the guests their choice of after dinner drinks.

"Byanntia produces its own spirits," asked Welsh.

"I can't imagine a planet that has both men and vegetation that will ferment that doesn't have at least beer," answered the elder Matson male. "We've got three families here that turn out beer, one that specializes in ale. No wine … no one's been able to get a decent enough grape crop. Good raisins, though."

"For the adventurous," offered young Joe Matson, "the Gutheries do bottle a passable whiskey-like fluid. It is generally held in reserve for extreme moments, but it is available."

After a moment of polite chuckles, both guests settled on trying two different Byanntian beers, offering to swap tastes with each other for comparison's sake. Once they had been served and taken their first sips, Shelby said;

"I used to be a very pleasant rancher's wife. Even though Joe here runs the day-to-day of Twin Feathers now, I still need to think like Jacob on occasion. I admit I've had to adopt some of his ways, and abruptness is one I've found particularly useful. That thought in mind, why don't we get down to you telling me just what's going on here?"

"Fair enough," answered Renni. "Why is it you folks think there's only one Gr'nar on the planet? Because the kuzzi told you so. Said he was 'the evil god of the Junsuka,' correct?" When the others merely nodded, the doctor continued.

"Okay, fine. But suppose that hungry worm wasn't really a god? Considering the fact your late husband sent it packing, I think that argues against deification for the Gr'nar. And, if it isn't a god, then it must be something mortal. And mortal things don't just spring into being. They need parents."

The Matsons simply stared, all their minds buzzing. When the kuzzi had finally explained the Gr'nar, told of how it returned to devour all in its path every sixty-four years, the transplanted Earthers to Byanntia had taken their word. Those native to the planet, it was assumed, would certainly know more about its history than newcomers to the world.

"I'm not sayin' you don't make sense," answered Stewart quietly. "But I can tell you this, the kuzzi weren't lyin'. They believe what they told us. And they should know."

"Yes," agreed Renni. "They should. We've talked to them as well. And oh yes, they absolutely believe there is only one Gr'nar, and that it appears every sixty-four Byanntian years. But if one just stops and thinks about it, that really doesn't make much sense."

"Calling us stupid," asked Joe in a tone half-way to belligerent.

"Distracted," interrupted Welsh, joining the conversation. "You were people settling a new world. You came here having been told there were no indigenous intelligent populations. You found one and you couldn't turn back. That meant you had the kuzzi to deal with, along with a thousand other problems. The natives told you there was only one Gr'nar. With flash floods and prairie fires and all the other inconveniences of life to deal with, once Jacob Matson dealt with the 'god of the Junsaka' most likely you were too busy simply trying to keep things going than to worry about than biologically back-charting some monster."

"But you folks aren't too busy to do so, right?"

"Tell me, Mr. Matson," answered Welsh, her tone sweet but edged, "is your plan to grow increasingly hostile toward us all night? We are here to help I hope you realize."

"No you're not," answered Shelby. "You're here for some reason all your own. Yes, we may get climate control out of the deal, but only because that's the cover for whatever you're really up to." When both the Matson's guests found themselves fumbling for an answer, Stewart said;

"Imagine that, Mom, government agents with a hidden agenda. Tell me again why you and Dad left Earth to come here?"

"All right," said Joe, waving his hand through the air in a cutting motion. "Let's not get down to where we're throwing things at each other. We might have our own foundry now, but plates are still expensive." Having cut through some of the tension with his slight bit of humor, the rancher added;

"Dr. Renni, my cynical side, inherited from my father and only slightly enhanced by my mother, here, tells me that you wouldn't have said as much as you have so far if you were up to something that was going to hurt us. That being the case, why don't you go ahead and tell us whatever else you're willing to tell us?"

"Thank you," answered the doctor, his attack of nervousness beginning to subside. "First, let me say that the idea of a weather control station is not a fabrication. The Rim Equity Board decided Byanntia should receive what they call Encouragement status. They set up the station, it 'encourages' planetary growth, helps keep the protein flowing ..."

"Allows them to ring the planet with satellites which they can use for all manner of U.P. business unrelated to Byanntia whatsoever—" When all turned to stare at Welsh, she demurely took another sip of her beer, then added;

"Well, are we being honest or aren't we?"

"Don't worry, Dr. Renni," said Joe, aiming a smile at Welsh as he spoke, "if we didn't already suspected that much we wouldn't be the kind of people that leave a world like Earth behind in the first place."

"You were born here, weren't you," asked Welsh, her face betraying honest puzzlement.

"Yeah, but homeworld pride runs deep around here. Anyway, why don't you folks go on and tell us—what's all this got to do with the Gr'nar?"

"I'm part of a team that follows leads like this wherever we hear about them in the galaxy," explained Renni. "If the Gr'nar really is a single entity, one capable of hibernating for decades on end, studying the biology of this thing could unlock secrets about longevity and other health issues

unimagined. Control of disease, of aging ... and the claims to its ability to travel underground at high speeds, invisibility—"

"Yeah, unique damn critters," mused Stewart.

"More than unique," answered the doctor, missing the edging tone in the younger Matson's voice, "far more. Think about it ... something that can travel underground—how would nature get around to developing invisibility as a trait for something that already can't be seen?"

"Hummmmmph, gotta admit I never thought about it that way," offered Joe, allowing an honest trace of wonderment to color his voice. Stewart nodded to his brother, saying;

"Yeah, huh—and, all that said, if it is a normal kinda beast, something that could be bred, or whose traits could be reproduced ... probably some tiny interest on the part of the military in there somewhere as well. Eh, doc?"

"Why, what an interesting idea," responded Renni, his sarcastic tone an admission that the youngest Matson might have a point. "I'll have to—"

The doctor paused as a tone emanating from his breast pocket alerted him to an incoming message. Excusing himself, Renni cued his earpiece, opening communications with the U.P. base camp. Although he was mostly only listening, the increasing excitement showing in his face drew the interest of his companion as well as the Matsons. Finally, after breaking his connection, he announced;

"Everybody, I have interesting news ..." The doctor allowed a moment to pass to build a bit of suspense, then said, "it seems our team has secured a Gr'nar."

Around the room, the members of the Matson clan allowed varying degrees of shock and concern to show in their faces. Although Jacob Matson had indeed defeated what had been thought to be the one-and-only Gr'nar, still no one had thought to be presented with another for decades. As the reality sank into their minds that there might be as many of the terrible monsters as there were any other life-forms on the planet, Renni offered;

"So, who's up for going to see it?"

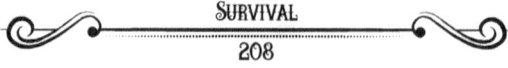

* * *

"Why are all the lights off," mused Renni as he brought one of the U.P. team flyers in for a landing. After several attempts to reach others in the ground party which only twenty minutes earlier had communicated with him over their find were met with silence, he said, mostly to himself;

"Now what are these idiots up to now?"

Stepping out of the flyer from the pilot's exit door, Renni abandoned electronics and simply called out several names, none of which elicited any kind of response. Shrugging his shoulders, the doctor then rounded the airship, opening the main exit door, allowing the others to disembark.

"Cat," said Renni, "you've got the mobile, get us some light, will you?"

As the other doctor tabbed several of the light towers into service, the scene that greeted the returning scientists and their guests was one that boiled fear and sent it screaming throughout the minds of the Byanntians. When Renni and Welsh had left several hours earlier, all had been as it had been since their arrival. Even when they had received their call earlier from the base camp, there had been nothing in the voices of those who had spoken over the open link to suggest anything was amiss.

"This is not good."

It was more than obvious to all that something had changed.

"That your idea of humor?"

Joe spat his words at Renni while simultaneously moving his mother back to the research team's flyer. When she protested, wanting to investigate, her eldest shoved her backward without concern, snapping;

"Investigate? Investigate what, mom? What in all the goddamned hells do you think there is here to investigate?" Shelby made to speak, but Joe would hear none of it. Shoving his mother roughly, he then lifted her bodily and tossed her inside the vehicle, shouting as he did so;

"Good God in Heaven. What more do you need to see? You got no memory all of a sudden? What can't you figure out from what you can see from right there?"

Shelby shook her head back and forth, her eyes closed. There was no denying what the evidence all around showed clearly. The Gr'nar had

returned. A circular disturbance in the ground, surrounded by a scarlet ring, showed clearly near one of the tables set up in the open air. The Matsons knew what that meant. Someone had been standing there, working at the table, perhaps tapping their foot. The Gr'nar, attracted to the sound they were making, their body heat—something—had come up from beneath them, burrowing quietly, quickly, and taken them. It had been fast, it had been final, and it had been bloody.

While Joe secured his mother in one of the flyer's comfortable passenger seats, Stewart caught hold of Renni's shoulder, asking him;

"It's awfully quiet here. How many people were here when you left? Did they have any other vehicles?"

"They did," came Welsh's voice from out of the darkness. "But they didn't get to them."

"What do you mean?"

Welsh played her handlight over the area before her. In the distance the wide beam reflected off several larger shuttle vehicles in the distance. The aircraft were sealed. While nearly everyone stared at the silent vehicles, Renni was working furiously at one of the monitor stations. Running his hands over the configuration pad, barking commands, he cursed the machine, screaming;

"No, goddamnit. No—it can't be. It can't. It doesn't make any sense."

"What doesn't make any sense," demanded Joe. Not turning from the series of screens he was studying, the doctor shouted back;

"I'm checking the vital monitors, they keep tabs on everyone in the team, heart rate, dehydration cycles, respiration, so on ... it's not ... it can't ..."

"What is it, Dave," screamed Welsh, her nerves beginning to strain, her eyes wide—wild looking. "What are you saying?"

"He's saying he can't find any of your friends," answered Joe from the flyer's main hatch. "He's saying none of them are breathing, or pumping blood—because they're all dead, like we're going to be if we don't get our asses out of here!"

Stewart reached Welsh, taking her gently by the shoulders. Tugging at her, moving her backward, she fell in step with him unconsciously,

her eyes straining to see out into the darkness. As she walked backward, guided by the youngest Matson, she screamed the names of others in their party. Nothing responded except the sound of the ever-constant prairie winds. As she continued to shout, Joe asked;

"Renni, that's a lot of names she's shouting. Just how many others were there in your party?"

"That's what doesn't make sense ... the readings ... if they were anywhere on the planet, the scanners would be able to link ... send back ... but, there's nothing—*nothing!*"

"How *many?*"

"But ..." the doctor turned, stared at the Matsons. His eyes watched Welsh being drawn backward toward the flyer, the information not actually processing within his brain. Even as Joe kept questioning him, Renni could only blather;

"It can't be ... the Gr'nar ... its capacity ... there were too many ..."

Finally, as Stewart reached the flyer, Joe jumped out, charging his brother with keeping their mother and Welsh inside as he went after Renni. The older Matson was able to walk straight up to the doctor without the shaken, blubbering man actually noticing his approach. Grabbing Renni with both hands, Joe stuck his face nose-to-nose with the doctor's, then shouted;

"How goddamned many people were here? How many of your people are missing?" Renni blinked once, then once more, finally whispering;

"Eighty-seven...there were eighty-nine of us...now, now...oh...ohhhh..."

As the enormity of what he was saying finally began to crystalize within the doctor's mind, Joe lead him back to the flyer. The rancher studied the ground as they walked, not knowing what he was watching for, but watching nonetheless. Leaving Renni to Stewart, Joe then slammed the main door shut and ran around to the other side. Each step he took rang within his head, a voice within his brain reminding him that he was sending out a dinner invitation with every jarring step.

Sliding into the pilot's seat, he slid the door shut and bolted it in one motion. Then, safely inside, Joe closed his eyes and allowed himself to

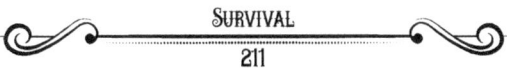

shudder. He had kept his wits about himself while they pieced together what had happened. He had made certain his mother was safe, had gotten everyone else on board, then gotten in himself. He had done everything just as his father would have.

"But," he thought, part of his mind forcing him toward shame, "dad wouldn't be shaking like a little girl now, though, would he?"

Making a fist, digging his nails into his palm to give his mind something else to complain about, he swallowed hard, then said;

"Eighty-seven people missing ... I guess this proves out that theory of yours, don't it, doc?"

"Wha—what do you mean, Mr. Matson?"

"Just what you said, guess there does have to be more than one of those damn things."

Joe went silent, working on getting the unfamiliar craft into the air. Stewart sat next to his mother who had her arms around Welsh, the two women holding onto each other. Stewart himself simply looked out the nearest window, watching the ground—eyes straining to catch the slightest disturbance. And David Renni, strapped in to a seat against the wall of the craft, held onto himself, held onto his belts, and fought desperately against the terror racing through his system, laughing at him for ever coming to a hell-hole like Byanntia.

***

Only three hours after their return to Twin Feathers, Joe and his mother, along with the two surviving U.P. scientists, were in New Dodge, trying to chair a meeting of all the Byanntian households. Stewart had been left behind to rouse the ranch's work force and to begin initiating those emergency procedures that had been established by his father years earlier for the time if, or when, the Gr'nar returned.

"Shelby," shouted Dennis Gutherie, "what the hell is all this about? I thought that damn digger weren't due back for decades. What is this shit?"

Although the word had been sent to every sentient group on the planet, representatives from all the original Earth families had not yet

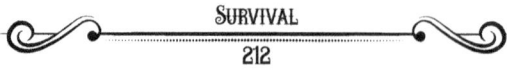

arrived. And, it had been noticed by all that no members of any of the kuzzi clans had shown up yet, either.

"It's her damn husband's fault," yelled out a voice from the back of the assembly. "Let the damn thing go—ain't that a ball'a shit. High and mighty Jacob Matson. Now we're all gonna die because—"

"You shut your flapper right now, Dwil Samper, or I will put a hurt on you ain't never going to be lifted." Joe had growled the words with menace, but had not raised his voice. Not giving Samper a chance to respond, he addressed the crowded town hall, saying;

"Listen up, everyone, we can call names and defame the dead later. I'll join in some, myself—*later*. Right now, however, we ain't got the time for it. Right now, we got trouble. You all know the U.P. landed a group here to maybe outfit us for weather control. We're getting that, so that's one good thing. But, their people were also here to study up on the Gr'nar."

A low murmur circled the room at the additional news. Happy to be able to distract some of the loose anger being generated away from the Matson name, Joe added;

"Now lissen up ... the U.P. sent close on ninety people here for this job. This morning they were all still alive. Right now, these two folks sitting here with me, Dr. David Renni and Dr. Catherine Welsh, they're all that's left." After giving the implication of what he had just said a moment to sink in, Joe added;

"I think it best we let Dr. Renni tell us whatever he can, especially concerning what he and his people have really been doing out in the desert, concerning the Gr'nar and all, then maybe we can start making some decisions before anyone else gets hurt." Standing, shaking slightly, the doctor said;

"I don't want to alarm anyone, but things ... ah, um ... they do seem to look bad." Several of the ranchers started to yell out accusations, others shouting back, more hurling additional anger at those already bellowing. Grabbing the chair next to him, Joe began banging it against the floor, hoping to restore order. Nothing helped until suddenly Renni simply stood up and screamed at the top of his lungs;

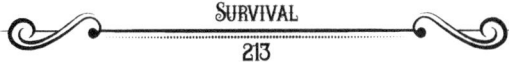

"PLEEEAASSSSEEEEEEEE—"

Everyone heard the plaintive screech, was shocked back to silence by it. Coughing from the strain to his voice, the doctor apologized for his shrill interruption, desperate to get his emotions back under control as he said;

"I know you are confused and frightened. Trust me, everybody, so am I. We all should be—and for good reason. First, let me tell you some things right up front. Mr. Matson was correct. Byanntia is getting a climate control station. That was always a given. To be honest, the satellites are already in place." As a curious murmur sounded throughout the room, Renni threw up his hands, admitting;

"Yes, yes, the whole notion of there being doubt about whether or not you would get the system was useful to the U.P. It worked as a perfect cover story so that my team could come here and do some research into what was and wasn't true about your Gr'nar."

Some in the crowd rumbled further at the admission, but none began another shouting match. Swallowing hard to keep his nerves steady, Renni started again.

"I mean, you have to understand, the idea that one creature could hibernate for decades, come out, slaughter entire populations, and then disappear ... it seemed a bit more myth than truth. Even considering some of the other things we've seen in the galaxy, it didn't really add up, biologically ... anyway, we were sent to find out what was fiction and what was not. Using core radars and seismographic sensors, we were able to formulate a lot of theories, but we needed to find a Gr'nar to be certain. Living, dead, partial remains, it didn't matter ... we just needed something to analyze."

"And you assholes did just that, didn't you," called out Ben Thornton, the head of the Thornton clan. "Woke the son'va bitch up, brought the damn worm back down on us—*again*—didn't you?"

Once more Joe thumped his chair, the noise heading off another shouting match. Giving Renni a signal to begin again, the doctor nodded, then indicated Welsh with one hand as he said;

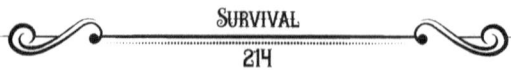

"While we've been talking, Dr. Welsh here has been trying to use our mobile hand monitor to patch into the camera system set up at our site. All we know at the moment is that everyone else who came here with us has disappeared. That's eighty-seven people whose life signs have stopped. It's almost certain that they're dead. How all this could—"

Before Renni could finish his thought, his colleague indicated that she had managed to get the two systems communicating with one another. The original technology the Byanntians had brought with them from Earth was now severely antiquated compared to what United Planet personal had at their disposal, but it was not impossible for an experienced technician to get artificial intelligences even further apart into harmony with one another. The doctor gave a hand signal for the lights to be lowered, then turned the floor over to Welsh, who said;

"All right, none of us yet knows what happened at our site. I do believe we would all like to." Pointing upward to the left, she added, "So, watch that monitor there, and I think we …"

As she pressed the last button necessary to start the playback from the main camera array she had reached, Welsh went as quiet as everyone else in the room. The doctor had programmed the playback to begin with any instance of a registered perimeter breech. Her efforts were astonishingly successful.

All eyes remained glued to the screen as the scene played out before them. It started simply enough—a slight vibrating of the ground. An audience not familiar with the Gr'nar might have missed the slight movement. None there in the New Dodge town hall did so, however. Not did they miss what happened after that, either.

Although the monitor image playing was a single angle shot, it was sufficient. The first thing it showed was the ground splitting open beneath a man working at one of the open air tables. Before he could even notice what was happening, the lower half of his body simply disappeared. His torso fell to the side, arms flailing, mouth working silently, and then, suddenly it disappeared as well.

All knew what they were seeing.

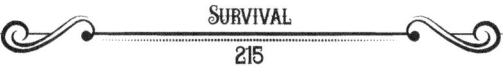

It was the Gr'nar. The thing that traveled underground. The invisible horror that could swallow a man in one or two bites. The hell-thing they had not expected to see again for half a century. As they watched, they saw others pulled down, torn to pieces, splattered across the landscape. By the time the carnage had ended, the single camera angle had allowed those gathered to watch fourteen people slaughtered. The room was deathly quiet when Welsh, her shaken voice near to breaking, asked;

"I can call up other of the cameras if ... I mean, if anyone cares ... if they ... need to–" Joe cut the woman off gently, saying;

"I think everyone here has the idea." As the lights were brought back up, a voice called out from the back;

"I do not believe anyone on this world needs reminding as to what it is that now stalks us once more."

The words came from a newcomer to the assembly, one who must have arrived after the lights had been lowered. Low, filled with a guttural, growling tone, all present knew it was a kuzzi that had spoken. Only one of the humans could identify him from his voice.

"Bentelii," called out Joe. "I was wondering if any of your people were going to show up." "Most," answered the towering feline form, "when invited to end of world, tend to respond. Now that your wretched kind has brought our god down upon yourselves once more, how could we not come to watch–and laugh?"

And then, the kuzzi warrior threw his head back, opening his mouth wide, exposing his yellowed fangs, and began to howl with mirth, as did his fellows.

***

"Quite an entrance you made last night."

"Oh, did you enjoy my performance? I do so try to please."

Joe stared at the large kuzzi seated across the table in the Matson family kitchen at the Twin Feathers ranch. Bentelii had leaned his long spear in the corner behind him. Many would not even have noticed it. The kuzzi did not like to draw attention to their weapons. They also did not like to be far from them.

Like all of his people, Bentelii's body was covered with a short coat of horizontally striped fur. The blue, black and grey markings were a natural camouflage that blended well with the alien landscape. His head was surrounded by a thick and glossy black mane. A single black stripe parted his forehead and muzzle, but stopped short of his hard, blue lips.

Most kuzzi males had very broad shoulders as well as chests that rippled with layers of muscles, and Bentelii was no exception. Eight foot, three, short-waisted, with powerful, backward jointed legs, he was a typical specimen of his people in every way save that he felt completely relaxed in human company. Of the three kuzzi who had gone into New Dodge the night before and then accepted the Matsons' invitation to return to Twin Feathers afterward, he was the only one to sleep inside the main house.

The meeting the evening before had gone late into the night. When the ranchers had insisted Bentelii and his fellows return home with them as their guests, they had accepted without hesitation. One reason was that no one anywhere on Byanntia was going to be comfortable with sleeping on the ground again until the current crisis was resolved—even eschewing the Matson home, the other kuzzi had still slept on a thick, concrete platform adjacent to the main barn.

Another reason for their acceptance was the simple fact that as any kind of hotel accommodations in New Dodge were limited at best, none of them were built for kuzzi occupancy. This was not through any type of racism. The native race of Byanntia were nomads. They did not care much for the indoors, nor did they maintain any permanent structures of their own. Outside of some simple forms of jewelry, they wore nothing on their bodies. They traveled to stay near the herds they hunted, and to keep ahead of the seasons.

"Want some coffee?"

"Every time I open my eyes."

Joe grinned. Bentelii and the eldest Matson male had been the first members of their races to become true friends. Many before them had communicated in a pleasant enough fashion, had worked together, traded, hosted each others families for meals and holiday events. Had, in other words, been good neighbors—made an effort to get along. With Joe and Bentelii, it had been different.

"You know," the rancher told his friend, passing him the handleless mug the kuzzi always used when he visited Twin Feathers, "you and your pals are lucky we were able to find a couple regions on this dirtball that would grow coffee."

They had become friends in an instant. Neither could say why. There had been no significant bonding moment—no special moment, no event shared, no secret bond. They had simply walked into each other's presence and that had been that. They had sensed immediately that there was something in the other worth knowing. "Ahhhhhh, yes," answered the kuzzi after downing a large, hot gulp. "And, are we equally lucky your fellows came here to bring Gr'nar down upon us?"

"Cutting right to the action, are we?"

"Considering what has happened, Joe, do you not think such is best?"

"Probably so. Your people have a plan?"

"The kuzzi clans are of several minds. Many plan to simply follow old ways. They already traveling to stone valleys, granite caves—"

"All the areas the Gr'nar can't travel," said Joe. Tipping his own coffee mug in his friend's direction, he added, "Of course, I guess I should make that 'a gr'nar,' not 'the' gr'nar, anymore." Setting his over-sized mug down, Bentelii asked;

"Do we know how many of them there are? My people are used to idea of only one gr'nar. But now ..."

"You saw and heard pretty much everything I did on that subject last night."

"And," the kuzzi said in a lower voice, staring at his friend, "do you trust what you saw and heard last night?"

"Why wouldn't I," asked Joe, honestly confused by the question.

"I watched your eyes, how they could barely stay focused on the screen. I think maybe new female pleases you."

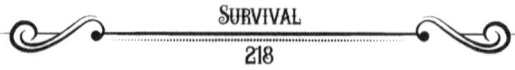

"Well, piss in the milk and call it good shootin'. What the hell does ..." Joe flustered slightly, then changed his tact, admitting;

"Yes, I am attracted to Dr. Welsh. She's good-looking, likes our beer and can talk about more than kison. What exactly has that got to do with anything?"

"Nothing, really," admitted the kuzzi. "Still trying to understand how you humans mate." When Joe simply glowered at his friend, Bentelii said;

"Very well, back to business. As I said, majority of kuzzi are headed for traditionally safe ground. The rest are of two minds. There are surprising number who want to fight, are waiting to see what you humans have in mind."

"And the others?"

"They think we should rise up against you interlopers and murder you all in your sleep. Appease gods, put things back to way they were."

Joe scratched behind his ear, his head tilted sideways. Finally snorting out a derisive blast of air, he said;

"I wish I felt surprise at that."

"Why should you," asked Bentelii, his fanged mouth shaping his race's equivalent of a grin. "I don't. So, what is big plan? How will mighty human race save poor helpless kuzzi from terrible monsters?"

"You are honestly such a pain in the ass," answered Joe, suppressing a smile. "And you know, I'd kick yours for you ... if you weren't as big as a house and made out of muscle."

"I'd probably deserve it."

And, with Bentelii's answer, both laughed loud enough to make certain no one else within the main house could possibly still be asleep. Getting himself under control, the kuzzi said;

"All right. Business. *Do* you people have any kind of plan?"

"Against four or five gr'nar?" Joe pulled at his chin. "Not really. We have the beginnings of a plan, something we were putting together when we thought there would only be one to deal with, like fifty-some years from now."

"Yeah?" Both of the friends' heads turned at the sound of a new voice. Walking into the kitchen, dressed in a gown Shelby Matson had loaned her, Catherine Welsh stifled a yawn as she added;

"I'd like to hear about that."

"Yes," added Bentelii, staring at the female, wondering about his friend's chances with her. "So would I."

***

The group preparing to hunt the gr'nar looked out across the open plane with more than a little trepidation. Yes, they had weapons as well as defenses. The Dortons, the raiders that had tried to steal their planet from them had left behind three heavily armed and armored assault vehicles. At the time of their deaths they had forfeited their body armor and personal weapons to their supposed victims as well.

Aside from these bits and pieces which had been kept in storage as communal property, to be used in times of defense, many private citizens had begun arming themselves during the years since that time. Ships of all sorts stopped on Byanntia, as well, and since the invasion several thousand firearms had been purchased by the homesteaders as well as by the kuzzi.

Originally the plan had called for volunteers to draw straws, the 'winners' getting the task of riding out across an open area on horseback to attract the attention of the Gr'nar. Once it was located, the surrounding forces would annihilate it once and for all, hopefully before it could devour any of the volunteers. With the possibility of a half-dozen gr'nars, however, the plan suddenly had become a far riskier proposition.

That was when Renni had offered a suggestion. Accessing the U.P. equipment remotely from Twin Feathers, the doctor was able to utilize the core radars and seismographic sensors they had brought to determine the location of the gr'nar horde. As he explained it;

"From what we saw on the feed from the base camp cameras, there are at least four of these things, possibly as many as six. Why there are more than ever before, why they've come back earlier than history says

they should, I have no idea. But, now that we have the equipment up and running, I should be able to guide you."

"And what exactly does that mean," asked one of the volunteers who had drawn a short straw.

"Everyone involved in the ambush has one of these ear-pieces," answered the doctor, pointing toward the small clip attached to his right ear. "All your receivers are numbered. They'll appear on my screen as moving numerals. So, if I see something coming toward, say, #3 from their left-hand side, I'll radio '#3—on your left.' Now, everyone will hear that, so everyone will know that something is coming from #3's left."

"Course," growled another of the volunteers, "you'll be sittin' safe and secure in a goddamned bunker while us assholes'll be puttin' our asses on the line."

"Personally," said Joe drily, "speaking as just another one of the assholes, I think I'd prefer the doc here be safe so he's only worrying about our safety and not his own."

"I will be," responded Renni. Then, fixing the man who had spoken out with a shaky, but determined glare, the doctor added, "and, just so we're clear with each other, I don't have to be down here, you know. I could've called in a ship to take me out of here. I ..."

"Save it, doc," snapped Joe, cutting off a conversation he could only see ending badly. Turning to the ambush crew, he said;

"Let's not waste anymore time. We don't know what the hell's gone wrong around here, but unless we plan on packin' it in, this is something we got to get done, and get done right. It seems we can't turn around on this goddamned planet without something new comin' along to tear us a new one. Well, okay—fine. Let it. Let it fuckin' try. We've taken all the shit this arm pit end of the galaxy can throw at us, and we'll take this, too. Am I right?" As a cheer went up throughout the assembly, Joe added;

"You're goddamned right I'm right. Now let's go stomp these things into paste and get back to enjoyin' the good life."

Cheers and gunshots loosed into the air had been the crowds response. Almost immediately thereafter the assault team moved forward.

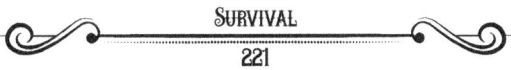

The site of the U.P. camp had been chosen as the first place to try and set an ambush for several reasons. First, the doctor's sensors had picked up subterranean activity near the camp. Second, that spot had been chosen in the first place as the U.P. main camp site because it was the place where Jacob Matson had defeated the Gr'nar years earlier. The idea made sense to the hardbitten Byanntians. Any good hunter knew a carnivore did not leave a hunting area until the game was played out. After the horrific toll the creatures had taken in that spot two nights earlier, it was simple logic to expect them to have not yet moved on.

The three assault vehicles had rumbled slowly into position first, situating themselves in a triangle the sides of which were roughly a mile each in length. After that, the various human and kuzzi gunmen who had volunteered to complete the three-sided box had taken up spots on boulders, or in whatever land vehicle they had available to them. Finally, with their guns in place, it was up to the quintet of volunteers to ride into the center of the trap and begin to act like the bait they were.

"Okay, you sums'bitches," snapped Mel Mosheberg, slapping his mount's hindquarters, "time to die!"

Following the foundry owner's lead, the others did the same, racing forward across the plane. Fear traveled through each man, tearing at their spines, freezing their blood. They thought of their lives cut short, bodies crushed, snapped in two. They thought of their loved ones, children without fathers, widows created, left lonely, looking for other men.

They thought on who would take their places, who would wear their clothing, spend their money, drink their whiskey. The ideas snaked within them, through their systems, poisoning their minds but driving away their fear, filling them with a rage powerful enough to keep them moving forward. And forward they rode, moment after moment, some not daring to watch anything but the ground beneath them, others unable to look downward at all.

"Doc," called out Joe into his throat mike, "anything?"

"Not yet," responded Renni. "They could be asleep, you know. They did eat a hell of a lot of people."

"It's been two days, though," cut in another one of the riders. "Shouldn't they be hungry now?"

"Shit, Lucas," called another, "damn things can sleep sixty years atta time. Who knows what makes these bastards tick?"

"Man has a point," added Mosheberg.

"Yeah, we're all geniuses here," responded Joe. Swallowing hard against the dust he and the others were raising, he added, "look, we're here, let's just do this. Fan out, guys. Let's start makin' some circles. See if we can wake these shitbags up."

"Breakfast time," screamed Mosheberg. "Kosher and otherwise. Come and get it!"

The five riders broke away from each other, all heading in different directions, following the loose plan they had agreed to earlier. If they reached the center of the triangle without incident, they would then move away from each other, slowing their pace while beginning to lead their mounts in circles. Nobody was to stop moving, but they had decided that if they did not elicit a response by the time they reached the center of the trap then they would continually slow their pace until at least one of them was unlucky enough to attract the gr'nars' attention.

All around them, the shooters waited tensely, watching—their own anxieties growing. Would the plan work? Even if it did, they would be trying to shoot invisible targets. Things that moved underground, came up only to latch onto something on the surface, and then pull it down to death. How exactly were they supposed to stop something like that?

Sweat trickled down across foreheads, leaking out from under hat brims, staining collars. Sand gnats buzzed, landing in the salty puddles, annoying—irritating. Distracting. Still, the shooters watched. And waited.

Why, they wondered—shooters and riders alike—were the gr'nar not responding? Not even one of them. It was not as if they had moved on yet. Renni's instruments was still showing seismic activity in the area. The five Byanntians who had drawn the short straws, who had bravely ridden out to face their dooms, were certainly doing everything they could to bring the monsters to the surface. Racing back and forth across the plane,

making their horses rear and stomp, several of them even unlimbering their bolt throwers and sending slugs into the ground.

For a long while, nothing happened. Then, just as Joe looked up, catching sight of what he thought was something hovering between the ground and the sun, the world tore itself apart in the one way no one could have possibly predicted.

* * *

"Now what do we do?"

The gr'nar had not acted as anyone thought they would. Years earlier, the first of the monsters to attack the surface after the arrival of the *Triumph* and the establishment of Byanntia's human colony had followed a specific pattern, one later confirmed by the kuzzi as what they had come to expect from the creature over the centuries.

"How could I have known? How could *anyone* have known?"

Even when more than one had attacked the U.P. encampment two days earlier, they had still done so in the manner the creatures had done so since the beginning of recorded history on the solitary world. They had broken the surface underneath or extremely near some living organism and then dragged it below the surface.

"Mr. Bentelii, forgive me if I'm repeating myself, but can I assume there is absolutely nothing in the records of your people, your oral tradition, anything that ..."

But this time, in the single instance anyone of the surface of Byanntia had ever wished to attract the attention of the hideous killing machines, the monsters had not acted as in the past. They had not only done the unexpected, but the unexplainable.

The unbelievable.

"Doc," answered the kuzzi, keeping his normal booming growl to a whisper, "no 'mister.' Just Bentelii. And you can repeat yourself all you care to. As for your question, I wish I had something to tell you, but ..." the large alien shrugged, holding his palm outward empty before him, his eyes as filled with honest confusion as anyone else present.

"Then that's it," sighed Mosheberg. "It's over. We're screwed."

"Unless this kuzzi bastard is lyin' to us."

Where one might have expected Bentelii to react to Ben Thornton's outburst, it was Joe Matson who rose from his seat. Crossing the short distance between himself and the speaker, he growled;

"Yeah, that's the answer, he's lyin' to us. He risked his life with us, was there at the triangle ready to die like any of us, just barely got away— *like* the rest of us—but what's that prove?" Standing over Thornton with balled fists, Joe raged;

"We all *know* how damn sneaky the kuzzi are. That's just the kind of low-dog trick one of them would pull. Put their own life on the line just so they could get an up-close view of some of us dyin'." Grabbing the man's shirt front, Joe jerked the fellow to his feet, screaming in his face;

"Of course, it meant sacrificing most of his own people, knowin' that all around this shitball of a world they were dyin' by the goddamned hundreds of *thousands*, but hell, it would be worth it—*right?*"

Joe was shaking Thornton severely when a pair of hands grabbed him from behind. The eldest Matson try to spin around, to attack whomever it was that was seeking to restrain him, grateful for something to strike out against, but he was held too firmly. As he struggled, swinging wildly, he heard his friend's voice say;

"I appreciate your support, my brother, but if we have any time left, this fool isn't worth any of it."

Joe forced himself to calm down after hearing Bentelii's words. He did not apologize to the man he had grabbed, nor did the other apologize to the kuzzi. Not that anyone was expecting them to do so. The men were a small splinter of survivors, all of them desperate, grasping at even the most insane of ideas to explain that through which they had just lived.

The gr'nar had finally attacked as the humans had hoped, but not in the fashion expected. Ironically, those who had ridden out expecting almost certain death were the only group spared on the face of the planet. The four to six beasts Renni had expected had torn through those situated along the edges of the killing zone, but they had not been the only ones to attack. All around Byanntia, wherever mammals of any kind

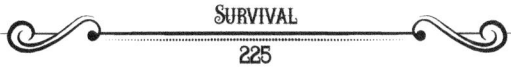

walked, the monsters had struck by the thousands. Possibly the hundreds of thousands.

And worse, they struck with a power unimagined.

Throughout the millennia, the kuzzi had been able to avoid the Gr'nar by hiding in caverns, or deep stone valleys, during the god-thing's feeding months. But not this time. This time, the horrors had burrowed upward through solid granite. They had found their way into the kuzzi's safe holes and they had destroyed them. The large blue-furred Byanntian natives, bottled up in caverns and deep canyons had, as Joe had screamed, been slaughtered by the hundreds of thousands—males and female, children and infants. And, the kuzzi had not been the only to die.

The gr'nar had attacked the humans as well. They had torn through settlements, ranches and factories. New Dodge had been reduced to burning rubble. Most every spot mankind had reached and claimed across the face of the planet had been struck by the creatures and left in ruin.

"It doesn't make any sense," moaned Renni quietly. The scientist had been next to useless since the handful of survivors had reached the spot where they had finally stopped running. It was in no way a place of safety. After finding out what had happened across the face of Byanntia, indeed, there was no spot imaginable that any longer could be thought of as secure from attack.

"It just doesn't make any sense."

In the center of the triangle, Joe and the other riders had watched in dumbfounded horror as the trio of armored vehicles had been shredded by the invisible monsters. Plate steel and titanium were ripped apart as easily as flesh. Two of the gr'nar had died when one of the heavy assault wagons had unexpectedly exploded—but they were the only ones. Fired upon, bombed, torched, none of the others—the hundreds of thousands of other gr'nars—had been stopped.

"Lissen up now, men," the speaker was old Doc Lieber, one of the other few survivors of the triangle massacre. "We've got to stop whining, and we've got to stop feeling sorry for ourselves. And we sure as goddamned

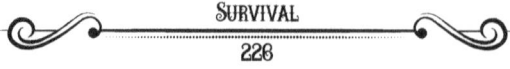

hell have to stop turning on each other." As the older man caught the attention of all the others present, he continued, saying;

"Now I ain't no kinda genius, but I know one thing. This all smells of a set-up to me. Ol' Ben might've been blowing smoke up his own ass when he accused Bentelii of lyin' about what the Kuzzi might or might not know about the gr'nar. But I do believe he was on the right track. Obviously the kuzzi don't know everything about the gr'nar."

"I'll agree that is obvious," seconded Bentelii. "And just so you can hear me say it, if I had any idea those bastards could eat through rock and metal, I'd would've had my ass on top of mountain or maybe in cloud, before I would've sat there waiting to die with rest of you."

And then, suddenly, listening to his friend's words, everything fell into place for Joe. The desperate band of survivors had been running for so long, he had forgotten the moment at the beginning of the attack when he had thought he had seen something. The fourteen men and the one kuzzi had run mindlessly for their lives for nearly an hour. Reaching the base of the nearest mountain range, they had then started climbing, and had not stopped until they had reached the plateau upon which they now hid, tired, hungry and frightened. Turning to Bentelii, Joe blurted;

"I think I know what's going on. I mean, I don't know ... can't explain how, or why ... but, I mean, I think—"

"Joe," growled Bentelii, his inhuman voice shot through with a hope the kuzzi could not have imagined even a moment earlier, "what is it? What are you trying to say?"

"When the gr'nar attacked us, everyone ... it happened all around the planet—right? It was coordinated. It was like a military strike. And unless I've been whacked in the head a mite too many times, I believe I know who made it happen."

Bentelii's eyes went wide with surprise, then narrowed to slits. Staring at his friend, he asked;

"Who?"

"The fa'lun."

***

Joe was more than a bit surprised when he discovered more than half of those assembled had not heard the story of his and Bentelii's encounter with the first race of Byanntia. While most of them listened with at least some small interest, none showed the intense concentration of Dr. Renni. After Joe had finished his telling of the moment when he had slain one of the flying creatures no other living being on the face of the planet had ever seen save for himself and his friend, Renni immediately began peppering the two of them with questions.

"Like the gr'nar, what makes you believe the one you killed was the only one on the planet? How long ago was that? Where are the remains? Are you certain that it was one of these fa'lun you saw in the sky? Did you only see one, or—"

"Doc," interrupted Joe, his head spinning trying to keep up with the questions. "Slow down. I know what I'm thinkin', but what's got you so stirred?"

"You said you knew what was behind the gr'nar attacks, claimed it was these fa'lun. The story you were told by Bentelii, that they were genetic geniuses, that they redesigned themselves for flight and then took to the skies ... I assume you're thinking they designed the gr'nar as well."

"That is what hit me. I remembered what you'd said about how there couldn't be just one of something, how there should really be more than one gr'nar. Well, when I saw something just hangin' in the air, watchin' us, it got me thinkin' ... I mean, if the fa'lun didn't have any problem with changin' themselves around, and if they had no scruples about guidin' the kuzzi into being nomads, steerin' them away from developin' the planet ... what was to say they might not put a safeguard in to keep the kuzzi docile?"

"What the hell are you talking about, Joe?"

"Mr. Mosheberg," responded the doctor, "he's saying the gr'nar are a weapon. These fa'lun, they come across as having been terribly paranoid as a race. Now, granted, all we have to go on is oral tradition, hearsay, but if these are facts—"

"If *what* are facts?"

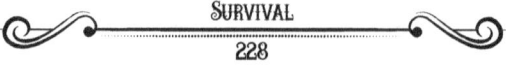

"Let's count them," offered Renni. "One, the fa'lun transformed themselves into almost a completely new species. Were they so in love with the idea of flight, or were they afraid to stay on the ground? That we don't know, but two, we do know they guided and molded the newly evolving kuzzi race—gave them language, civilization, and their nomadic way of life." As some of the others stared at the doctor with curiosity, he explained;

"Nomads just wander, they don't create great empires or mighty weapons, they just exist—year in, year out. In other words, they don't grow into a threat to anyone."

"And three," growled Bentelii, "if you stick something like gr'nar in ground, no permanent life looks like good idea. If we had begun building cities, sooner or later, along would come gr'nar to ... to keep us in our place."

The sixteen stared at each other, past each other, sitting on the ground in silence. Before their current discussion had begun, they had contacted whomever they could, trying to estimate the extent of the attack. The first thing that had stunned them was that the devastation had been worldwide. The gr'nar had surfaced in a thousand spots—a hundred thousand for all anyone knew.

The monsters had attacked everywhere. Farms had been devastated. Their main city and all their towns were in ruins. In short order, any kind of structure, any and all the changes humanity had wrought across the face of the land were all in flames. The kuzzi had fared no better.

Before the debacle of the trap had been set, hand radios had been spread across the globe to the various native tribes so that they might be able to know what was happening. The reports that had come back from the kuzzi were as horrifying as any others.

Even after all the years since the *Triumph* had first landed, three days earlier no more that four thousand human beings were to be found on Byanntia. The Kuzzi, on the other hand, had numbered in the millions. As best the sixteen lost souls hunkering in desperation could determine, however, at that point in time no more that one or two hundred thousand sentient beings remained alive on their world.

"So," started one of the ranchers who had yet to speak, "so what? You got your handful of facts there, science boy. So what're we supposed to do with 'em? You tell me, just what the hell do we do now?"

"I'll tell you what we do," answered Bentelii. The thought of endless kuzzi corpses strewn across the planes—torn apart, devastated—laughed savagely in the back of his mind. Feeling his anger growing, overwhelming him, the warrior stood, staring into the sky as he snarled;

"We find fa'lun, and we kill them back!"

***

The sixteen survivors had formulated the simplest of plans. They would return to the U.P. base camp. Once they had regained their wits, one of Thornton's sons had suggested that since the initial gr'nar attack had been followed by a two day period of inactivity, that perhaps the monsters had once more eaten their fill.

"It makes sense," Renni had admitted, his tone one of irritated respect toward the young kisonboy who had essentially done his thinking for him. "I don't propose we make foolish targets out of ourselves, but it is likely we've got a similar two-day bit of breathing time available to us."

"Then," Joe had suggested, "let's goddamned well make the most of it."

The fifteen humans and their one kuzzi ally reached the shattered scientific base without incident. Once there, the forces divided along what all hoped were sensible lines. Four men each were given the three larger shuttles which had been left undisturbed by the creatures. They were to then set out in different directions to search for survivors of either Byanntian race who could then be transported to a high point in the western mountains.

After that, Stewart Matson was to stay behind in the camp with Renni to assist him in piecing together enough of the doctor's equipment to be able to direct Joe and Bentelii as they used the smaller U.P. flyer to search out the fa'lun. Renni had explained that much of the equipment they had been using to search underground could be easily adapted to check for life signs atop mountains or in the air as well.

When the group had first arrived, most of the men had gone straight for the flyers to make certain they were all still airworthy. The remaining few busied themselves gathering supplies. Some of those rations they uncovered were used to prepare a hasty meal for all concerned, but the majority of it was divided among the shuttles to be distributed among those survivors they might manage to find.

Knowing they were working under the clock and realizing they could not know for certain how much time they had, the group had rallied to get underway as quickly as possible. In less than an hour two of the shuttles were already gone, searching out survivors. Before another hour the third had departed as well.

"How we comin' on this thing, Stew?"

"We might have it in a few minutes," responded the younger Matson. As Joe nodded, his brother added, "you done checking out the flyer?"

"Yeah. She'll do to get me and Bentelii into the air. After that it'll be up to you two to find us somethin' to chase after."

Stewart looked down toward the ground, rubbed a hand against his pants, then turned his head as he asked;

"Still no word from mom yet?"

Joe shook his head in response. Stew nodded slightly, then shrugged, not able to pull any words from himself. His brother understood—did not know what to say, either. Struggling for something positive, he offered;

"Couldn't raise anyone at all at Twin Feathers. Doesn't necessarily mean the worse, though." When Stewart turned, looking hopeful, Joe offered;

"You know how mom's just never got in the habit of taking a com with her. Even if she did, these damn gr'nar done wrecked so much, could be all the towers are down. Could be hundreds of folks callin' and we can't hear none of them."

"It's possible," admitted Stewart. Taking a deep breath, he added, "That Welsh lady, she could be all right, too, you know."

Joe smiled. Only a few years previous his younger brother would have been maneuvering to make time with the off-worlder simply

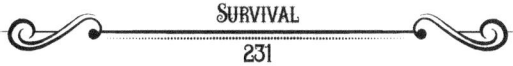

because he knew Joe was taken with her. After the death of their brother and father within a short space of time, however, the two had changed toward one another.

"Guess even mules like us can grow up some," he thought. Aloud, though, he said only;

"That'd be nice. She and mom kinda took to one another. Maybe they're lookin' out one for another." Stewart was about to comment when Renni called out to the two Matsons.

"I think we've got something."

Suddenly Joe felt himself going cold all over. Byanntia boasted very few airships. If the doctor had found something in the skies, there was little doubt as to what it could be. Calling out to Bentelii, he said;

"How about it, coffee-hound, ready to try flyin'?"

"Not really," admitted the kuzzi. "But tracking down and killing those who chained my race, then threw it to its death? For that I am ready." The warrior slung his long spear over his shoulder, then added;

"Although, it is true, I do wish we had some coffee."

The pair boarded the last remaining flyer and were airborne moments later.

***

Joe and Bentelii had been in the air for slightly under two hours when Renni's radio message came through. The doctor had been scanning the air with the U.P. equipment he and Stewart had jury-rigged, keeping a dead fix on the flying objects he had spotted earlier. Finally, those object had stopped flying.

"You're sure of the site," asked Joe. He wanted to laugh, but settled for a dry chuckle and a sad shake of his head.

"Yes," Renni assured the rancher. "All of them, they've been landing there one after another. Granted, the equipment we're using isn't designed for this kind of work, but considering the limited stature of Byanntia's airborne wildlife, I can't imagine we're mistaken."

When Bentelii gave his friend a quizzical look, Joe told him;

"The damn fa'lun, care to guess where the miserable sons'a bitches are gatherin'?"

"The Kelin."

Joe nodded. The Kelin was the tallest peak in the mountain range the kuzzi knew as the Kelin Heights. It was the place where Joe Matson had killed what Bentelii had believed must have been the last of the fa'lun years earlier. The irony of the situation did not escape either of them.

"Got some more news for you." Stewart's voice sounded happier than it should have. Without waiting to be asked, the younger Matson added;

"Stragglers have been turning up. Got two here that you might want to hear from."

As Joe listened, wondering—hoping—two voices came over the ship's speakers. First was that of his mother, followed by that of Catherine Welsh. The rancher bit back the first wave of emotion threatening to swallow him, then suddenly shoved the familiar aside bruskly as an inspiration sprang forward into his conscious mind. Cutting the two women off, he said;

"Excuse the bruskness, but I just had what I'm hopin' is a good idea." As Bentelii looked on with curiosity, Joe explained;

"Those weather satellites you people put in place, are they operational?" When Welsh assured him they were, he asked, "how hard would it be to make it rain? How long would it take? How heavy could you get it flowin'?"

"That would depend. Where would you want it to rain?"

"Everywhere."

"A world-wide storm?" The climatologist shuddered at the idea. "It's not ... I mean, it *may* be possible, but the consequences, I can't say what the results ... it—"

"Listen to me, Catherine, nothing matters except ... can you do it?"

Joe's voice came through the speaker at the U.P. base camp in a low, cold tone. Welsh caught a look in the eyes of the rancher's mother which made her choke back her automatic response. Swallowing hard, she breathed in and out several times, then said;

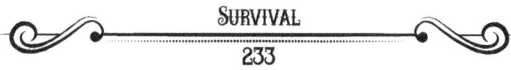

"Yes, I could do it. But, you have to understand, it would be a terrible strain on the atmosphere. And ... once it got started, a heavy rain, covering the planet ... such things have only been done under terraforming situations. It would be very hard—no. Not hard ... it would be impossible to stop. To control."

"Meaning it would never end?"

"Meaning it would end when it wanted to, and we wouldn't be able to do much about it."

Joe looked over to his old friend. Bentelii was already staring at him, his head tilted slightly to the side. The kuzzi's eyes were filled with puzzlement, but only until his companion turned to face him. Once their eyes locked, the large warrior smiled grimly, then nodded his consent. Giving his friend a smirk meant to convey a "what the hell" attitude, Joe responded to Welsh, telling her;

"That, you beautiful stack of pancakes, will have to do. Get it started. We're about thirty miles off from the Kelin. I want the sky pukin' water by the time we get there."

Welsh excused herself to set the necessary machinery into operation. As she did, Shelby asked her son exactly what he thought he was doing.

"Bentelii and I are going to land atop the Kelin. Before we left we filled this thing with weapons and explosives. If we can drive all the fa'lun inside somewheres, we can just blow the damn bastards to Hell and be done with them. Never did rain much here on Byanntia. My bet is these bastards don't like it much."

"You could accomplish that without drowning the planet."

"That's true, Mom. But it ain't gonna be long before the fa'lun's damn attack dogs go hungry again. Reports so far make it sound like there's not all that many of us left—human or kuzzi."

"But ..."

Worms don't like rain, Mom. I'm thinkin' we'd better try drownin' the goddamned things off while we got the chance."

Shelby Matson sat before the small silver microphone, unable to speak. She did not want to lose another son. Could not bring herself to

happily send him off into danger. But, damnably, she knew he was right. Like his father before him—her husband—she knew he was right. Knew they had run out of options. Had run out of time.

"Joe," she said finally, her voice straining to crack, her will an iron rod preventing it from doing so, "I won't waste what we don't have with a lot of chatter. I'm just going to tell you two things."

"Go ahead, Mom."

"All I want to say is, I love you. And ... that your father would have been proud enough to bust. Now, go on, get it done. Burn every last one of those evil goddamned bastards and leave 'em to ruin."

Joe signed off and turned the flyer toward the Kelin Heights. Both he and Bentelii were amazed to see the sky already darkening over, thick cloud banks building as far as the eye could see. The rancher set their speed at a gentle cruise, wanting to make certain all the fa'lun were back to their headquarters or city or nest or whatever it was they had atop Byanntia's highest mountain before their ship was anywhere near it. As he did so, his friend stretched as best he could within the confines of his cramped seat, then said;

"Hummpph, and I thought my mother was tough."

Joe turned slightly so he could give his friend a grin. As he did, Bentelii grinned back at him, asking;

"Stack of pancakes?" The rancher blushed slightly, answering;

"Hey, I like pancakes."

"Well ... who doesn't?"

And then, the two went silent as the first raindrops began to splash against their cockpit window.

***

Joe and Bentelii gave the fa'lun four hours after they arrived at the base of the Kelin range to finish flocking before they moved on their lair. It had been nearly three hours since the last of the enigmatic aliens had arrived through the terrible downpour, prompting the rancher to say;

"I don't see any reason to wait any longer."

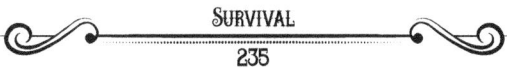

"I agree. Those not here are not coming. Now all we have to do is kill them."

"Yeah," agreed Joe. "Any ideas on that?"

"No." The kuzzi said the word harshly, not so much out of defeat, but out of fear his friend might have an idea which would leave him looking bad. Knowing Bentelii's mind as well as his own, the rancher smiled, admitting;

"Me, neither. We got choices, but they ain't good ones."

"Such as...?"

"Well, we could just blow the mountain top. I'm fairly certain we could level the thing with what we're packin', but ..."

"But there is no guarantee we will get them all—yes?"

"Yeah," agreed Joe. "Not knowin' what's goin' on in there, what their set-up is, we could maybe not even get most of then."

The rancher lowered his head, then stared out through the cockpit's windshield. The view had not changed. Water drops the size of olives were splattering against it so harshly he could not see even the nose of the shuttle, let alone beyond it. He wished they had some other option, but remembering his father's words, "wishing don't get it done," he frowned, then admitted;

"No, without gettin' a look inside, gettin' some kind of idea of what gives in there, I don't see how we can risk it."

"Then ..." Bentelii took his own long look out at the torrents of rain lashing their ship. The kuzzi were only feline in the most superficial of senses, cats being the mammals they resembled the most as humans did simians. Still, the idea of allowing himself to become soaking wet did not appeal to him. To do so on a treacherously steep mountainside in the worst rainstorm in the history of his world was even less desirable to him. Still, he broke off staring out the window, exhaled harshly, then finished;

"In we go."

Joe had landed the flyer in the center of a relatively flat expanse on the Kelin. Although at a slight angle, the ship's emergency grapples were more than adequate to keep it solidly in place despite the torrential

downpour. The last radio message the pair had been able to receive indicated that the storm had indeed circled Byanntia. As best Welsh's instruments could tell them, the entire world was covered by clouds, that even at the poles lightning was splattering down across the planet's meager glaciers.

No more reports would be coming to them, however. The machinery at the U.P. base had been abandoned when one of the shuttles had come to remove Welsh and the others. After only four hours the water level around Byanntia had already reached several inches.

Joe was amazed at the speed, but the climatologist had assured him that a world such as his, arid as it was, was not made to absorb much new moisture. It did not possess the proper strata to direct run-off. The last things the rancher was told were the locations to where the shuttles had been moving Byanntia's survivors, and the fact that Twin Feather's was already more than a foot deep in water.

"If we survive," his mother had told him, "there won't be anything familiar to go back to."

"Well, you always said you wanted to redecorate some day ..."

Shelby gasped slightly, but before she could speak, Joe cut her off, saying quietly;

"Goodbye, Mom."

After that he had Bentelii had waited until finally the moment had come when further delay seemed pointless. Staring out the cockpit window, however, neither one could see any kind of sensible approach to their problem. They had loosely discussed simply entering the fa'lun's stronghold and slaughtering them all. Both were still eager to do so, but the "how" of it had slowed them considerably. Finally, though, Bentelii spoke.

"I know why you can not voice an idea. It is because only sensible plan involves me going down and you staying above. Tell me I am wrong and I will most happily listen."

The kuzzi warrior was correct. The rain was coming down far too violently for anyone to climb down the face of the mountain unaided. One of them would have to remain above, keeping the other's descent line

secure. And Bentelii, far stronger, gifted with thick claws on both his feet and hands, was the logical choice.

"Besides," he told his friend as he slung an automatic rifle over his shoulder next to his customary spear, "in all our world, you are only one to kill fa'lun. Making us look bad."

Joe nodded, suppressing a grin, then followed Bentelii outside. The pair worked together to secure one end of the cable they had brought to their flyer's front landing gear. After that, Joe handed the kuzzi a com-link, telling him to test it to make certain they could hear each other over the storm. The device had been built for a standard human head, but it finally slipped begrudgingly into place once the warrior shifted his mane.

The test proved the pair had a reasonable chance of staying in communication, although they would be relying more on the visual feed Joe would be receiving since the link could not reach the kuzzi's mouth, ear and eye at the same time. Deciding they could make do with Joe being able to hear his friend, and see what he could see, Bentelii nodded then began making his way over the rain-slick edge of the cliff face.

The warrior worked his way slowly. He was not afraid of heights, but he did not enjoy being wet. Nor did he enjoy being cold. The deluge being called down by the satellites, especially at the altitude the pair had landed, was frightfully chilly, only ten degrees above the point where it would be coming down as snow, instead.

Bentelii clamped his jaws firmly shut, refusing to shiver, to allow his teeth to chatter. Hand over hand he lowered himself—slowly, carefully. He would not hurry and court disaster. He would not panic and invite failure. The fa'lun had engineered his people, as they had the entire planet. The kuzzi had been kept simple and backward as a strategy, condemned to pastoral ignorance because their "betters" had felt safer that way.

"Well, I hope you feel safe now," thought Bentelii, his brain pulsing with anger. "I hope you are sitting contentedly within your mountain, never dreaming of what is coming. I hope you are ready for my face to be last thing you ever see."

The kuzzi slipped then, both his feet sliding out from under him. Before he could compensate, his body swung outward away from the mountain. Holding onto the cable as tightly as he could, Bentelii fell backward toward the Kelin, slamming against it hard enough to knock all the air from his lungs. Maintaining his grip, he scrambled wildly with his feet, slipping against the slick stone, digging at the cliff face until one of his feet caught hold. While he regained his breath, Joe's voice sounded in his ear.

"Ben! You okay?"

"Just shaken." The kuzzi lifted his head just enough to catch sight of the rancher's silhouette staring down at him from above. Comforted by the knowledge his friend was watching, he said;

"When this is over, you owe me biggest cup of coffee there is."

"When this is over," answered Joe, "if there is any coffee left on this soggy planet, it's all yours."

Bentelii returned to his descent in silence. The rain continued to slam out of the sky, coming down in such vicious waves that in only minutes he could no longer see the ledge above, or his friend. Loosing strength in all his limbs, beginning to feel light-headed from the chill stealing through his muscles, the kuzzi closed his eyes for a moment, forced his breath in and out rapidly a dozen times, then whispered to himself;

"Rest of it, all the way—*now!*"

Pushing off from the cliff wall with his powerful legs, Bentelii flew outward about six feet, and then loosened his grip that he might slide down the cable freely. Grabbing hold tightly after a drop of some fifty feet, he ground his teeth together from the burning pain of the sudden friction. He did not cry out, however, nor did he regret the move for upon inspection he found he was a mere seven feet above the entrance to the fa'lun stronghold.

The warrior rested against the cliff wall, panting heavily—shivering as well. His hands aching, head beginning to throb from the cold, he swallowed hard and then began to move downward once more. In less

that five minutes he had reached the opening in the cliff face. What he saw was not what he had expected.

Atop the cliff, Joe's eyes went wide as the com-link revealed what Bentelii had found. Somehow they had both been hoping that the fa'lun had regressed when they took to the skies, had lost their scientific skills as they had lost their interest in the world below. Such was not the case.

The aerial race's arrogance and contempt for their neighbors showed through in their lack of either sentries or other restraints against entry. The fa'lun had not conceived that anyone could possibly follow them to their stronghold. It was their only failing, however. From the vantage point Bentelii had chosen, the view he sent back to Joe was a terrifying sight.

The fa'lun had not abandoned their science, but simply moved it aloft. From what the kuzzi could see, the entire mountain top was honeycombed with an array of rooms. He saw hints of gardens, aquatic hatcheries, and open living quarters in the background. In the foreground, however, he saw something far more disturbing.

"You see it," he whispered, struggling to keep his voice low. "Don't you, Joe? That is what I think it is—yes?"

The rancher agreed with his friend's assessment. From the look of things in the vast open area below Bentelii, the fa'lun were preparing for war. Whether they knew the rain occurring outside was artificial or not, they knew it would drown their main attack force, and so they were preparing another. As best the horrified onlookers could tell, the fa'lun were stockpiling incendiary bombs, ones they could carry by hand.

Could drop by hand.

The pair's suspicions were proved out when the fa'lun actually tested one of the devices in a deep crevasse. The effects they could see, as well as the ecstatic reaction of the fa'lun told them all they needed to know.

"There are far more of them than we suspected, Joe."

"I know."

"They are better armed than we had hoped. And far more vicious."

"We've underestimated them at every turn," Joe answered. Watching the thousands of fa'lun move about their massive stone arboretum,

floating gracefully or flitting at top speed, the rancher's heart sank further. Creatures of such speed could not be shot from the sky. Could not be turned by human hand even if their population had not been decimated. Determined not to give in, he said;

"It's true beyond denyin'. But we still have time. We can get 'em. You just shimmy on back up here and let's get—"

"Joseph ..."

The rancher froze. No one called him by his full first name. Even his mother did not do so anymore. Deep inside himself he knew what his friend was about to do. Not able to accept it, he said;

"No—listen to me, we can—"

"We can not," Bentelii cut him off. Not raising his voice, the kuzzi said, "already rain begins to lighten. You know they will attack when it stops. And, if they are allowed to leave this place, then everyone dies."

"But ..."

"Everyone, my friend."

Joe Matson went quiet. He knew it had to be. Knew there was no way around the plain and horrible truth staring both of them in the face. Huddled underneath their flyer, freezing as Bentelii had frozen, still holding onto the cable no longer needed, the rancher felt the last of his world crumbling. Unslinging the automatic weapon he had brought with him, the kuzzi whispered;

"Years ago, I told you it was good thing you killed one of them. Now, I shall do most glorious thing."

Clicking off the weapon's safety, Bentelii stood up out of the shadows and began to move forward. He could see the spot he needed to reach, was confident he could make it in a single leap. Flexing his legs, making certain his descent had not left him too weak for the last task he needed to perform, he said;

"Get in ship, fly to your stack of pancakes."

Cocking his weapon, the warrior prepared himself.

"Make her yours. Make babies."

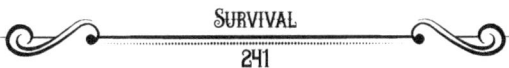

Knowing there was nothing else to do, Joe cut loose the cable from the landing gear and hurried back inside the ship.

"And when you have a son, name him Bentelii ..."

As Joe ignited the power chamber, his best friend moved to the back of the ledge from which he would make his attack so as to be able to get the running start he needed. Then, as he began to move, he screamed—

"And let him know he was named for greatest damn bastard who ever lived!"

As Joe lifted off, his com-link was filled with the sound of non-kuzzi screams, followed by a thundering roar which preceded the destruction of the upper third of the Kelin by only five seconds.

EPILOGUE

ALTHOUGH THE SATELLITE-PRODUCED STORM HAD ENDED ONLY nineteen hours after it had begun, the effects of it had been tremendous. The Byanntian sea level had risen to a point nearly twenty feet higher than ever before reached. Two years after the end of both the gr'nar and the fa'lun, it was still nearly two feet higher than previous. None of the survivors cared much one way or the other.

"Bring that little monkey over here, let her daddy see her."

Sadly for commerce, the kison herds had been eliminated along with the gr'nar. United Planets made noises about penalties for missed shipments at first, but with two U.P. representatives testifying that if the citizens of Byanntia had not acted as they had every single soul on the planet would have been slaughtered, such ideas were quietly shelved. Along with the kison, more than two million kuzzi and human corpses, or at least, pieces of corpses, had littered the swirling waters, giving more than a bit of credence to their testimony.

"Don't call your daughter a monkey, Joe, she doesn't look nearly enough like you to deserve a name like that."

Oddly enough, the tens of thousands of tons of flesh and blood and organs encouraged a meteoric rise in aquatic life around the planet. Although even two years after the Great Purge, as the events passed had been labeled for posterity, no official deal had been brokered, it did appear that the Byanntia Corporation was going to be able to renegotiate its old contracts substituting tonnages of fish in the place of beef.

"Sassin' me," said Joe, smiling, leaning back against one of the support beams of his home. Watching Catherine walk forward carrying their little girl, he added;

"That's what I get for listenin' to a kuzzi. I could of married me a proper wife, instead of ending up with some sharp-tongued—"

Catherine cut her husband off by dropping the baby into his arms, telling the girl;

"Go on, pee on daddy. Apparently he needs cooling off some."

U.P. thought it would be able to make heavily one-sided deals with the survivors due to the fact they would need so much assistance. But, when the rescue ships had landed, detailing how much of their futures the Byanntians would need to mortgage away to be rescued, human and kuzzi alike had turned their backs on such benevolence.

"She wouldn't do that," Joe assured his wife. Holding the girl up above his head, swinging her back and forth in the gentle sea breeze the way she adored, he added;

"Not until you were out of sight, anyway. She loves me, you know."

"Yeah, true," agreed Catherine. Looking out over the ocean, watching the fleet leaving for that day's fishing, she smiled as she watched her husband play with their little Bentelii, telling him;

"But that's just because she doesn't know any better."

It had taken decades, and death in all its varied guises, but the inhabitants of Byanntia had become a community at last. Those kuzzi who survived were not so petty as to not realize their race would have perished without the humans. And, none of the planet's non-feline residents was foolish enough to believe they could survive without the aid of the kuzzi.

Thus, the handful of sentient life which still walked Byanntia— the eight thousand, five hundred and ninety-seven who had survived everything a cruel cosmos had to hurl at them—had come together as no

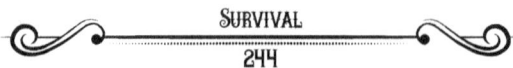

others had anywhere else. Rebuilding the major settlements of New Dodge and Oklahoma Flats, the two races now acted as one.

They fished the seas together. Hunted game in the hills together. They planted crops and build and created and lived together, sharing all misfortune and all rewards.

They were not kuzzi. They were not human.

They were Byanntians.

And they would remain so—

Forever.

BIOGRAPHIES

MIKE MCPHAIL–EDITOR

Author and graphic artist Mike McPhail is best known as the editor of the award-winning *Defending The Future* (DTF) series of military science fiction anthologies. In his current role as a freelance project administrator for Dark Quest Books, he produces not only the DTF series, but also David Sherman's *DemonTech* and *18th Race trilogy*, Phoebe Wray's, *Jemma Saga*, and a number of stand alone works. www.defendingthefuture.com

As a member of the Military Writers Society of America, he is dedicated to helping his fellow service members (and deserving civilians) in their efforts to become authors, as well as supporting related organizations in their efforts to "help those who have given their all for us." www.milscifi. com

C.J. HENDERSON –AUTHOR

CJ Henderson is the creator of both the *Piers Knight* supernatural investigator series and the *Teddy London* occult detective series among many others. He has written over 70 books and/or novels, hundreds and hundreds of short stories and comics and thousands of non-fiction pieces. He is a master of hardboiled suspense as well as raucous comedy, and is not shy about saying so even when sober. For more on this truly fascinating teller of tales, he encourages all to stop in at www.cjhenderson. com. He promises free short stories and more humility.

JACK DOLPHIN–AUTHOR

Jack Dolphin is a New York-based freelance writer and filmmaker. His periodic forays into fiction have appeared in *Hardboiled* and *New Mystery* magazines and in the anthologies *100 Crooked Little Crime Stories*, *Steam*

Powered Love and *The Dead Walk Again*. His other interests include hiking, urban archaeology, 60's soul music and the Brooklyn Cyclones baseball team. He has one wife, one daughter and one cat Ñ each a stunningly beautiful example of the type Ñ and sees no reason to add any more to the collection.

ROBERT E. WATERS–AUTHOR

Robert E. Waters has been publishing fiction professionally since 2003, with his first sale to *Weird Tales*, "The Assassin's Retirement Party." Since then, he has sold over 25 stories to various online and print magazines and anthologies, including stories to *Padwolf Publishing, The Black Library, Dragon Moon Press, Marietta Publishing, Dark Quest Books, Mundania Press, Nth Degree/Nth Zine*, and the online magazine *The Grantville Gazette*, which publishes stories set in Baen Book's best-selling alternate history series, *1632/Ring of Fire*. His first novel, *The Wayward Eight: A Contract to Die For*, set in the gaming universe Wild West Exodus, was published in 2014. Robert also co-edited the anthology *Fantastic Futures 13*, published in 2013 by Padwolf Publishing. From time to time, he also writes short fiction reviews for *Tangent Online*. He also served for seven years as an assistant editor for *Weird Tales*. Robert is currently living in Baltimore, Maryland with his wife Beth, their son Jason, their cat Buzz, and a plethora of tropical fish who like to play among the ruins of a sunken Spanish Galleon. His website is www.roberternestwaters.com.http://www.roberternestwaters.com/

JAMES CHAMBERS–AUTHOR

James Chambers' tales of horror, crime, fantasy, and science fiction have been published in numerous anthologies and magazines, and *Publisher's Weekly* described his collection of four Lovecraftian-inspired novellas, *The Engines of Sacrifice*, as "chillingly evocative." His other books include the novellas *Three Chords of Chaos*, as well as *The Dead Bear Witness* and *Tears of Blood* (the first two volumes in the Corpse Fauna series), and the story collections *Resurrection House* and *The Midnight Hour: Saint Lawn Hill and Other Tales* with illustrator Jason Whitley. His stories have appeared in the award-winning *Bad-Ass Faeries* and *Defending the Future* anthology series as well as *Allen K's Inhuman, Bare Bone, Chiral Mad 2, Clockwork Chaos, Deep Cuts, Fantastic Futures 13, The Green Hornet Chronicles, In an Iron Cage, Mermaids 13, The Spider: Extreme Prejudice, To Hell in a Fast Car, Walrus Tales*, and many other publications. He has edited and written numerous comic books including *Leonard Nimoy's Primortals* and the critically acclaimed "The Revenant" in *Shadow House*. He is a member of the Horror Writers Association and the recipient of the HWA's 2012 Richard Laymon Award. He is online at www.jameschambersonline. com and https://www.facebook.com/ThreeChordsOfChaos.

BRUCE GEHWEILER-AUTHOR

Bruce Gehweiler is an author, speaker and the host of the "Rabid Alien Radio" YouTube Channel investigating astounding new information about ancient mysteries and our paranormal universe. His books include *Where Angels Fear* and *Breaking into Fiction Writing* both co-authored with C.J. Henderson. His short fiction appears in books including, *Crypto-Critters Volume I & II, Hear Them Roar, The Dead Walk Again, Barbarians at the Jumpgate*, and *Lai Wan, Tales of the Dreamwalker*. Bruce is a former publisher, editor and book packager and was the lead consultant for the bestselling children's Christmas book project *The Elf on the Shelf.* His eighteen years in the publishing industry and lifetime of investigative research into the paranormal make him a popular guest at conventions and as a speaker. Contact Bruce at brucegmp@yahoo.com to book him for lecture or convention appearances.

MORE TITLES FROM MOONDREAM PRESS

Copper Dog Publishing LLC

OUR IMPRINTS:

Pumpkin Hill Press

To find out more about our imprints
and our upcoming releases, visit our website:
www.CopperDogPublishing.com
or our Facebook page:
www.facebook.com/copperdogpublishing

www.ingramcontent.com/pod-product-compliance
Lightning Source LLC
Chambersburg PA
CBHW060545260626
47161CB00003B/1067

* 9 781943 690091 *